Annis Lee Wister

Erlach Court

Annis Lee Wister

Erlach Court

ISBN/EAN: 9783743311244

Manufactured in Europe, USA, Canada, Australia, Japa

Cover: Foto ©Andreas Hilbeck / pixelio.de

Manufactured and distributed by brebook publishing software
(www.brebook.com)

Annis Lee Wister

Erlach Court

POPULAR WORKS FROM THE GERMAN,
Translated by MRS. A. L. WISTER.

The Alpine Fay. By E. Werner. 12mo. Extra cloth. $1.25.

The Owl's Nest. By E. Marlitt. 12mo. Extra cloth. $1.25.

Picked Up in the Streets. By H. Schobert. 12mo. Extra cloth. $1.25.

Saint Michael. By E. Werner. 12mo. Extra cloth. $1.25.

Violetta. By Ursula Zöge von Manteuffel. 12mo. Extra cloth. $1.25.

The Lady with the Rubies. By E. Marlitt. 12mo. Extra cloth. $1.25.

Vain Forebodings. By E. Oswald. 12mo. Extra cloth. $1.25.

A Penniless Girl. By W. Heimburg. 12mo. Extra cloth. $1.25.

Quicksands. By Adolph Streckfuss. 12mo. Extra cloth. $1.50.

Banned and Blessed. By E. Werner. 12mo. Extra cloth. $1.50.

A Noble Name; or, Dönninghausen. By Claire von Glümer. 12mo. Extra cloth. $1.50.

From Hand to Hand. By Golo Raimund. 12mo. Extra cloth. $1.50.

Severa. By E. Hartner. 12mo. Extra cloth. $1.50.

The Eichhofs. By Moritz von Reichenbach. 12mo. Extra cloth. $1.50.

A New Race. By Golo Raimund. 12mo. Extra cloth. $1.25.

Castle Hohenwald. By Adolph Streckfuss. 12mo. Extra cloth. $1.50.

Margarethe. By E. Juncker. 12mo. Extra cloth. $1.50.

Too Rich. By Adolph Streckfuss. 12mo. Extra cloth. $1.50.

A Family Feud. By Ludwig Harder. 12mo. Extra cloth. $1.25.

The Green Gate. By Ernst Wichert. 12mo. Extra cloth. $1.50.

Only a Girl. By Wilhelmine von Hillern. 12mo. Extra cloth. $1.50.

Why Did He Not Die? By Ad. von Volckhausen. 12mo. Extra cloth. $1.50.

Hulda; or, The Deliverer. By F. Lewald. 12mo. Extra cloth. $1.50.

The Bailiff's Maid. By E. Marlitt. 12mo. Extra cloth. $1.25.

In the Schillingscourt. By E. Marlitt. 12mo. Extra cloth. $1.50.

At the Councillor's; or, A Nameless History. By E. Marlitt. 12mo. Extra cloth. $1.50.

The Second Wife. By E. Marlitt. 12mo. Extra cloth. $1.50.

The Old Mam'selle's Secret. By E. Marlitt. 12mo. Extra cloth. $1.50.

Gold Elsie. By E. Marlitt. 12mo. Extra cloth. $1.50.

Countess Gisela. By E. Marlitt. 12mo. Extra cloth. $1.50.

The Little Moorland Princess. By E. Marlitt. 12mo. Extra cloth. $1.50.

TRANSLATED FROM THE GERMAN

OF

OSSIP SCHUBIN

BY

MRS. A. L. WISTER

PHILADELPHIA

J. B. LIPPINCOTT COMPANY

1889

CONTENTS.

CONTENTS.

ERLACH COURT.

CHAPTER I.

EXPECTED GUESTS.

ERLACH COURT,—a vine-wreathed castle, not very imposing, on the Save,—a pleasant dining-room, with wide-open windows through which thousands of golden stars are seen twinkling in the dark blue of a July sky, while the air is laden with the fragrance of acacia- and linden-blossoms. Beneath a hanging lamp, around a table whereon are finger-bowls and the remains of a luxurious dessert, are grouped six persons,—the master of the house, Captain von Leskjewitsch, his wife, and his seven-year-old son and heir, Freddy, a Fräulein von Gurlichingen, whose acquaintance Frau von Leskjewitsch had made twenty years before and whom she had never since been able to shake off, and two gentlemen, Baron Rohritz and General von Falk.

The general is the same youthful veteran whom we have all met before in some Viennese drawing-room or in some watering-place in Bohemia,—accredited throughout Austria from time immemorial as excellent company, dreaded as an incorrigible gossip, and notorious as a thorough idler. He often boasts that in thirty years he has never once dined at home; he might add, nor at his own expense. He is never positively invited anywhere, but since he has never been turned out of doors he is met everywhere. Absolutely free from prejudice in his social proclivities, he is equally at home in aristocratic society and in the world of finance; in fact, he rather prefers the latter; the dinners there are better, he maintains.

In spite of his seventy years, he is still as erect as a fir-tree,—dressed in the most youthful style,—occasionally, although with a half-ironical smile, alludes in conversation to 'us young men,' and dances at balls with the agility of a boy.

Baron Rohritz, who is scarcely six-and-thirty, already ranks himself, on the contrary, for the sake of his personal ease, with the old men. Tall and slender, with delicate, clearly-cut features, he is a remarkably distinguished figure, even in the circle to which he belongs. Although his moustache is brown, his hair is already very gray, which women find extremely interesting, especially since there is said to be some connection between this premature change of colour and an unfortunate love-affair. The finest thing about his face is his deep-set blue eyes; but since he uses an eye-glass, is near-sighted, and often nearly closes his eyes, there is something haughty in his look, which produces a chilling effect. When he smiles his expression is very attractive, but he smiles only rarely, and shows to the best advantage in his treatment of dogs, horses, and children.

Fräulein von Gurlichingen, commonly called Stasy,—the diminutive of her baptismal name, Anastasia, and a play upon her perpetual state of ecstatic excitement,—is an old maid, who was once accounted a great beauty, and in consequence is fond of wearing golden bands around her romantically frizzed curls. Her languishing, light-blue eyes were once compared to forget-me-nots sprinkled with sugar, and her complexion is suggestive of Swedish kid dusted with violet powder. She was young twenty years since, and has forgotten to stop being so. She once nearly married a prince of the blood, and has lately been jilted by an ‘infantry-officer. She has come to Erlach Court to recover from this last blow, perhaps in hopes of eventually obtaining a recompense for the loss of the captain.

Little Freddy is a very pretty, spoiled child, in a sailor suit, with bare legs very much scratched; and the master and mistress of the house are two genial people, who eight years previously, both having outlived the bloom of their early illusions, although she was only six-and-twenty and the captain thirty, had "patched together their tattered lives," which means that they had married each other, not so much in the hope of being happy themselves, as in that of making two other fellow-beings miserable.

Although, however, they had thus married for pique, and though each had brought to the union nothing save a remnant of unfortunate love for somebody else, although they quarrelled with each other continually, they got along together not much worse than two-thirds of the married people whose union has been the result of passionate attachment.

All were waiting for the after-dinner coffee, which the mistress of the mansion, in dread of spots, never allowed to be served in the drawing-room, except on state occasions. Its appearance was unpardonably delayed to-day, and the famous Erlach Court sociability was beginning to degenerate into yawning ennui.

With the exception of Baron Rohritz, who had been occupied the entire time in gazing with half-closed eyes into the clouds of blue smoke from his cigar, all present had done their best to enliven the prevailing mood: the general had told anecdotes from the 'Fliegende Blätter,' Freddy had succeeded in producing a particularly charming noise by running a wet forefinger around the rims of various wineglasses, Fräulein Stasy had suggested a poetic comparison between dry storms and the tearless anguish of a stricken heart, and the married pair had squabbled with special earnestness about the most diverse matters, first about the potato-rot, then about a problematical constitution for Poland; and yet the conversation had failed to become fluent.

For a few minutes an oppressive silence had prevailed; the husband and wife, usually equal to any emergency in this direction, had ceased even to quarrel. The ticking of the watches was almost audible, when the servant brought in on a salver the contents of the post-bag which had just arrived.

While the captain hastily opened a newspaper, that he might read aloud to the nervous Stasy, with a harrowing attention to details, the latest cholera bulletins, Frau von Leskjewitsch leisurely opened two letters: the first came from a Trieste tradesman and announced the arrival of a late invoice of the best disinfectants, the second apparently contained intelligence of some importance. After she had read it, Frau von Leskjewitsch laid it, with a pleased expression, upon the table.

"Children," she exclaimed,—it was a habit of hers thus to apostrophize people well on in years, for, except Freddy, who was not yet eight, and the general, who dyed his hair, all present were more or less gray-headed,—" children, our circle is about to receive an addition; my sister-in-law has just written me that she accepts our invitation and will arrive here to-morrow or the day after."

"Bravo!" exclaimed the captain, who on hearing this news quite forgot to go on teasing Stasy, and suppressed three entire cholera-telegrams. "I shall be delighted to see my little niece."

Freddy said, meditatively, "I should like to know what my aunt will bring me."

The rest of the party received the joyful tidings without emotion, partly because the long-looked-for coffee at that moment made its appearance, and partly because of the other three Stasy alone had any personal acquaintance with the Baroness Meineck—as the captain's sister was called—or her daughter. After the coffee had been cleared away, and whilst the master and mistress of the house were arguing outside in the corridor, most uselessly and most energetically, as to the train by which the expected guests would arrive, the general, who was playing his usual evening game of tric-trac with Rohritz, sighed,—

" Our comfort is all over."

Rohritz raised his eyebrows inquiringly: "Do you mean that in honour of these fresh guests we shall be obliged to put on a dress-coat at dinner every day?"

" Not exactly that," said the general; " the ladies

themselves are not too much given to elegance; but"—the general's face lengthened—"we shall be obliged to be cautious in our conversation."

Rohritz smiled significantly. "Double sixes!" he exclaimed, throwing the dice on the green cloth and moving his men with cunning calculation on the backgammon-board.

Meanwhile, the garrulous general continued, without waiting to be questioned: "Leskjewitsch is patient with his sister, and is excessively fond of his niece, but, between ourselves,"—he chuckled to himself,—"Leskjewitsch is a fool!"

If anything gave him more satisfaction than to live at the expense of others, it was to be witty, or rather malicious, at their expense. Rohritz thought this bad form, and was silent.

" I do not know the ladies personally," the general went on, rubbing his hands, " but for originality"— here he tapped his forehead with his forefinger— " neither mother nor daughter is far behind the captain. The mother is an old blue-stocking, and has been travelling all over the world for the last ten years, collecting materials for an historical work upon the Medicines, or whatever you choose to call them——"

" The Medici, perhaps ?" Rohritz interpolated.

"Very likely; I only know that there was an apothecary in the family, and that there were pills in their scutcheon, and that the worthy Baroness's work is to be eight volumes long," said the general.

Stasy, who had been leaning back in a luxurious arm-chair, moved to tears for the hundredth time over the last chapter of 'Paul and Virginia,' her favourite book,—the death of the heroine, she said, touched her especially because she could so easily fancy herself in Virginia's place,—now laid her book aside, since her tears seemed to arouse no sympathy, and joined in the conversation:

"You are talking of the Meinecks?"

"Yes. Are you personally acquainted with the ladies?" asked the general.

"Yes,—not very intimately, though. I always held myself a little aloof from them, but last summer we were at the same country resort,—I was with a sick friend at Zalow,—and I saw something and heard a great deal of the Meinecks."

"And are all the strange things that are said of them true?" asked the general.

"I really do not know what is said of them," replied Stasy, "but it certainly would be difficult to exaggerate their peculiarities. The Baroness, unfortunately too late in life, has arrived at the conclusion that the continuance of the human species is a crime. One of her manias consists in giving *à tort et à travers*, wherever she may chance to be, short lectures, gratis, upon the American Shakers and their system. But, with all her zeal, she has

hitherto succeeded in making but few proselytes.
Even her elder daughter, who was for some years
a fanatical adherent of her mother's doctrines, lately
married an artillery-officer. Stella, the younger
sister, whose acquaintance you are to make, dis-
likes having a brother-in-law in the artillery. The
Baroness's distaste was not for the quality of her
son-in-law, but for marriage itself. She appeared
at the wedding in deep mourning, and but for the
remonstrances of her relatives the invitations to the
ceremony would have been engraved upon black-
edged paper, like notices of a funeral."

"Ah! And the second daughter,—hm—I mean
the one expected here?"

"She will not hear of marriage, and is studying
for the stage."

"Indeed?" said Baron Rohritz.

The general moved a little nearer him, and, with
a mischievous twinkle of his green eyes, whispered,
"Between ourselves, I would not trust any girl
under sixty—he-he-he!—in the matter of marriage.
This Stella is hardly an exception; she probably
imagines she can make a very good match from
the stage—he-he!"

Rohritz shrugged his shoulders.

Stasy continued: "I really am sorry for Stella:
under other circumstances she might have been
very nice, but as it is she is dreadful. Two years
ago she had a craze for horsemanship: she used to

tear about for hours every day upon an English blood-horse which she had bought for a mere song because it was blind of one eye. Since the Meineck finances did not, of course, warrant a groom, and the Meineck arrogance could not accept the attendance of any one of the young men of the place,—and I know from the best authority that several kindly offered themselves as her escort,— she rode alone, and in a habit—good heavens!— patched up by herself out of an old blue cloth sofa-covering,—just fancy! One day the Baroness was more than commonly in need of money,— perhaps to publish a new volume of history or to repair a tumble-down chimney,—who knows?—at all events the horse was sold to a farmer in the neighbourhood. Stella cried for a week over her loss. Now the horse is quite blind, and draws an ash-cart; and when the little goose sees him she kisses his forehead."

"Ah! *besoin d'aimer!*" chuckled the general. "Hm—hm!"

"Three times a week she goes to Prague,—of course without any chaperon,—and takes singing-lessons from a long-haired music-master who predicts for her a career like Alboni's. Heaven knows what will be the end of it. The Meineck temperament is sure sooner or later to show itself in the child. Her father's mode of life scandalized even his comrades, and her aunt——surely

you know about Eugenie von Meineck, the captain's
old flame——"

She stopped short, for at this moment the captain himself entered the room, and, turning to
Rohritz, said, "I'm glad, old fellow, that your
stay in Erlach Court is to be brightened up a
little."

"I assure you that no change is needed to make
my visit to you most agreeable," Rohritz rejoined,
courteously.

The captain bowed: "Nevertheless you cannot
deny that your pleasure may be increased, and you
are still young enough to enjoy the society of a
pretty and clever girl."

Rohritz bit his lip; he had a very decided,
although quite excusable, dislike for what are
called clever young women. Stasy turned up her
nose.

"Do you think the little Meineck clever—*mais
vraiment* clever, *spirituelle?*" she asked.

"She is full of bright, merry ideas, and what a
pretty girl says is apt to sound well," the captain
replied, dryly.

"Do you think her pretty?" Stasy drawled; she
never could make up her mind to call any girl
pretty.

"Pretty? She is charming, bewitching!" the
captain declared, in an augry crescendo.

Just then his wife appeared, much provoked

at some particularly shocking misdeed on the part
of the maid to whom had been intrusted the arrangement of the guest-chambers, and she asked,
" What is the matter ?"

" A difference of opinion with regard to your
niece Stella, Katrine dear," Anastasia said, sweetly,
leaning back with a languishing air among the
cushions of her arm-chair and touching her finger-
tips together. " Your husband thinks her so very
beautiful."

" Oh, my husband always exaggerates," Frau
von Leskjewitsch remarks.

" I never said very beautiful; I did not even
say beautiful: I simply said charming," the captain
shouts.

" She is pretty. There is something very attractive about her," his wife assents, " and my husband finds her especially charming because she
looks like his old flame, Eugenie Meineck. For
my part, this resemblance is the only thing about
Stella that I do not like. I am sorry that even in
her features alone she should remind one of her
aunt."

" A rather indelicate allusion on your part,"
growls the captain, whose brown cheeks had
flushed at his wife's words.

As his wife always declared, he had never got
out of roundabouts, which suited him but ill, for
he was an unusually tall, broad-shouldered man,

with very handsome, clear-cut features, and a face tanned and worn by war, wind and weather, but recognizable as far as it could be seen as that of a southern Slav.

"Extremely indelicate," he repeats, with emphasis.

"I think it ridiculous never to outlive disappointments," says Frau von Leskjewitsch, who ever since she was a girl of eighteen had assumed the air of a matron of vast worldly experience, —"extremely ridiculous," she adds, with comic mimicry of her husband's reproachful intonation. As she spoke she slightly threw back her head crowned with luxuriant hair gathered into a simple knot behind, half closed her eyes, and stuck one thumb in the buff leather belt that confined her dark-blue linen blouse at the waist. Baron Rohritz, an experienced connoisseur of the female sex, had stuck his eye-glass in his eye, and was gazing at her without a shadow of impertinent obtrusiveness, but with very evident interest. Without being handsome, or taking the slightest pains to appear so, she nevertheless produced a most agreeable impression. According to the Baron's computation, she was about thirty-four years old, and yet her tall slender figure had all the pliancy of early youth. Her every motion was characterized by a certain energy and determination that possessed an attraction in spite of being foreign to the generally received opinion as to what constitutes feminine grace. The eyes, shadowed by long black lashes, that looked forth from her pale, oval face were full of intelligence and constantly varying expression, her features were fine but not regular, and her laugh was charming.

"Yes," she repeated, "I insist upon it, there is nothing more ridiculous than the inability to have done with one's disappointments. Good heavens! I freely confess to myself, and to the world at large, that the worthy man with whom I was wretchedly in love for four years was one of the vainest, most insignificant, most egotistical and uninteresting geese that ever lived."

"You were not in love with him," declared the captain, who did not seem to be quite free from a certain retrospective jealousy. "You were simply under the domination of an *idée fixe*."

"As if the passion of love were ever anything save an *idée fixe* of the heart!" retorted Frau von Leskjewitsch; "and an *idée fixe* is a disease; while it lasts it is well to be patient with it, but when it is over one ought to thank God and get rid of the traces of it as quickly as possible. That you never did, Jack: you were always like the belles of society, who cannot make up their minds to burn up their old ball-dresses and other trophies or simply to throw them away. They stuff their trunks full of such rubbish, until there is no room left for their honest every-day clothes. Throw it away, and the sooner the better!"

"What has once been dear to me is forever sacred in my eyes," said the captain, solemnly.

"Yes, and consequently you drag about with you through life such a heap of old, dusty, battered illusions that I really cannot see where you find the strength to hold fast to one healthy vital sensation. Bah! painful as it is, one must bury one's dead in time!"

"I prefer to embalm mine," the captain rejoined, with dignity.

"Let me congratulate you upon your collection of mummies," said his wife.

"You have no capacity for veneration," the captain declared.

"Because I disapprove of whining *ad infinitum* as homage to a vanished enthusiasm,—ridiculous!" said Katrine.

"Don't quarrel, my doves!" Stasy entreated, clasping her hands after a child-like fashion.

"We have no idea of doing so," the mistress of the house replied, good-humouredly. "We never quarrel. Our complaint is a chronic difference of opinion. What were we really talking about?"

"About illusions," remarked Baron Rohritz.

"Oh, that was merely a side-issue,—only an after-piece," said Frau von Leskjewitsch, bethinking herself. "What was the starting-point of our discussion?—Oh, yes: we were speaking of my little niece."

"Perhaps you can show us a photograph of her," said Anastasia.

"Yes, yes." And Frau von Leskjewitsch began an eager search in a small gilt cottage which had once been a bonbonnière and now served as a receptacle for photographs. In vain. Upon a closer examination several of the photographs were found to be missing. Little Freddy confessed with a repentant face that he had cut them up to make winders for twine. His mother laughed, kissed his sleepy, troubled eyes, and sent him to bed. Thus Baron Rohritz was left to draw from fancy a possible likeness of Stella Meineck.

CHAPTER II.

BARON ROHRITZ.

Stasy had vented so much malice upon Stella that Rohritz had involuntarily begun to think well of her. After he had retired, in the watches of the night, and was trying in vain to be interested in a volume of Tauchnitz, his thoughts were still busied with her. "Poor thing," he reflected, "there must be something attractive about her, or Les and his wife would not be so devoted to her. And, after all, what did that venomous old maid's accusations amount to?—that she has an antipathy for artillery-officers,"—Rohritz as a former cavalry-man shrugged his shoulders indulgently at this weakness,—"and that she wants to go upon the stage. That, to be sure, is bad. I know nothing in the world more repulsive than girls of what are called the better classes who are studying for the stage."

And Rohritz recalled a certain officer's daughter whom he had once met at an evening entertainment, and who in proof of her distinguished talent had declaimed various 'selections.' He had been quite unable to detect her talent, and had spoken of her contemptuously as an hysterical tree-frog. The appellation had met with acceptance and had been frequently repeated.

The remembrance of the officer's bony daughter lay heavy on his soul. "Yes, if Stella should remind me in the least of that hysterical tree-frog, I really could not stay here much longer," he thought, with a shudder. "And in any case I cannot but regret these last pleasant days. That old dandy and the faded beauty were bad enough, but they could be ignored; while a young girl— and a relative, too, of the family—— Pshaw! at all events I can take my leave."

With which he put out his candle and went to bed.

What it was that was dear to him in the sleepy and very uninteresting life at Erlach Court it would be difficult to say. Perhaps he prized it as chiming in so admirably with the precious ennui which he had brought home from America ten years previously, and which had since been his inseparable companion. It was such a finished, elegant ennui; it never yawned and looked about for amusement, never in fact felt the least desire for it, but looked down in self-satisfied superiority upon those childish mortals who were actually capable of being irritated or entertained upon this old exhausted globe.

He was proud of this kind of moral ossification, which was gradually paralyzing all his really noble qualities.

" 'Tis a pity!" said Leskjewitsch, whose youth was still warm in his veins, and who declared that he had never been bored for half an hour in his life, except upon a pitch-dark night in winter at some lonely outpost when he had been delayed on the march; and although the honest captain was a demi-savage and "still in roundabouts," we cannot help repeating his words with reference to Rohritz, " 'Tis a pity!"

Yes, a pity! Who that saw Edgar von Rohritz —his mother had bestowed upon him his melodramatic name in a fit of enthusiasm for Walter Scott and Donizetti,—who that saw him to-day could believe that in his youth, under a thin disguise of aristocratic nonchalance, he was far more sentimentally inclined than his former comrade Leskjewitsch? But sentiment had fared ill with him. After having overcome, not without a hard struggle, the pain of a very bitter disappointment, his demands upon existence were of the most moderate description, and this partly to spare himself useless pain and partly from caution lest he should make himself ridiculous. He kept his heart closely shut; and if at times sentiment, now fallen into disgrace with him, softly appealed to it, entreating admission, he refused to listen. He was no longer at home for sentiment.

About twenty years since he had begun his military career in the same regiment of dragoons with Jack Leskjewitsch, and when hardly five-and-twenty he had left the service and travelled round the world, perhaps because change of air is as beneficial for diseases of the heart as for other maladies.

For years now he had made his home in Grätz, whence he took frequent flights to Vienna. He was but moderately addicted to society, so called. He never danced; at balls he played whist, and dryly criticised the figures and the toilettes of the dancers. He had the reputation of being a woman-hater, and accordingly all the young married women thought him excessively interesting. He was held to be one of the best matches in Grätz, wherefore he was exposed to persecution by all mothers blest with marriageable daughters.

Wearied of this varied homage, he had gradually withdrawn from society, and had even relinquished his game of Boston, when one day a report was circulated that he had suddenly lost almost all his property through the negligence of an agent. All that was left him—so it was said—was a mere pittance. Since he never contradicted this report, it was thought to be confirmed. The mothers of marriageable daughters discovered that he had a disagreeable disposition, and that it would be very difficult to live with him. One week after this sad report had been in circulation, he observed with a peculiar smile that during this space of time he had received at least half a dozen fewer invitations to dinners and balls than usual. Shortly afterwards meeting a friend in the street who offered him his sincere condolence, he replied, with a twirl of his moustache,—

"Do not trouble yourself about me: I assure you that it is sometimes very comfortable to be poor!"

The news of his sadly-altered circumstances penetrated even to the secluded Erlach Court, and Captain Leskjewitsch, who learned it from a casual mention of it in a postscript to a letter from a comrade, was exceedingly agitated by it. He ran to his wife with the open letter in his hand, exclaiming, "Ah çà, Katrine, read that. Rohritz has lost every penny! Under such circumstances he must need entire change of scene for a time. We must invite him here immediately,—immediately,—that is, if you have no objection."

For a wonder, the quarrelsome couple were perfectly at one on this point.

"I shall be delighted to see him," replied Katrine. "Invite him at once; that is, if you are not afraid of his making love to me."

The captain's face took on an odd expression. "There is no danger of your allowing a stranger to make love to you," he muttered. "Your disagreeable characteristic is that you will not allow even me to make love to you."

Katrine raised her eyebrows: "I have an aversion for *rechauffées.*"

The captain took instant advantage of his opportunity: "You certainly cannot expect to be the first woman who I—hm!—thought had fine eyes?"

But Katrine was very busy with her household accounts, and consequently she had no time at present to indulge in her favourite amusement, a lively discussion.

"Don't agitate yourself, my dear," she rejoined, "but go and write a beautiful letter to Rohritz;

and do it quickly, that it may go by to-day's post.
Shall I compose it for you ?"

"Thanks, I think I am equal to that myself,"
the captain replied, with a laugh. "Upon my
word, a poor dragoon has to put up with a deal
from so cultivated a woman."

As he turned to go, Katrine called after him:
"I warn you beforehand that I have a weakness
for Rohritz. All the rest is your affair. I wash
my hands of it."

Nothing so aroused Katrine Leskjewitsch's sarcasm as the problematical conscientiousness of
those young wives who combine a decided love for
flirtation with a determination to cast all the blame
for it upon their husbands, posing in the eyes of
the world as suffering angels at the side of black-
hearted monsters. Her ridicule of such women
was sharp and plentiful.

"A deuce of a woman!" the captain murmured
as he betook himself to his library and—rare effort
for a dragoon—indited a letter four pages long to
his old comrade.

His friend's epistle, strange to say, touched Rohritz. It was so cordial, so frank, and so warmly
sympathetic, such a contrast to the formal assur-
ances of sympathy which he met with elsewhere,
that he accepted the invitation extended to him,
and made his appearance at Erlach Court a week
afterwards.

He had been here now for three weeks, and had been really content, especially during the early period of his visit, when he had been alone with his host and hostess. The arrival of the general and Stasy had somewhat annoyed him, and the news of the approach of another detachment of guests—consisting, moreover, of a mother and daughter—positively irritated him. Good heavens! another mother, another daughter! Was there then no spot upon the face of the globe where one could be safe from mothers and daughters?

CHAPTER III.

THE ARRIVAL.

A TELEGRAM had finally announced the arrival of the Meinecks by the 10.30 morning train at H——, the nearest railroad-station, tolerably distant from Erlach Court.

It is almost noon; the captain and Freddy have driven over to the station to meet the guests, and the rest of the family are on the terrace outside of the dining-room. The hostess, dressed as usual with puritanic simplicity in some kind of dark linen stuff, deliciously fresh and smelling of lavender, is leaning back in a garden-chair, diligently crochetting a red-and-white afghan for her little son's bed. The general, in a very youthful felt hat adorned with a feather, is chuckling in a corner over a novel of Zola's. Anastasia is fluttering gracefully hither and thither, fancying the while that she looks like a Watteau. In pursuance of her lamentable custom of wearing her shabby old evening-gowns in the country in the daytime, she has donned a much-worn sky-blue silk with dilapidated tulle trimming, and is surprised that her faded splendour appears to fail to dazzle those present.

"Life is pleasant here, is it not?" asks Katrine, looking up from her crochetting at Rohritz, who faces her as he leans against the balustrade of the terrace. "I am trying my best to induce my husband to leave the service and retire to this place. He is still hesitating."

"Hm! Do you not think that for a man of his temperament existence at Erlach Court would be a trifle monotonous?" is Rohritz's reply.

"He can occupy himself," Katrine makes answer, shrugging her shoulders.

"If I mistake not, you have rented the farm at Erlach Court?"

"Yes, thank heaven!" Frau von Leskjewitsch admits, with a smile. "Farming is usually a very costly taste for dilettanti. But he has entire control over the forests and the vineyards; they would

give him plenty to do; and then he is an enthusiastic horseman, and the roads are very fine."

· Rohritz is silent, and thoughtfully knocks off
the ashes from his cigar with the long nail of his
little finger. He cannot help thinking that Katrine
Leskjewitsch, exemplary as she may be as a mother,
has her faults as a wife. Jack Leskjewitsch is not
yet eight-and-thirty, and she is prescribing for him
a life suited to a man of sixty.

"It is certainly a pity to cut short his career,"
Rohritz remarks, after a while, "especially since
he passed so brilliant an examination for advanced
rank last year."

"Yes, his talent is indubitable," Katrine assents:
"one would hardly think it of him. He devotes
but little attention to study, as I can testify, and
I certainly did not coach him, as did the wife
of an unfortunate captain who passed the same
examination." The corners of Katrine's mouth
twitched. "What do you think was the end of the
united efforts of husband and wife? Two weeks
after barely and laboriously passing his examination the worthy man was a maniac. In fact, no
fewer than seven of my husband's fellow-students
in that course lost their reason. 'Tis odd how
much ambitious incapacity one encounters in this
world! Jack does not belong in that category,
however. He adores the service, but he has not a
particle of ambition."

All this is uttered with a seemingly woful lack of interest.

" 'Tis a pity that she does not sympathize more fully with Les," Rohritz thinks to himself; but all he says is, "And yet you would have him relinquish his career?"

"A cavalry-man who looks forward to a career ought not to marry," Katrine maintains. "Probably you can recall the delights of a military, nomadic existence for a family, particularly in those holes in Hungary. Such hovels!—a stagnant swamp in front, a Suabian regiment installed in the rooms, and no sooner have you got things into a civilized condition than you have to break up to the sound of boot and saddle. In one year I changed my abode three times. I could have borne it all so far as I was concerned, but there was the child. Freddy became subject to attacks of fever, so I bundled him up and brought him here. He recovered immediately, and I wrote to my husband that he must choose between his family and the army."

"That was to the point, at least," said Rohritz.

"Yes. He was apparently offended, and did not answer my letter for a month. Then he was seized with a longing for—for the child. He alighted in the midst of our solitude like a bomb at Sevastopol. Of course we were charmed to see him, and he was so delighted with Erlach Court that he was quite ready to turn his back on the service. I, however, do not approve of hasty decisions, and so I advised him to postpone his change of vocations——"

"His resignation of a vocation," Baron Rohritz interpolated.

"What a hair-splitting humour you are in to-day!" Katrine rejoined, with a shrug,—"to postpone for a while his—resignation, if that pleases you. So he obtained leave of absence for a year. Hm!—I am afraid he is beginning to be bored. I cannot understand it. You must admit that we are charmingly situated here."

"Indeed you are."

"The estate is in good order," Katrine went on, "and we have no neighbours."

"A great advantage."

"So it seems to me. One of the most disagreeable sides of an army life was always, in my opinion, the being forced into association with so many unpleasant people. Most of my husband's comrades were very agreeable, unusually kindly, pleasant men, but to be forced to accept them all, and their wives into the bargain without liberty to show any preference,—it was simply odious. I am a fanatic for solitude; the usual human being I dislike; but you cannot throw everybody over, however you may desire to do so,"—with a glance over her shoulder towards Stasy and the general.

c

"I beg you will make no application to yourself of my remark."

"Much obliged." Rohritz bowed. "I confess I began——"

"No need of fine phrases," Katrine interrupted him. "You know I like you. And in proof of it—you may have heard that we want to pass the winter here; it will be delightful! entirely lonely, —shut off from civilization by a wall of snow,— Christmas in the country,—the children from three villages to provide with gifts,—the castle quite empty, except for our three selves and Freddy! Well, in proof of my genuine friendship I invite you to share with us this charming solitude. Will you come? Say you will." Dropping her work in her lap, she offers him both her hands.

"A curious creature! She treats me like an aged man, and moreover considers herself sufficiently elderly to dispense with caution in her intercourse with the other sex. An odd illusion for a woman still extremely pretty," Rohritz thinks; and, occupied with these reflections, he does not immediately reply.

"You decline?" she asks, merrily. "I shall not throw away such an invitation upon you a second time."

"They are coming! they are coming!" Stasy exclaims, clapping her hands childishly and tripping to and fro in much excitement.

"I do not hear the carriage," Katrine rejoins, looking at her watch. "Besides, it is not time for them yet."

"But I hear something in the avenue—— Ah, please come, dear Edgar," Stasy entreats.

Rohritz does not stir.

"Baron Rohritz!" in an imploring tone.

"What can I do for you, Fräulein Stasy?"

"Your opera-glass—be quick!" And, while Rohritz reluctantly rises to go for the desired optical aid, Stasy lisps, "Not at all over-polite; quite like a brother: just what I enjoy."

"It is they," Katrine exclaims. "The carriage is just turning into the avenue. Let me have it for a moment,"—taking from his hand the glass which Rohritz has just brought. "Yes, now I see them quite distinctly."

A few minutes later the rattle of approaching wheels is heard. The two ladies and the general hasten down to receive the guests. Rohritz discreetly withdraws to his apartment, and from behind his half-drawn curtains watches the arrival. The carriage stops, the captain springs out to aid two ladies to alight. At first Rohritz hears nothing but a hubbub of glad voices, sees nothing but a confused group, the general standing on one side with a polite grin on his face, and Freddy giving vent to his joyous excitement by performing a war-dance around the party.

When the situation at last becomes clear, he perceives a very handsome old lady in a close black travelling-hat, a pair of blue spectacles shielding her eyes from the dust, and wearing a dust-cloak which may once have been black, while beside her—he adjusts his eye-glass in his eye—assuredly Stella does not remind him of the 'hysterical tree-frog' of frightful memory, but of some one else, for the life of him he cannot remember whom. He looks and looks, sees two serious dark eyes in a gentle childlike face beneath the broad brim of a Kate-Greenaway hat, a half-wayward, half-shy smile, charming dimples appearing by turns in the cheeks and at the corners of the mouth, a delicately-chiselled nose, a very short and rather haughty upper lip, beneath which gleam rows of pearly teeth, and for the rest, the figure of a sylph, rather tall, still a little too thin, and with a foot peeping from beneath her skirt that Taglioni might covet.

He looks and looks. No, Stella certainly does not remind him of the 'hysterical tree-frog,' but as certainly she recalls to his mind something, some one—who is it? who can it be?

An unpleasant surmise occurs to him, but before it can take actual shape in his brain the impetuous entrance of the captain has banished it.

"Come to the drawing-room, Rohritz, and be presented to the ladies," he calls out. "By the

way, what means this wretched idea of which
Stasy informs me? She says that you are going
back to Grätz immediately."

"The fact is, my lawyer has summoned me,"
Rohritz replies; "but—hm!—I fancy the matter
can be settled by letter. At any rate, I will try
to have it so disposed of."

"Bravo!"

CHAPTER IV.

STELLA.

FREDDY has been terribly disappointed; instead
of the bonbonnière, the snap-pistol, or the story-
book, among which three articles he has allowed
his expectant imagination to rove, his aunt has
brought him Sanders's German Dictionary.

"I hope you will like it," Stella remarks, with
emphasis, depositing the voluminous gift upon the
school-room table. "We had to pay for at least
five pounds of extra weight of luggage in the
monster's behalf, and moreover it has crushed flat
my only new summer hat. 'Tis a great pity."

Freddy, who, although hitherto rather puny and
delicate in body, is mentally, thanks to clever qualities inherited from both his parents, far in advance of his age, and already thinks Voss's trans-

lation of the Odyssey entertaining, turns over the leaves of the three volumes of the Dictionary without finding them attractive.

"I put in a good word for the child," Stella says, with a laugh, to the captain, who with his friend Rohritz happens to be in Freddy's school-room, "but mamma insists that it is of no consequence; if it does not please him now, it will be very useful to him in future. Never mind, my darling," she adds, turning to her little cousin, who, with a sigh and not without much physical effort, is putting the colossal Sanders on his bookshelves; "it certainly presents an imposing spectacle, and I have a foolish thing for your birthday, the very finest my limited means could afford." As she speaks she strokes the little fellow's brown curls affectionately.

"Stella, Stella, where are you loitering?" a deep voice calls at this moment, and the girl replies,—

"In a moment, mamma, I am coming!—I have to write a letter to a Berlin publisher," she says by way of explanation to the two men, as she leaves the room.

*   *   *   *   *   *   *

The evening has come. Dinner is over. All are sitting in more or less comfortable garden-chairs on the terrace before the castle, beneath the spreading boughs of a linden, now laden with fragrant blossoms.

The stars are not yet awake, but the moon has risen full, though giving but little light, and looking in its reddish lustre like a candle lighted by day; the heavens are of a pale, greenish blue, with opalescent gleams on the horizon. The sun has set, twilight has mingled lights and shadows, the colours of the flowers are dull and faded. Around the castle reigns a sweet, peaceful silence, that most precious of all the luxuries of a residence in the country. The evening wind murmurs a dreamy duo with the ripple of the stream running at the foot of the garden, and now and then is heard the heavy foot-fall of a peasant returning from his work to the village.

Baroness Meineck is holding forth to her hostess, who listens patiently, or at least silently, upon the subject of the cholera-bacilli and the latest discoveries of Pasteur. To Rohritz, who, will he nill he, has had to place his hands at the disposal of the arch Stasy as a reel for her crewel, the Baroness's voice partly recalls a sentinel and partly a tragic actress; she always talks in fine rounded periods, as if she suspected a stenographer concealed near. While the quondam beauty, with a thousand superfluous little arts, winds an endless length of red worsted upon a folded playing-card, he glances towards the spot where Stella is telling stories to Freddy, and involuntarily listens.

Since the Baroness, perhaps because she has

reached some rather delicate details in her medical treatise, sees fit to lower slightly her powerful voice, he can hear almost every word spoken by Stella. ˙If he is especially susceptible in any regard, it is in that of a beautiful mode of speech. What Stella says he is quite indifferent to, but the delightful tone of her soft, clear, bird-like voice touches his soul with an indescribably soothing charm.

"Now that's enough. I do not know any more stories," he hears her say at last in reply to an entreaty from her little cousin for "just one more."

"No more at all?" Freddy asks, in dismay, and with all the earnestness of his age.

"No more to-day," Stella says, consolingly. "I shall know another to-morrow." She kisses him on the forehead. "You look tired, my darling! Is it your bedtime?"

"No," the captain answers for him, "but he could not sleep last night for delight in the coming of our guests, and he is paying for it now. Shall I carry you up-stairs—hey, Freddy?"

But Freddy considers it quite beneath his dignity to go to bed with the chickens, and prefers to clamber upon his father's knee.

"You are growing too big a fellow for this," the captain says, rather reprovingly: nevertheless he puts his arm tenderly about the boy, saying to Stella, by way of excuse, " We spoil him terribly:

he was not very strong in the spring, and he still enjoys all the privileges of a convalescent,—hey, my boy?" By way of reply the little fellow nestles close to his father with some indistinct words expressive of great content, and while the captain's moustache is pressed upon the child's soft hair, Stella takes a small scarlet wrap from her shoulders and folds it about his bare legs.

"'Tis good to sleep so, Freddy, is it not? Ah, where are the times gone when I could climb up on my father's knees and fall asleep on his shoulder?—they were the happiest hours of my life!" the girl says, with a sigh.

"But, Baron Rohritz, pray hold your hands a little quieter," the wool-winding Stasy calls out to her victim. "You twitch them all the time."

"If you only knew how glad I am to see you all again, and to spend a few days in the country," Stella begins afresh after a while.

"Why, do you not come directly from the country?" the captain asks, surprised.

"From the country?—we come from Zalow," Stella replies: "the difference is heaven-wide. Yes, when mamma thirty years ago bought the mill where we live now,—without the miller and his wife, 'tis true,—because it was so picturesque, it really was in the country, or at least in a village, where besides ourselves there were only a few peasants, and one other person, a misanthropic widow who lived at the very end of the hamlet in a one-story house concealed behind a screen of chestnut-trees. I have no objection to peasant huts, particularly when their thatched roofs are overgrown with green moss, and misanthropic widows are seldom in one's way. But ten years ago a railway was built directly through Zalow, and villas shot up out of the ground in every direction like mushrooms. And such villas, and such proprietors! All *nouveaux riches* and pushing tradesfolk from Prague. A stocking-weaver built two villas close beside us,—one for his own family, and the other to rent; he christened the pair Giroflé-Girofla, and declares that the name alone is worth ten thousand guilders. He also maintains that the architecture of his villas is the purest classic: each has a Greek peristyle and a square belvedere. It would be deliciously ridiculous if one were not forced to have the monsters directly before one's eyes all the time. The worst of it is that one really gets used to them! Dear papa's former tailor has built himself a hunting-lodge in the style of Francis the First directly on the road, behind a gilded iron fence and without a tree near it for fear of obscuring its splendour. Like all retired tradesfolk, the tailor is sentimental. Only lately he complained to me of the difficulty experienced by cultivated people in finding a fitting social circle."

"Do you know him personally, then?" the captain asks, with an air of annoyance.

"Oh, yes, we know every one to bow to," says Stella. "In a little while we shall exchange calls: I am looking forward to that with great pleasure."

"What do you think of such talk, Baron?" Stasy asks under her breath.

Baron Rohritz makes no reply: perhaps such talk is to his taste.

Meanwhile, Stella goes on in the same satirical tone: "As soon as some one of these æsthetic proprietors has come to a decision as to where the piano is to stand, we shall certainly be invited to admire the new furniture. Then mamma will look up from her books and say, ' I have no time; but if you want to go, pray do as you please.' Mamma never cares what I do or where I go." Stella's soft voice trembles; she shakes her head, passes her hand over her eyes, and runs on : " Even the walks are spoiled; one is never sure of not encountering a picnic-party. They are always singing by turns ' Dear to my heart, thou forest fair,' and 'Gaudeamus,' and when they leave it the ' forest fair' is always littered with cold victuals, greasy brown paper, and tin cans. It is horrible! I detest that railway. It snatched from us the prettiest part of our garden; there is scarcely room enough left for ' pussy wants a corner,' and now mamma has rented half of it and the ground-floor of the mill to a family from Prague for a summer residence."

"I do not understand Lina," the captain says, with irritation. "You surely are not reduced to the necessity of renting part of your small house for lodgings."

"Mamma wanted just two hundred guilders to buy Littré's Dictionary,—the fine complete edition. Moreover, I think you are under a mistake with regard to our resources. I detest the railway, but if it had not bought of us, two years ago, a piece of land on which to build a shop, I hardly know what we should be living upon now. Ah, if poor papa could see how we live! He could not imagine a household without a butler or a lady's-maid. Mamma dismissed the butler at first upon strictly moral grounds——"

Anastasia von Gurlichingen casts down her eyes. "Did you ever hear anything like that, Baron Rohritz," she asks, "from a young girl?"

Rohritz shrugs his shoulders impatiently, and Stella goes on quite at her ease:

"He was always making love to the cook, and the lady's-maid was jealous and complained of it. Then the lady's-maid was dismissed, for pecuniary reasons; then the cook, for sanitary considerations: one fine day she nearly poisoned us all with verdigris, her copper kettles were so badly scoured. Her place was never filled, for in the interim, that

is, while we were looking for a new *cordon bleu,*
mamma discovered that a cook was a very costly
article and that we could get along without one.
Our last maid-of-all work was a dwarf not quite
four feet tall, who had to mount on a stool to set
the table. Mamma engaged her because she
thought that her ugliness would put a stop to love-
making——" Stella breaks the thread of her
discourse to laugh gently; her laugh is like the
ripple of a brook. "But real talent defies all
obstacles. Mamma's experiment made her richer
by one sad experience: she knows now that not
even a large hump can make its possessor im-
pervious to Cupid's arrows."

The captain laughs. Stasy's disapprobation has
reached its climax; she twitches impatiently at the
worsted she is winding from Rohritz's hands.

"What would papa say if he could see it all?"
Stella says, in a changed voice.

"Do you still grieve so for your poor father,
mouse?" the captain asks, kindly, perceiving that
the girl with difficulty restrains her tears at the
mention of her dead father.

"You would not ask that, uncle, if you knew
what a life I lead," she replies, in a choked voice.
"Yes, it is amusing enough to tell of, but to
live—— There is no use in thinking of it!"
She bends slightly above her little cousin, whose
head is resting quietly upon his father's shoulder.

"He is sound asleep," she whispers, brushing away a fluttering night-moth from Freddy's pretty face,—"poor little man!"

"It is growing cool," Katrine declares, glancing anxiously towards Freddy in the midst of the Baroness's interesting discourse upon the latest achievements of medical science, and then, rising, she leaves her sister-in-law to go to her little son, saying, "Give me the boy, Jack. I will carry him up-stairs."

"What! drag up-stairs with this heavy boy? Nonsense!" says the captain.

Whereupon Freddy wakes, rubs his eyes, is a little cross at first, after the fashion of sleepy children, but finally says good-night to all and goes off, his little hand clasped in his mother's.

"Here is some one else asleep too!" says Katrine, as she passes the general, who is sitting with his arms crossed and his head sunk on his breast.

"Can you tell me, Jack, whether mummies ever have the rheumatism?" she asks. "Indeed, you had better waken him. I will have the whist-table set out.—And you, sweetheart," she says to Stella, "might unpack your music and sing us something."

While Stella amiably rises to go with her aunt, and the Baroness makes ready to follow them, murmuring that she must unpack the music herself, or her manuscripts will be all disarranged, Stasy turns to Rohritz:

"What do you say to it all? Did you ever hear such talk from a well-born girl? Such a conversation! Some allowance, to be sure, must be made for her."

But Rohritz simply murmurs, "Poor girl!"

"Yes, she is greatly to be pitied; her training has been deplorable!" sighs Stasy, and then, lowering her voice a little, she adds, "The colonel——"

"What Meineck was he?" Rohritz interrupts her, impatiently. "There are four or five in the army,—sons of a field-marshal, if I am not mistaken. Was he in the dragoons or the Uhlans?"

"Franz Meineck, of the —— Hussars," says Jack.

"The one, then, who distinguished himself at Solferino and got the Theresa cross?" Rohritz asks.

"The same," replies the captain.

"I do not know why I imagined that it must have been Heinrich Meineck. It was Franz, then." He adds, with some hesitation, "I did not know him personally, but I have heard a great deal of him. He must have been a charming officer and a delightful comrade, besides being one of the bravest men in the army——"

"He was particularly distinguished as a husband," Stasy exclaims, with her usual frank malice.

"We will not speak of that, Fräulein Stasy," says the captain. "My sister's marriage was certainly an insane, overwrought affair, and Franz gave his wife abundant cause for leaving him; but of the two lives his was the ruined one."

CHAPTER V.

AN EXPERIMENT.

YES, of the two lives the colonel's was the ruined one; wherefore, in spite of all the evident and great fault on his side, the sympathies of every one were in his favour,—that is, of all his fellows who knew life and the world, and who were ready to give their regard and their sympathy to men as they are, instead of, like certain great philosophers, reserving their entire store of commiseration for those exquisitely correct creatures, men as they should be.

When they made each other's acquaintance in Lemberg at Lina's father's, General Leskjewitsch's, Franz Meineck was twenty-six and Lina Leskjewitsch thirty-two years old. Nevertheless the world—the world that was familiar with these two people—wondered far more at her fancy for him than at his falling a prey to her fascinations.

She had from her earliest years been an exceptionally interesting girl, and a position as such had always been accorded her without any effort on her part to obtain it, for in spite of all her whims and eccentricities no one could detect in her a spark of affectation or pretension. She was altogether too indifferent to what people said of her ever to pose for the applause of the crowd. Her egotism, fed as it was by the homage of those around her, led her to yield to the prompting of every caprice, and since she was very beautiful, and could be excessively fascinating when she chose,—since, moreover, her father held a distinguished office under government,—she was dubbed original and a genius where other girls would have been condemned as eccentric and unmaidenly.

Always keenly alive to intellectual interests, she was, by the time she had reached her twenty-fifth year, a confirmed blue-stocking; she studied Sanskrit, and was in correspondence with half the scientific men in Europe. Moreover, she was by no means 'sicklied o'er with the pale cast of thought,' but full of wit and spirit. She swam like a fish, venturing alone far out upon river or lake, and rode with the boldness of a trained equestrian, without even a groom as escort. She had always disdained to dance; at the only ball she had ever been induced to attend she had been merely an on-looker. She could not comprehend how there could be any pleasure in dancing, she remarked, with a contemptuous glance towards the whirling couples: it was either ridiculous, or childish, or else positively disgusting.

Her contempt for love-making was as pronounced as for dancing. The homage of the young exquisites of society bored her inexpressibly; it was absolutely odious to her. She often boasted that in her life she had had but three loves,—Buonaparte, Lord Byron, and Machiavelli.

All her acquaintance, more especially the feminine portion of it, were astounded when a report was suddenly circulated that she was smitten with Franz Meineck, a simple, fair-haired hussar, with nothing to recommend him save his handsome face and his fine chivalric bearing.

It was easy to see what attracted him in her,— her rich brunette beauty, and, in strange contrast with it, the cold, defiant bluntness of her air and manner, the nimbus of originality that surrounded her, the fact that towards all other men her indifference was well-nigh discourtesy, while to him she was amiability itself. But what she, she of all girls in the world, could find to attract her in him,—this was what puzzled the brains of all the wiseacres in Lemberg.

But that he pleased her no one could deny, least of all she herself. Once, after a dinner at which Meineck had been her neighbour, a very cultivated and interesting friend asked her how she could possibly find any entertainment in that superficial hussar. She replied, with a shrug, that she found it much more amusing to hear a superficial hussar talk than to see a distinguished philosopher masticate his food, which according to her experience was the only entertainment afforded by great scientific lights at a dinner.

While, however, Meineck's love for her was, from the very beginning, of an enthusiastic, passionate nature, the inclination she felt for him was at first very gentle in character.

For her he was but a child; the idea that her relations with him could end in marriage would have seemed more mad and improbable to her than to any one else. Her demeanour towards him was always friendly; she would rally him good-humouredly, and anon treat him with a kindliness that was almost maternal. There was nothing in her manner to suggest her being in love with him.

Towards the end of February, when some treacherously mild weather heralded, as all prophesied, a cold windy March, Lina allowed her youthful adorer to be her escort in long rides on horseback. Here he was in his element, and greatly her superior in spite of her Amazonian skill. It was after one of these expeditions, when she reached home with eyes sparkling and cheeks slightly flushed, that she suddenly had an attack of terror. She knew that, accustomed as she had been for so long to absolute freedom, she must sooner or later find any fetters galling; she did not wish to marry.

The next day, without informing any one save her nearest of kin of her intention, she left Lemberg and retired to a small estate near Prague, where after her independent fashion she was often wont to stay for months alone with an old gardener and her maid.

It was a pretty, romantic spot, formerly a mill. A venerable weeping-willow stood beside it, its branches trailing above the antiquated mansard roof; a little brook rippled past it, gurgling and sobbing between banks of forget-me-nots and jonquils on its way to the larger stream. In this particular March, however, jonquils and forget-me-nots were still sleeping soundly beneath the snow, and the brook was silent. The February prophets were right: March was terribly cold. Long icicles hung from the eaves of the mill, almost reaching its windows, and the weeping-willow was clad in a fairy-like robe of glistening snow.

Lina sat from morning until evening like a kind of feminine Doctor Faust among bookcases, retorts, and globes in a spacious, dreary room, trying to work and longing ' to recover herself.' Then one day Meineck made his appearance at the mill. She received him with a great show of gay indifference, sitting at her writing-table and playing with her pen by way of intimating that any prolongation of his visit was undesirable. He perceived this. Embarrassed, confused by the sight of the scientific apparatus that surrounded him on all sides, he sat leaning forward, his sabre between his knees, in an arm-chair from which he had been obliged to remove a Greek lexicon and two volumes of the 'Revue,' and stammering all sorts of childish nonsense while he gazed at her with adoring eyes. She wore a perfectly plain gown of dark-green cloth fitting her like a riding-habit, and her hair, which curled naturally, was combed back behind her ears and cut short. He found this mode of dressing her hair charming, and his heart throbbed fast as he noted the magnificent fall of her shoulders. In his eyes she was incomparably beautiful; hers was the majestic loveliness of the unattainable. He often saw her thus afterwards in his dreams, and in his death-agony her image hovered before him again, noble, undefaced, as it was impressed upon his heart at this interview.

Later on he wondered how he found courage to speak, but—he found it. He sued for her hand, he wooed her passionately with words that could not but move her. She refused him. He would not accept her refusal. She stood her ground bravely, frankly confessing to him that it cost her an effort to repulse him, but that she must do it to insure the peace of mind of both. Apart from her dislike of resigning the freedom of her existence, she thought it unprincipled to give heed to the pleading of a poor exaggerated lad who was led away in a moment of romantic enthusiasm to offer his hand to a woman so much his elder.

There were such full, warm, cordial tones in her deep voice! Sight and hearing failed him. He knelt before her, kissed the hem of her garment, and promised at last to be content for the present if she would allow him to speak again at the end of six months. By that time it would be manifest that his love was not merely momentary romantic enthusiasm.

She laid her beautiful slender hands upon his shoulders, and said, kindly, "Dear lad, if after six months you are still so insane as to covet an elderly bride, we will discuss the matter again. And now adieu!"

He pressed his lips upon her hand so passionately that she suddenly withdrew it, and the colour mounted to her cheeks; he had never seen them flush so before. His eyes fathomed the depths of her own: she turned her head away.

"*Au revoir!*" he said, and withdrew, bowing gravely and profoundly.

There was something of triumph in the rhythm of his retreating footsteps; at least so it seemed to her as she listened to the sound as it died away in the distance. He walked as though his feet were shod with victory. Indignation possessed her. Her strong nature defended itself vigorously against the influence of this beguiling insidious force which had taken captive her heart and threatened to subdue her reason. In vain! The hand which his lips had pressed burned, and suddenly there glided through her veins, dreamily, lullingly, a something inexpressibly sweet, something she had never experienced before,—a delicious yet paralyzing sense of weariness. She started, and sat upright; then, gathering together the papers on her writing-table, she tried to work. In vain! The pen dropped from her fingers. She rose hastily and went to take a long walk. Her feet sank deep in the melting snow; the air was warm, and the south wind rustled among the trees and shrubbery, whispering mysteriously along the crackling surface of the frozen brook. Her weariness increased; she had to retrace her steps.

She went to bed earlier than usual that evening, and tried to think of grave subjects; but sweet, long-forgotten melodies haunted her heart and brain: she could not think; and at last she fell asleep to the sound of that fairy-like music within her soul.

In the middle of the night she awoke. The

moon shone through her window directly upon her bed. She listened. What sound was that? A merry uproar like the triumphal note of spring— the swift rushing of the brook—ascended to her windows. The ice was broken.

And in slow, monotonous cadence the falling of the drops from the melting snow on the roof struck upon her ear.

" Ah," she sighed, " the spring has come !"

*   *   *   *   *   *   *

He constantly wrote her letters full of chivalric fire and enthusiastic devotion. She never answered them. Then the war of 1859 broke out. One of her brothers informed her that Meineck had had himself transferred from the show-regiment—one but little adapted to service in the field—to which he had hitherto belonged to another which had been ordered to the front. A short time afterwards she received from the young hussar the following note :

" In spite of the horror with which the loss of life inseparable from every campaign inspires me, I rejoice in the war. I rejoice in the opportunity of proving to you at last that I am worth something in the world. Grant me one favour: send me a line or two, or only a curl of your hair, or some little trinket that you have worn,—anything belonging to you that I can take with me into action. I kiss your

dear hands, and am, as ever, with profound esteem
and intense devotion,

"Your   F. Meineck."

She clasped her hands before her face and sobbed
bitterly. And she, who all her life long had jeered
at such sentimentality, cut off one of her curls, enclosed it in a small golden locket, and sent it to
him with the following words:

"Dear lad,—

"You burden me with a great responsibility.
There was no need for you to plunge neck and
heels into this campaign to prove to me that you
were worth something. I send you herewith the
trifle for which you ask: may it carry a blessing
with it! God bring you safe home, is the earnest
prayer of your faithful friend,

"Karoline Leskjewitsch."

June passed. The earth languished beneath the
burning sun. Pale, feverish, and sleepless, Karoline
Leskjewitsch dragged through the endless summer
days, scraping lint,—she felt unfit for any other occupation,—and reading with hot, dry eyes the lists
of the dead and wounded.

One day she found his name in the list of the
dead. She was crushed, utterly annihilated. A few
hours afterwards, however, she received a letter

from her brother, stating that the report of Meineck's death was a mistake; he was in Venice,
severely wounded. She could not tell how it was,
but on the same evening, almost without luggage,
without telling any one of her plans, she started
off with her old maid, and two days later arrived
in Venice and was conducted by her brother to the
room where the wounded man lay.

Pale, wasted, with dishevelled hair and sunken
features, he lay back among the pillows. Too
weak to stir, he could only greet her with a bliss-
ful smile.

She wore a black Spanish hat with large nodding
feathers. As she entered she took it off, and, going
to his bedside, she said, " I did not come merely to
see you, but as a Sister of Charity, and I shall stay
with you until you are well again."

He replied, in a voice so weak as to be scarce
audible, "To make me well a single word will
suffice : say it !"

She hesitated for a moment, and then, stooping
over him, she pressed her lips to his.

Who that saw them together ten years later could
have believed it ? No marriage was ever more romantic than theirs at first. His case was considered
hopeless. The two physicians whom she questioned
as to his condition declared his recovery impossible.
Resolutely setting aside all opposition, she was married to him immediately, that she might nurse him

devotedly and be enabled to support him in the dark hour of the death-struggle.

At the end of ten weeks the physicians acknowledged that they had been mistaken. Not only was he out of danger, but he had well-nigh recovered his former strength and vigour. Early in October the pair took their wedding-trip to Bohemia. In matters of sentiment Franz was a poet to his finger-tips, and he scorned the idea of the usual journey with his bride from one hotel to another. They spent their honeymoon in the old mill at Zalow.

On many a fresh, dewy, autumnal morning the peasants saw the two tall figures strolling through the forest where the leaves were rapidly falling. She who had hitherto carried herself so erect now walked with bent head and with shoulders slightly bowed, as if scarcely able to bear the weight of her great happiness.

They would wander unweariedly about the country for hours: they ransacked all the old peasant dwellings for antiquities, and they chose the spot for their graves in a picturesque, romantic churchyard. And when the light faded and they returned home, they would sit beside each other in the twilight in the spacious room where he had wooed her, and where now all the literary and scientific apparatus had given place to huge bouquets of autumn flowers filling the vases in every corner. The bouquets slowly changed colour, the

cornflowers paled and the poppies grew black, in
the darkening night; and something like profound
melancholy would possess the lovers,—the sacred
melancholy of happiness. With her hand in his,
the wife would tell her husband of the mild March
night in which the joyous sobbing of the brook had
wakened her, calling to her that spring had come.

"Believe it or not, as you please," Meineck was
wont to say, often with a very bitter smile, in after-
years, "I am really that fabulous individual, hitherto
sought for in vain, the man who never, during the
entire period of his honeymoon, was bored for a
single quarter of an hour."

He took up his profession again; she would not
hear of his resigning from the army for her sake.
When he proposed it she clasped her arm tenderly
about his neck and said, "Inactivity would ill become you, and I want to be proud indeed of my
husband. I have but one duty now in life, to make
you happy," she gently added.

He was fairly dizzy with bliss. Was it possible,
he sometimes asked himself, that an angel had actually descended from heaven to nestle in his heart
and to conjure up for him a Paradise on earth?
Her caresses gained in value from the fact that she
was not so softly docile as other women, that now
and then he had to overcome in her a certain
acerbity and harshness.

"A woman and a horse must both be possessed

of amiable possibilities of obstinacy, or we take no pleasure in them," he declared.

She bloomed afresh after her marriage. Her features, which were rather marked, grew softer, and had the freshness of those of a girl of eighteen. Her hair, which at his request she allowed to grow, curled in soft rings about her brow. Every one noticed how very beautiful she had grown; and he too, they said, had gained much since his marriage. His moral and intellectual stand-point was loftier. She refused to have an interest which he did not share; she expended an immense amount of acuteness in discovering what would arrest his attention in whatever she was reading, and either repeated it to him or read it aloud.

The idea of playing the love-sick girl at her age was odious to her,—ridiculous; she wished to be his friend, his trusty comrade; but withal she spoiled him by a thousand delicate attentions far more than the youngest wife would have done. She exhausted her ingenuity in rendering his life delightful. She was not fond of going much into society; therefore she made his home attractive to his comrades. The entire regiment adored her, from the colonel to the youngest ensign. The women alone hated her. It was intolerable, they thought, that a blue-stocking should presume to eclipse them with the other sex.

What became of all this bliss? It vanished little

by little, as the snow slowly subsides, filtering into the ground.

*   *   *   *   *   *   *

"I know myself," she had said to him when he wooed her; "I know myself: my paralyzing weakness will pass away, as will your intoxication."

But his intoxication, after all, lasted longer than her weakness.

After they had been married about five years, their second daughter, Estella, was born. The mother's health was terribly undermined for a while. Franz surrounded her with the most loving care, but she no longer took any pleasure in it. The fitful, unnatural glow kindled so late in her heart slowly died away; her illusions faded, her passion cooled. Nothing was left of the young spring deity of her imagination who had roused her heart from its cold wintry sleep, save a good-humoured, ordinary man whose society offered her no attraction and whose tenderness wearied her.

Then came the campaign of '66. When he left her she contrived to shed a couple of tears, and during the fray in Bohemia her conscience pricked her terribly, but when the truce was proclaimed she was quite indifferent as to the length of his absence; it might have been prolonged *ad infinitum*, for all she cared. When he came home at the end of half a year his conscience was laden with a first infidelity. She had written an essay upon Don John of Austria.

From this moment the downward course was rapid.

If he could but have had a comfortable attractive home, he might perhaps have clung to it; he might have felt that he had something to live for, something to prevent, as he afterwards expressed it, his 'going to the devil.'

But he daily felt more and more of a stranger beneath his own roof, and his wife did nothing now to induce him to stay there; on the contrary, his presence bored her,—a fact which she did not always conceal.

For a little while he restrained himself, and then——

All the brutal instincts of his nature asserted themselves, and he took no pains to subdue them.

*   *   *   * .   *   *   *

One joy, however, was his all through this dreadful time,—his youngest daughter. He never took much pleasure in the elder of the two: she had inherited all her mother's caprice, without any of her talent.

But little Stella was indeed a darling.

When she was between one and two years old, at a time when his comrades, although but rarely, still met at his house at gay little suppers, he would go up to the nursery, where the child lay in bed, and if she happened to be awake and laughing at his approach he would take her in his arms just as she was in her little white night-gown and cap and carry her down-stairs to display her. She would obediently give her hand to every guest, but was not to be induced to unclasp the other arm from her father's neck. He petted and caressed her while his friends praised his pretty little daughter.

When she had grown larger, she was always the first to run to meet him on his return home from parade. Often in winter when his cloak was covered with snow she would shrink away with a laugh, exclaiming, "Oh, papa, how cold! I cannot touch you."

"Come here," he would say to her, and, opening his cloak, he would gather her up in his arms. "'Tis warm enough here, mouse, is it not?" And as she clung to him he would close the cloak about her, and she would thrust her hands through the opening in front and peep out, supremely happy.

She often remembered in after-years how delicious it had been to nestle against her father's broad chest, protected in the darkness, and look out into the world through a narrow crack.

He it was who gave her her first alphabet-blocks, more as a toy than by way of instruction. She ran after him continually to show him the words she had spelled out with them, taking especial delight in long learned expressions of which she did not understand a syllable. One of the first words she put together upon his writing-table as she sat upon his knee was 'phosphorescence.'

He laughed, and told the officers of it at the riding-school. Poor fellow! He was secretly ashamed of his wretched home and his matrimonial failure, as well as of the miserable part he played in his household. As he could not speak of anything else, he talked of his child.

*   *   *   *   *   *   *

His wife's article upon Don John of Austria appeared meanwhile in 'The Globe,' and, unfortunately, attracted considerable attention. One critic compared the author's brilliant style to that of Macaulay. ·From that moment she lost the last remnant of interest in her house and family.

The praise which her article received went to her head; she recalled how when a young girl she had been called a genius, and how it had been said that if she only chose to take the slightest pains she could excel George Sand as an author, Clara Schumann as a pianiste, and Rachel as an actress. Yes, if she only chose! Now she did choose. She tried her hand in every department of literature, devised plots for tragedies and romances, and wrote essays upon every imaginable social problem, without achieving any really finished or useful result. She herself was quite dissatisfied with her efforts, but she never ascribed their imperfection to any want of capacity, but always to the fact that the free flight of her fancy was cramped by her domestic cares. Possessed by the demon of ambition, she turned aside from everything that could absorb her time or hinder her in the mad pursuit of her chimera. Social enjoyment did not exist for her: she secluded herself entirely from society. If her husband wished to see his comrades he could find them at the club.

Her household went to ruin. It was long before Meineck ventured to remonstrate with his highly-gifted wife; but at last scarcely a day passed without crimination and recrimination between the pair. In spite of his faults and aberrations from the right path, he was exquisitely fastidious in his personal requirements and a martinet in his love of order; his wife's slovenly habits and the disorder of her household disgusted him.

"Good heavens! who," he sometimes asked, angrily, "could put up with such untidy rooms? —all the doors ajar, the drawers half open and their contents tossed in like hay; the servants dirty and ill trained, and the meals served in a way to destroy the finest appetite! Even the children are neglected."

There came at last to be terrible scenes, in which Meineck would shout and swear and now and then shatter to pieces some chair or ottoman that stood in his way, while his wife sat motionless at her writing-table, now and then uttering some cold, cutting phrase, her pen suspended over her paper, longing for the moment when she should be left alone ' to work.'

Yet at intervals there were still moments when she would seize the helm of her neglected household, would set things straight, and would preside in tasteful attire at a well-ordered table. Her inborn elegance upon such occasions could not but excite admiration, and for a few hours, sometimes for a couple of days, she would expend her talent upon what alone employed it worthily, in promoting the comfort of those about her.

Upon such occasions Meineck would torment himself with self-reproach, would take upon himself the entire fault of her shortcomings, and would, so far as she would permit him, show her the most devoted attention. Scarcely, however, did he begin to have faith in the sunshine when it vanished.

Moreover, these seasons of wondrous amiability on Karoline's part grew rarer and briefer,—particularly when she could not but acknowledge that her literary career by no means developed so brilliantly as she had hoped from the success of her Don John of Austria. She sought the cause of this, as has been said, not in the insufficiency of her own talent, but in the cramping nature of her domestic circumstances.

*　　*　　*　　*　·　　*　　*　　*

One evening—Stella was about eleven years old—Meineck came home intoxicated. Chance willed that both his wife and his daughters saw him in this condition.

The next day at the mid-day meal he was rather uncomfortable in their presence, and consequently talked more and faster than usual, assuming that air of bravado which some men are sure to adopt when they are particularly embarrassed. His affected self-possession vanished very soon, however. His wife merely bestowed upon him a cold greeting, and then entered into an absorbing conversation with Franziska, the elder daughter, upon some abstruse point of English law. She and the girl both avoided looking at him, and sat bolt upright, with virtuous indignation expressed in every feature.

He turned from them to his loving little Stella. She was sitting, pale and with downcast eyes, before an empty plate. Poor little Stella! she too had been affected by the scene of the evening before. What business was it of hers? Was he the only man in the world who had ever been so overcome? Was that chit to school him? For the first time in her life he spoke harshly to her: "What is the matter with you? Why do you not eat? Are you ill?" And, beckoning to the servant, he put something upon her plate.

She took up her knife and fork obediently, but she could not swallow a morsel, and the big tears fell upon her plate. He saw them perfectly well, although he pretended not to look at her.

When the others had retired and he sat alone at the comfortless board, his head leaning on his right hand, his left drumming a tattoo on the table, as he reflected upon his squandered life, suddenly a little arm stole around his neck and two tender childish lips were pressed to his temple. He started: it was Stella! He took her on his knee and covered her head, her neck, even her little hands, with kisses, and his tears fell upon her brow. Neither of them ever forgot that moment.

*   *   *   *   *   *   *

Soon after this the husband and wife agreed so far as to find their life together intolerable, and they parted by mutual consent. Of course the mother took the children; what could Meineck have done with them? The legal divorce, with which she threatened him if he did not accede to a voluntary separation, would undoubtedly have assigned them to her. He was to be allowed to spend two weeks of every year beneath her roof to see the children. These arrangements concluded, she set out for Florence to collect materials for a history of the Medici,—which she never wrote.

In the spring he went to her at Meran. His position in her household was so painful, however, that he did not stay all the allowed time: he felt disgraced even in his little Stella's eyes; she seemed estranged from him.

He never came to be with them again. He often sent his daughters beautiful presents, and wrote them long, affectionate letters, but he made no further attempt to see them.

Years passed. Meineck had risen to the rank of colonel; his wife meanwhile had tramped all over the map with her daughters, from Madrid to Constantinople, to collect historical material for all sorts of projected essays. She was now at her mill in Zalow, partly because her finances were at a low ebb, and partly because she intended at last to begin her great work. This work upon which she had settled definitively was 'The Part assigned to Woman in the Development of Universal History.'

Franziska, who, oddly enough, could no longer agree with her mother, was lodging in Prague with the widow of a government official who rented a few rooms to teachers and bachelors, and preparing herself in a bleak little apartment to pass her final examinations. Poor Stella, who had meanwhile shot up into a tall miss of eighteen, went to Prague by railway three times a week in summer and winter, always alone, to take lessons,—read everything she could lay hold of, from Milton's 'Paradise

Lost' to Hauff's 'Man in the Moon,'—and tramped about the country escorted by a very savage white wolf-hound.

It was in November, and the ground was covered with snow, when a letter arrived from the colonel in Venice to his wife and daughters. He had been ordered to a southern climate on account of an affection of the lungs which had not yielded to a course of treatment at Gleichenberg, and he had now been in Venice for a month. If his daughters would consent, the letter went on to say, to come to cheer his loneliness for a while, he would do his best to make their stay in Venice agreeable to them.

Franziska declared that she could not possibly interrupt her studies at this time; Stella announced that she was ready to set off on the instant. Her mother hesitated to allow her to travel alone, and looked about for a suitable escort for her, but Stella declared that she needed none. Had she not been to Prague continually alone by the railway? and where was the difference in going to Venice, except that it was farther off? Moreover, there were carriages for ladies only. It never occurred to this valiant young person, trained to economy as she had been by her learned mother, that she could travel otherwise than second-class.

Her mother enjoined it upon her not to waste her time in Venice, and instead of a luncheon stuffed a 'Histoire de Venise' into her travelling-bag. The girl bought her ticket, attended to her luggage herself, and then mounted cheerily into a much overheated railway-carriage and was borne away.

CHAPTER VI.

A RUINED LIFE.

How she rejoiced in the prospect of seeing him again, looking forward to the joy of nestling tenderly in his arms and telling him how she had longed for him during the many, many years, and how she had lain awake many a night telling herself stories of him,—that is, recalling every little incident in her memory with which he was connected!

She did not recall him as she had last seen him, old before his time, with dark rings around his bloodshot eyes and deep wrinkles at the corners of his mouth, gray and worn; no, she saw him with fair curls and a merry, kindly look, sometimes in his dazzling hussar-uniform, but oftener in his blue undress-coat with breast-pockets. She could not possibly call him up in her memory without an accompaniment of the rattle of spurs and sabre.

She saw his shapely, carefully-tended hands; she distinctly remembered the fragrance of Turkish tobacco, mingled with the odour of jasmine, with which all his belongings were saturated.

For her he was always the brilliant young officer who had muffled her in his cloak when she ran to meet him.

How long the journey seemed to her at first! Then she was suddenly assailed by a strange timidity: when the conductor took her ticket and announced that the next station was Venice she began to tremble.

The train stopped; the conductor opened the door. With her heart throbbing up in her throat, she looked out, but saw no one whom she knew. No, her father had evidently not come to meet her! Could he have failed to receive her telegram? She noticed a gray-haired man in civilian's dress, with a crush-hat, and delicately chiselled features wasted by illness, and large hollow eyes, peering about as if he were looking for some one. A cold, paralyzing pang shot through her: his look met her own. While he had lived in her memory as a brilliant young officer, she had always been for him the undeveloped child of twelve, with tightly-stretched red stockings, and a short shapeless gown,—something that could be taken on his lap and caressed. But this daughter advancing towards him was a young lady, who could pass judgment upon him, a judgment that could not be bribed, like that of a child, by caresses. He asked himself, with a shudder, how much she knew of his life, and whether she were capable of forgiving it, forgetting, in his dread, that a woman will forgive everything in the man whom she loves, be he husband, brother, or father, save cowardice and dishonour,—and as far as regarded the *point d'honneur* the colonel's worst enemy could find nothing of which to accuse him.

"Papa!"

"Stella!" Instead of clasping her in his arms, he kissed her hand. "How are they all at home?" he asked, embarrassed. "Is your mother well? and Franzi?"

"Oh, yes! They both gave me all sorts of kind messages for you. Franziska, unfortunately, could not come with me, for she could not interrupt her studies at this time."

What frightfully correct German she spoke! Had they robbed him of his little Stella? His annoyance increased.

"Where is your maid?" he asked.

"Maid? I have none. Oh, we have not had a maid for a long time."

"You came all the way alone?" the colonel exclaimed, in dismay,—" all alone?"

"Yes. You have no idea how independent and practical I am."

The colonel frowned; he would rather have found his daughter spoiled and helpless; but he said nothing, only asked about her luggage to hand it over to the porter of the Hotel Britannia, and then offered her his arm to conduct her to the gondola which was waiting for them. Arrived at the hotel, they got into the elevator to be taken to the third story, and they had as yet scarcely exchanged three words with each other.

The pretty little *salon* into which he conducted her looked out upon the Grand Canal and past the church of Santa Maria della Salute upon the Lido. The room was pleasantly warm, and in the centre a table was invitingly spread, the teakettle singing merrily, flanked by a flask of golden Marsala and a bottle of Bordeaux. A prismatic ray of sunshine fell across the neat creases of the snowy table-cloth.

" Oh, how delightful !" cried Stella, and her eyes sparkled, while in her delicate and softly-rounded cheek appeared the dimple for which her father had hitherto looked in vain.

" I had a little breakfast made ready for you, thinking that you might perhaps have had nothing very good to eat upon your journey," said he.

" I have eaten nothing since I left home but biscuit, because I disliked going to the railway restaurants," she declared.

And the colonel rejoined, " *Tiens !* not entirely a

strong-minded female yet, I see," and as he spoke he helped her take off her long brown paletot. "If I am not mistaken," he said, examining the clumsy article of dress, "this is an old army-cloak."

"Indeed it is, papa," she replied, proudly,—"one of your old cloaks: I had it altered by our tailor in Zalow, because it reminds me of old times." And this was all she could bring herself to say of the myriad charming and loving phrases she had prepared. "It is a great success, my coat. Do you not like it?" she asked.

"Candidly, no," he made reply. "Nevertheless I am greatly obliged to it for proving to me that, even in the clumsiest and ugliest garment ever devised by human hands to disfigure one of God's creatures, my daughter is still charming."

She cast down her eyes with a little blush and was suddenly ashamed of her threadbare adaptation of which she had been so proud. Kindly, but still with some hesitation, he put his hand upon her shoulder and said, "You will let me look a little more closely at my daughter."

A warm wave of affection suddenly surged up in her heart.

"Do not look at me, papa; only love me," she exclaimed, and, throwing her arm around his neck, she nestled close to him. "You cannot imagine how rejoiced I was to come to you."

And the poor wretch reverently bent his sad, weary head above his child's golden curls, and repentantly acknowledged to himself that he had not deserved so great mercy.

*   *   *   *   *   *   *

When daylight had faded and the lanterns at the base of the old palaces flared up, casting reddish reflections to break and glimmer upon the surface of the lagunes, the colonel lit the lamp and put paper and writing-materials upon the table before Stella.

" Write a few lines to your mother, my darling, and thank her for sending you to me." Then, while Stella was writing, he sat opposite to her for a while in silence, his head thoughtfully leaning on his hand. At last he began: " Stella, I have an impression that you live now in a very modest way at home. Do you know the state of your mother's finances ?"

" Low," said Stella, laconically.

" Hm ! I really do not know how much is necessary to maintain two daughters; perhaps I do not send her enough for you. She ought to have let me know. I do not wish that my children should be pinched, as—as——"

" As they seem to be from the looks of my shabby wardrobe," Stella said, with a laugh. " Well, we are not quite so badly off, after all. If it be a question of buying books or curios, we can always

scrape the money together; but if one wants a pair
of new boots, the purse is empty."

The colonel tugged discontentedly at his moustache.

"I beg you to write to Franzi and ask her if she
needs money," he began afresh. "I am, to be sure,
living now upon my capital, but your share is secured to you, and I shall not last long."

At first his meaning escaped her; she gazed at
him with wide eyes; then, as she comprehended at
last, the pen fell from her fingers, and she burst into
a flood of tears.

"Hush, hush, my darling; do not torment yourself beforehand. Perhaps I describe my condition
to you as worse than it really is," he said, leaning
tenderly over her, and, putting his hand beneath
her chin, he looked deep into her dark eyes. "If
sunshine can make a man well I am all right."

*   *   *   *   *   *   *

No, it was too late,—too late! His physical
strength could never be restored, his lungs nothing could heal; but with his child beside him his
soul and heart gained health and strength. Since
those first fair years of his married life, he had
never been so happy as now, although he seldom
quite forgot that he stood on the brink of the
grave.

Once, on a damp muggy November evening in
a Viennese suburb he had seen a drunkard stag-

gering along the wall in a narrow street, quite unable to find his way. A policeman was just about to take him into custody, when a little girl, muffled in rags and with a pale wizened face, suddenly appeared beside him out of the darkness, seized him by his red, trembling, swollen hand, and called in a hoarse, anxious voice, without impatience or harshness, but not without authority, 'Father, come home!' And the drunkard, who had paid no heed to the jeers of the passers-by, nor to the admonition of the policeman, hung his head, and without a word followed the weak, helpless little creature like a lamb. The colonel had stood and looked after them until the darkness swallowed them up. He recalled distinctly the girl's thin yellow braids, her long chin, the sordid red-and-black plaid shawl which she wore about her shoulders, and the worn old laced boots, far too big for her little feet and coming half-way up her naked little blue legs, and continually in her way as she walked.

The little episode had made a painful impression upon him for a time, and then he had forgotten it. Now it arose in his memory, but transfigured, and as, clasping his daughter's hand, he went on to his grave, he compared himself in his secret soul with the drunkard led home by the child.

*　　*　　*　　*　　*　　*　　*

He was very ill. Unaccustomed to spare himself, and without any real pleasure in life, he had increased his malady by months of entire want of care and nursing, until his physicians had insisted that a summer should be spent at a sanitarium in Gleichenberg. Partially restored, he had immediately, in direct opposition to all advice, re-entered the service. The autumn manœuvres had brought on an inflammation of the lungs. How very ill he was never entered his mind, in spite of his speech to Stella. He thought he should live a couple of years longer, and his great dread was lest he should be pensioned off before the time because of his invalid condition. The pains that he took to maintain an upright military bearing aggravated all the evils of his case.

There were a number of distinguished Austrians in the Hotel Britannia, some few of them invalids, most of them gay and pleasure-loving and well pleased to spend a few weeks amid picturesque surroundings and in pleasant society. The colonel was beloved by all, and they eagerly welcomed his pretty daughter,—even the ladies, whom the colonel consulted as to the necessary reform in the girl's wardrobe. She sat with her father in the midst of them all at the upper end of the table, the lower end, where the other inmates of the hotel were crowded together, being the subject of much merry scorn and stigmatized as 'the menagerie.' Compassion for the daughter of the

dying man deepened the sympathy called forth by
the young girl's grace and charm. Old gentlemen
rallied her upon her conquests, and the young
men paid her devoted attention. She had a special
friend in the handsome black-eyed prince Zino
Capito, who had an unusual share of time to bestow upon her since the latest mistress of his affections, the famous Princess Oblonsky, had just departed for Petersburg to take possession of the
effects of her husband, suddenly deceased. He
daily sent Stella magnificent flowers with which
to adorn the hotel apartments for her father.
"Invalids are so fond of flowers," he would say,
with a smile that displayed his brilliant white
teeth. And when the weather was fine and the
colonel felt well enough, he would invite them to
take a sail in his cutter upon the blue Adriatic.

The colonel often spoke of his wife, longing to
see her. The last *liaison*—that which had been the
cause of a definite separation between himself and
his wife, had robbed him of his self-respect, had disgraced him in his children's eyes, and had snatched
from him every vestige of peace of mind—had
dissolved itself more than two years before. The
recollection of it disgusted him, but, like all men
who have no future, he gladly allowed his thoughts
to stray into the distant past. The wife from whom
he had parted, elderly, learned, with her slovenli-
ness and irritability, he had forgotten; his memory

f

preserved the bride, in her light dress, bending above his couch of pain; he saw her on his marriage-day in the flood of sunlight which streaming through the tall window of his sick-room invested with a glorious halo the golden cross upon the improvised altar.

One sunny day, as he was sailing in the Grand Canal in a gondola with Stella, he pointed to a beautiful old palazzo.

"There is where I lay wounded in '59, when your mother came to nurse me. Those windows there were mine."

In the evening of the same day, while Stella was writing to her mother and he lay half dozing on a lounge, he suddenly said, "Stella, do you think your mother could make up her mind to come to Venice with Franzi for a few weeks? She need not be in the same house with us, if that would bore her, but—— Tell her how much it would please me to see her; and," he added, with an embarrassed smile, "tell her I am really very ill: perhaps that may induce her to come."

He awaited the reply to this letter with feverish eagerness. In a week there arrived a package of rather insignificant notices of a work of his wife's, just published at her own expense; two weeks later the answer to the letter appeared.

"Well, what does your mother say?" asked the colonel, as he observed Stella deciphering the almost illegible document. "Read it aloud to me," he insisted : "you know everything that goes on at home interests me. Is she coming ?"

But Stella, with tears in her eyes, and a burning blush, stammered, "A letter must have been lost. This one never even mentions our plan !"

The colonel turned away and looked out of the window at the East India steamship.

" 'Tis a pity !" he sighed, in an undertone, after a while. "I should have liked to ask her forgiveness."

*   *   *   *   *   *   *

Although upon Stella's arrival, when he felt better, he had spoken continually and with apparent satisfaction of his approaching death, from the time when he began to decline rapidly he avoided all reference to his condition. The doctor visited him daily, sometimes oftener, and would drink a glass of sherry with him while recounting his brilliant exploits in the way of restoration to health of patients whose condition was even worse than the colonel's. But after a while he grew less confident, and at last towards the end of April he proposed an operation for the relief of the lungs. The colonel eyed him fixedly, and sent Stella out of the room.

"How long a time do you give me ?" he asked. "Be frank. I am a soldier, and not afraid to die."

"Under the circumstances, a couple of months."

" I understand. Say nothing to my daughter, but let matters take their course. It is all right."

That evening he sat writing for an hour, never stirring from his writing-table. Suddenly he grew restless, and ended by tearing up what he had written.

" Stella, come here !" he called; and as she came to him, " Don't cry, darling,—it distresses me so that I lose my wits; and I need them all. I wanted to write out my will; but it is useless. Your little property is secure, and you must divide the rest: I cannot show you any partiality. It is terrible to think of dying here, but, if it must be, do not leave me in Venice, in a strange country. Bury me near you in Zalow,—your mother knows the spot; she will bear with me in the churchyard." He took a little golden locket from his breast-pocket. " Take care of that," he said : " it is the locket your mother sent me in the campaign of '59, and she must hang it around my neck before they lay me in the grave. Beg her to do this. Do you understand, Stella ?"

She sat opposite him at the little round table, very pale, but perfectly upright and without a tear, just as he would have had her.

" Yes, papa."

*   *   *   *   *   *   *

The next day was her birthday.

He gave her a golden bracelet to which was attached a crystal locket containing a four-leaved clover.

"I cannot show you any partiality in my will," said he, "but wear that for my sake, darling. And if ever heaven sends you some great joy, say to yourself that your poor father prayed the dear God that it might fall to your share!"

*   *   *   *   *   *   *

One day the colonel received a letter bearing a Paris post-mark which seemed to depress him greatly. All day after receiving it he was thoughtful and taciturn. In the evening he wrote a long letter, pausing from time to time to cough sadly. As he folded it, Stella observed that he enclosed money in it. After apparently reflecting for a while, he drew from a case in his pocket a photograph of Stella which had been taken in Venice, gazed at it lovingly for a moment, seemed to hesitate, and finally enclosed it also in the envelope with the letter. Looking up, he became aware of his daughter's curious gaze, and suddenly grew confused. He sealed his epistle with unnecessary care, and then all at once reached both hands across the table and clasped Stella's between them, saying,—

"You are wondering to whom I am sending my darling's picture? To my youngest sister, your aunt Eugenie. Do you remember her? Yes? You used to love her, did you not?"

"Very much, papa; but—I thought she was dead."

The colonel turned away his head; after a moment he drew Stella towards him, and said, softly, "She is not dead: I cannot tell you about her,—do not ask me. But—do not be hard to her, and if you should ever meet her, speak a kind word to her, for my sake."

*　　*　　*　　*　　*　　*　　*

He still went daily below-stairs in the lift to take his meals, but he now dined at a small table alone with Stella, after the *table-d'hôte* in the spacious, lonely dining-hall. His frequent attacks of coughing made him shun society. He dreaded annoying others.

"I am no longer fit to mingle with my kind, Stella," he would say. "My poor little butterfly, it is tiresome to have such a father, is it not?"

She, apparently, did not find it so. She desired nothing beyond the privilege of taking care of him, although she could be little more than a weak, helpless child. By day she cheered him with her lively talk, and at night if he stirred she was beside his bed in an instant in her long dressing-gown, her little bare feet thrust into slippers, supporting him in her arms if he coughed. Outside the moon shone full above the church of Santa Maria della Salute. Up from the garden was wafted the odour of roses and syringas, while above the swampy atmosphere of the lagunes, and mingling with the plash of waters at the base of the old palaces, floated sweet, sad melodies,—the songs of the evening minstrels of Venice,—

"Vorrei baciar i tuoi capelli neri,"

and

"Penso alla prima volta in cui volgesti
Lo sguardo soave in sino a me !"

Sometimes she would fall asleep sitting beside his bed, her head resting on his pillow.

*   *   *   *   *   *   *

She grew to look like a shadow, so pale and worn did she become. He did all that he could to prevent her from coming to him at night, even threatening to employ a nurse, but the threat was never fulfilled.

In fact, he needed very little care but such as her affection insisted upon giving him; he was never confined to bed, only grew more and more inclined to rest on a lounge during the day. He was very thoughtful of others, and required but little service at their hands up to the very last, only seldom demanding any assistance in dressing. He grew nervous and restless, longed for change, yearned for his home with the fervent desire of a dying man. Before his mental vision hovered the picture of the old mill, with its old-fashioned garden, the small sparse forest with feathery underbrush at the foot of the knotty oaks, and the gray waters of the stream that wound through the autumn mist between bald stony banks. He felt an insane desire to see it all once more. For a long time he endured this yearning in silence, not venturing to express it; his wife had repulsed all advances of his too decidedly. But, good heavens! he needed so little room, he would not trouble her much; and then, besides, he was an old man, ill unto death: his demands upon her personally were restricted to a kind word now and then, a sympathetic pressure of the hand!

Meanwhile, he grew worse and worse. Other complications heightened the peril in which he stood from the original disease. He complained that he could no longer endure the food at the hotel. His physician, who, like all physicians at health-resorts, avoided as far as possible the annoyance of having his patients die on his hands, strongly advised a change of air.

Utterly dejected, his face turned away from her, the dying man begged Stella to ask her mother if he might come home.

But Stella had already asked, and shortly afterwards an answer was received. The Baroness wrote that now, as ever, she was prepared to do her duty,—to receive him, and take care of him. The mill was always open to him.

How he rejoiced in the prospect of home! He tried to help in the packing, but he was too languid. From his lounge he looked on while Stella managed it all, and now and then with a smile he would call her to him, only to stroke her hands and look into her dear, loving eyes.

At last they set out. It was Easter Monday, in the latter half of April; the bells were all ringing solemnly, and dazzling sunshine lay upon the dark waters of the lagunes.

All their acquaintance at the hotel surrounded the father and daughter as they stepped into their gondola. The little vessel was filled with flowers, farewell tokens to Stella, and from the balconies of the hotel many a white kerchief waved adieu to the travellers.

*   *   *   *   *   *   *

At first they journeyed by short stages, sometimes taking a roundabout route for the sake of better lodgings at night, stopping at Villach and at Grätz. Then the colonel grew anxiously eager to be at home; he could no longer restrain his impatience. From Grätz he insisted upon making one journey of it, during which they had to change conveyances frequently. Every one was kind, showing all manner of attention, to the sick man and his pretty, loving, tender daughter. With every hour he became more weak and miserable. The last change they made he could scarcely manage to descend from the railway-carriage: two porters were obliged to help him into the other coupé.

It was one of those first-class half-coupés for three occupants. Stella had not been able to procure for him, as hitherto, an entire carriage, and we all know how deceptive is the ease of those half-coupés.

The girl propped her father up with rugs and cushions so that he found his position tolerable, and he fell asleep. The afternoon passed, and twilight came on. Greenish-yellow tints coloured the horizon, and a small white crescent gleamed above the darkening earth. Through the open window of the coupé came the warm, balmy air of the spring. Sometimes there mingled with the acrid, searching odour of the undeveloped foliage the full, sweet fragrance of some blossoming fruit-tree. A scarcely perceptible breeze swept gently and caressingly over the meadows, and lightly rippled the surface of the large quiet pond past which the train rushed. Here and there the level landscape was dotted by a village,—long barns and hay-ricks covered with blackened straw, grouped irregularly about some little church or castle among trees white with blossoms or pale green with opening leaf-buds.

The colonel slept on. Suddenly Stella perceived that she had lost her bracelet,—the one with the four-leaved clover. She moved with a sudden start. The colonel awoke.

"Where are we?" he asked.

"In an hour we shall be at home: it is only

three stations off," she said, soothingly, with a beating heart.

He bent his head, folded his hands, and prepared to wait patiently. But it was impossible: a deadly anguish assailed him. He looked round in despair like some trapped animal.

"I am ill!" he cried. "I cannot tell what ails me. I never felt so before!"

He coughed convulsively, but briefly, then tried to move the cushions so that his head might find a more comfortable resting-place.

"Take more room, papa; lay your head in my lap," Stella entreated, tenderly.

He did so. He laid his head on her knees, and, taking her hand in his, held it against his cheek. The feverish unrest which had hitherto throbbed throughout his frame subsided, giving place to a delicious desire to sleep. For the last time the vision rose upon his mind of the drunken father being led home by his little girl; then all grew indistinct. He dreamed; he thought he was staggering painfully through a bog, when some one took him by the hand and led him across a narrow bridge beneath which gleamed dark, slowly-flowing water. He looked down; it was Stella who was leading him, but Stella as a little three-year-old child, with her simple little white night-cap tied beneath her chin, her rosy little bare feet showing beneath the hem of her white night-gown.

The bridge creaked beneath him; he started and awoke.

"Are we at home?" he asked, scarce audibly.

"Almost, papa."

He pressed her hand to his lips.

The twilight deepened; a dark transparent mist seemed to veil the sky; the heavens showed as if through thin mourning crape; the broad shining edges of the ponds and pools were dim; the crescent moon grew brighter.

The train whizzed along faster than ever, swaying from side to side on the sleepers. Suddenly Stella felt her father start violently; then he heaved a brief sigh, like that which one gives when surprised by anything unexpectedly delightful, or when one is suddenly relieved of a heavy burden. Then all was quiet,—quiet,—still as death! She bent over him and listened. In vain! She felt his hand grow cold and stiff in her own. A sudden anguish took possession of her. She was afraid in the darkness. Meanwhile, the lamp in the coupé was lighted. Its crude, yellow light fell upon the colonel's face.

Was he asleep, or—— She held her own breath to listen for his. Her heart beat as though it would break; no longer able to control her distress, she called, "Papa!" then louder, "Papa! Papa!" He did not answer.

The night-moths fluttered in through the open

window and circled about the lamp; the fragrance of the blossoming cherry-trees filled the air; a cracked church-bell in the distance hoarsely tolled the Ave Maria.

In an undertone Stella prayed 'Our Father;' but in the midst of it she burst into a convulsive fit of sobbing: she stroked and caressed the cold cheeks, the thin gray hair, of the dead. She knew that before many minutes were over he would be taken from her, and with him everything dear to her in life.

Onward rushed the train. The fiery sparks flew like rain past the windows; there was a shrill whistle,—then a stop. The journey's end was reached.

*   *   *   *   *   *   *

Her mother and sister had come to the station to meet them. When the conductor opened the door, Stella sat motionless, her father's head resting upon her knees.

It was dark. The stars gleamed in the blue-black heavens.

Mute and pale as the dead, the Baroness walked with Franziska and Stella behind her husband's corpse the short distance between the station and the mill. Some awkwardness on the part of the bearers released one arm of the dead man, and the hand fell and trailed on the earth. With a quick impetuous movement his wife took it in her own, pressed the cold, dead hand to her lips, and held it clasped in hers the rest of the way.

They laid the body in the fresh, white bed, fragrant with lavender and orris, which had been prepared for the sick man in the corner room he had so loved, and in which the Baroness had placed a bouquet of white hawthorn in honour of his arrival.

Two candles were burning at the head of the bed.

Stella, who had, as it were, turned to marble, moving and speaking like an automaton, suddenly grew restless. She seemed to have forgotten something, and then looked for and found the locket which the colonel had given her for her mother, and which she had ever since worn around her neck. Very distinctly and monotonously she repeated the dying man's message and request as she handed the locket to her mother.

"He begs you will hang this around his neck before they lay him in the grave; and once he said he should have liked once more to ask your forgiveness."

The Baroness took the little case from her child's hand. She grew paler than ever, and her eyes were those of one startled by an inward vision of a long-forgotten past. The hawthorn shed a delicious fragrance; outside, the breeze of spring sighed among the weeping-willows, the brook gurgled and sobbed.

All in an instant the old, gray-haired woman's hands began to tremble violently.

"Leave me alone with him for a moment," she softly entreated; and Stella slipped away.

In the terrible week ensuing upon that wretched evening the Baroness treated Stella with an unvarying and altogether pathetic tenderness; in that week Stella learned to comprehend what an irresistible charm this woman had been able to exercise,—learned to understand how longing for her, even after years of separation, had gnawed at the heart of the dying man.

Then, to be sure, everything ran its old course, with the sole exception that the widow never uttered in the presence of her children one unkind word with regard to their father, but often alluded before them to his fine qualities.

CHAPTER VII.

A RAINY EVENING.

It has been raining all the afternoon,—it is raining still. The inmates of Erlach Court are house-bound. Freddy, because of disobedience, and in consequence of his sneezing thrice during the afternoon, has been sent to bed early and sentenced to a dose of elder-flower tea. His elders, instead of spending the evening, as usual, in the open air, are assembled in the drawing-room.

Stasy has for the twentieth time finished 'Paul and Virginia,' and is now devoting herself to another kind of literature, Zola's 'Joie de vivre,'—of course only that she may testify to the horror with which such a book must inspire her. Every few minutes she utters an indignant 'no!' in an undertone, or holds out the book to Katrine, one hand over her blushing face, with "That is really too bad!" Katrine, however, shows no inclination to participate in her horror; she waves the book aside, saying, "I do not care to read everything," and goes on crochetting at the afghan which is to be ready for Freddy's approaching birthday.

The Baroness Meineck, meanwhile, is playing chess, the only game which she does not despise, with the general; and the captain is idling.

Hitherto Stella has been singing to her own accompaniment, for the entertainment of the company, the pretty Italian songs she caught from the gondoliers on the Canal. She is still sitting at the piano, but she has stopped singing. Her slender hands touch the keys of the instrument, playing softly now and then a couple of bars from a Chopin mazourka, as she looks up at Rohritz, who, with both elbows on the top of the piano, leans towards her, talking.

" How interested Rohritz seems in his talk with Stella ! he is quite transformed," Leskjewitsch remarks.

"He must answer when he is addressed," Stasy rejoins, sharply, looking up from her ' Joie de vivre.'

" If he does not like to talk to the girl he can go away," the captain observes.   " She has not nailed him to the piano."

" He-he ! she nails him with her eyes.   Do you not see how she ogles him ?" Stasy replies, with a giggle.   " I wonder what he is telling her."

" He is talking of Mexico, and of the phosphorescence of the tropical seas," the captain says, curtly.

" Indeed ? nothing more sentimental and personal than that ? Since, then, it is not indiscreet, I think I will listen."   And, clapping to her book, Anastasia stretches her long thin neck to hear.

It is very quiet in the large apartment; except for the monotonous drip of the rain outside, and the click made by setting down the pieces on the chess-board, there is nothing to interfere with those who wish to listen to the conversation at the piano.

" Knowing only the poor little sparks which you have seen twinkling through our Northern ocean on warm September evenings, you can form no idea of the gleaming splendour of the tropical seas, Fräulein Meineck.   The nights I spent on the deck of the Europa on my Mexican voyage I never can forget," says Rohritz.

Stella, who has hitherto shown a genuine interest in all he has told her, suddenly assumes a whimsically wise air, and, striking a dissonant chord, asks, "How old were you then?"

"I really do not understand——" he remarks, in some surprise.

"Oh, there is no necessity for your understanding,—only for replying," she rejoins, very calmly.

"Twenty-four."

It is one of her peculiarities, the result of her desultory and imperfect training, that she often plunges into a discussion of topics which every well-trained girl should carefully avoid.

"Twenty-four," she repeats, thoughtfully; then, pursuing her inquiries, "And were you in love?"

He laughs in some confusion.

"You are putting me through an examination."

"I allow you the same privilege," she declares, magnanimously. "Your answer sounds evasive. Apparently you were in love. I merely wanted to know, that I might judge how large a percentage of romance I must deduct from your description. All things considered, I can no longer accord any genuine faith to your account of the phosphorescence of the tropical seas; when people are in love they see everything as by a Bengal light."

This sententious remark of course induces Rohritz to put the laughing inquiry, "Do you speak from experience, Baroness Stella?"

"Certainly," she replies, with a convincing absence of embarrassment. "I have been through it all with my sister: she saw her artillery-officer by a Bengal light, or she never would have left science in the lurch for his sake, for, heaven knows, he was just like all the rest, except that in addition—he played the piano. Just fancy! an artillery-officer playing the piano!—Wagner, of course! Two dogs and a cat of ours went mad at the sight. But Franzi assured me that her artillery-officer's touch reminded her of Rubinstein. So you see how trustworthy your descriptions are."

Rohritz laughs good-humouredly, then says, "Even if I admit that on board the Europa I still had a little touch of the disease you mention, I must maintain that the delirious period had passed."

"Hm! one thing more," says Stella, pursuing still more boldly the devious path upon which she has entered. "I must know this precisely. Were you in love with a married woman? *Un homme qui se respecte* is never in love except with a married woman,—at least in all the novels."

"Stella!" Stasy calls, horrified.

Even Rohritz, who has hitherto listened very patiently to Stella's nonsense, seems unpleasantly affected by this speech of hers. He looks penetratingly into the young girl's eyes, and becomes aware that he is gazing into depths of innocence.

Before he has time to say anything, Stasy calls out, in a shocked tone,—

"Stella, you are frivolous to a degree——"

Stella blushes crimson ; her eyes fill with tears ; she makes awkward little motions with her hands upon the keys, and plays a couple of bars from Thalberg's Étude in Cis-moll.

"Frivolous?—frivolous? But, Anastasia, I was only jesting," she murmurs, and, turning to Rohritz as if for protection, she adds, "It needed very little logic to guess that, for if you had been in love with a young girl there would have been no need for you to be unhappy and to go sailing about on tropical seas to distract your mind : you could simply have married her."　.

"But suppose the young girl would not have him ?" the captain asks, merrily.

Stella looks first at Rohritz, then at her uncle, and murmurs, "That never occurred to me."

A burst of laughter from the captain—laughter in which Katrine joins heartily and Stasy ironically—is the reply to this confession.

"Acknowledge the compliment, Rohritz ; come, acknowledge it," Leskjewitsch exclaims in the midst of his laughter.

But Rohritz maintains unmoved his serious, kindly expression of countenance.

"It is not given to even the greatest minds to contemplate all possible contingencies," he says, dryly.

The Baroness Meineck, absorbed in her game, has heard little, meanwhile, of what has been going on about her; she now suddenly remembers that it is incumbent upon her to attend to her daughter's training.

"I suppose you have been uttering some stupidity again, Stella," she observes, coldly; "you are incorrigible!"

"Poor mamma, she really is to be pitied," Stella sighs, her sense of humour asserting itself in spite of her; "she has no luck with her children. Her clever daughter *commits* stupidities, and her silly daughter *utters* them. Which is the worse?"

CHAPTER VIII.

A LOVE-AFFAIR.

IT rains the entire ensuing night, and far into the forenoon of the next day. The hollows worn in the stone pavement of the terrace are filled with water, and form little brown ponds. The buff-coloured castle has become orange-coloured, and looks quite worn with weeping. The lawns reek with moisture, and the Malmaison roses are pale and draggled. Drowned butterflies float on the surface of the pools, and fantastic wreaths of mist curl about the foot of the mountains on the farther side of the Save. No sun is to be seen amid the gray-brown rack of clouds.

At last the rain falls more slowly; the chirp of a bird makes itself heard now and then; a white watery spot in the gray skies shows where the sun is hiding; slowly it draws aside the veil from its beaming face, and between the torn and flying masses of cloud the heavens laugh out once more, blue and brilliant.

Tempted forth by the delightful change in the weather, Katrine, Stasy, and Stella venture out to take their daily bath in the Neuring. In its normal condition the Neuring is a clear, sparkling stream, flowing freely over its pebbly bed in constant angry attack upon diverse fragments of rock which look in magnificent disdain upon its impotent assaults. A bath in the current between the largest of these fragments of rock, where for the convenience of the bathers a stout pole has been fixed, is a great favourite among the delights of Erlach Court.

. One shore of the stream slopes, flower-strewn and verdant, nearly to the water's edge, and here stands a roughly-constructed bath-house, from which wooden steps lead down into the water.

Stella is sitting, in a very faded bathing-suit of black serge trimmed with white braid, on the lowest of these steps, gazing sadly into the stream.

"I certainly did behave with unpardonable stupidity yesterday," she says, twisting her golden hair into a thick knot and fastening it up at the back of her head with a rather dilapidated tortoise-shell comb.

"When do you mean?" asks Stasy. "At lunch, or in the evening, or early this morning?"

"Yesterday evening, in the drawing-room," Stella replies, somewhat impatiently.

"That talk with Rohritz was a little reprehensible," Katrine says, with a laugh.

"In your place, after having been guilty of such a breach of decorum, I could not make up my mind to look him in the face," Stasy declares.

She slips into the water before the others, and is now trying, holding by the pole between the rocks, to tread the waves. The water hisses and foams, as if resenting her trampling it down.

"Was it really so bad, Aunt Katrine?" Stella asks, changing colour.

Katrine leans towards her, gives her a kindly pat on the shoulder, lifts her chin caressingly, and says,—

"Well, your remarks were certainly not extraordinarily pertinent, but I hardly think that Rohritz took them ill. 'Tis hard to take things ill of such a pretty, stupid, golden butterfly as you."

With which Katrine cautiously sets her slender foot among the yellow irises and white water-lilies on the edge of the water.

" It was terrible, then,—it must have been terrible if even you thought it so!" says Stella, as the tears rush to her eyes, and drop into the stream at her feet.

" Don't be a child," Katrine consoles her : " the matter was of no great consequence."

" Certainly not," Stasy adds, rather out of breath from her exertions. " What he thinks can make no kind of difference to you, and he assuredly will not report elsewhere your very strange remarks. Probably they interest him so little that he will soon forget all about them."

"Come and take your bath; you are wonderfully averse to the water to-day," Katrine calls out to the girl, who still sits sadly upon the wooden step, lost in reflection. "Indeed you need not take your stupidity so much to heart: it would have been nothing at all, if there had not been rather an odd story connected with Rohritz's sudden voyage across the ocean."

" Ah !" exclaims Stella, paddling through the water to her aunt, who, clinging to the pole, is now enjoying the current. " Really, something romantic ?" she asks, curiously.

" There was nothing romantic in the affair save his way of taking it," Katrine says, with a dry smile, "and therefore the remembrance of this piece of his past may be particularly distasteful to him."

"Ah, but it was a married woman, was it not? Do tell me!" Stella entreats, burning with curiosity.

"No, Solomon," Katrine replies: "it was a young, unmarried woman, not so very young either, about twenty-six or twenty-seven, well born, a Baroness von Föhren, a Livonian with Russian blood in her veins, poor, ambitious, prudent, and just clever enough to entertain a man without frightening him. I saw her once, and but once, at the theatre; she was very beautiful, and I took an extraordinary dislike to her. I am always ready to applaud Judic in *opéra-bouffe*, and on *grand prix* day in the Bois it interests me exceedingly to observe the *dames aux camellias* through my opera-glass; but nothing in this world so disgusts me as demi-monde graces in a woman who ought to be a lady."

"I think you are a little severe in your judgment of Sonja. She was not irreproachable in her conduct," Stasy, who has for years maintained a kind of friendship with the person under discussion, here interposes,—"not irreproachable, but——"

In all that touches her extremely strict ideas of propriety and fitness, Katrine understands no jesting.

"Her conduct was not only 'not irreproachable,' it was revolting!" she exclaims. "If she interests you, Stella, I can show you her photograph; at one time you could buy it everywhere. She was

made to turn a young fellow's head. With regard
to women men really have such wretched taste."

"Oho, Katrine! That sounds as if you said it
par dépit," Stasy says, archly.

"I do not in the least care how it sounds,"
Katrine rejoins.

"Ah, tell me about Baroness Föhren," Stella
entreats.

"There is not much to tell. He had a love-affair
with her——"

"A love-affair!" The words fall instantly from
Stella's lips, as one drops a burning coal from the
hand.

"Yes," Katrine goes on. "It happened in Baden-
Baden, where the Föhren was staying with a relative of hers. Rohritz paid her attention, and something or other gave occasion for a scandalous report. In despair at having compromised the lady
of his affections, Rohritz instantly proposed to her,
and informed his father of his determination to
marry her. The old Baron, a man of unstained
honour, and imbued with a strong feeling of
responsibility in maintaining the dignity of the
Rohritz family, was rather shocked by this hasty
resolve, and, viewing the affair from a far less
romantic and far more sensible point of view than
that taken by his son, made inquiries into the
reputation of the lady in question, and—I cannot
exactly explain it to you, Stella, but the result of

his investigations was that he informed Edgar that he need be troubled by no conscientious scruples on behalf of this adventuress, and that he positively refused his consent to the marriage."

" And then ?" asks Stella.

" I do not know precisely what happened," says Katrine. " Jack told me all about it lately with characteristic indignation, but I did not pay much attention. The affair dragged on for a while. Edgar, who was then most romantically inclined, would not resign the Föhren, corresponded with her,—how I should have liked to read those letters!—finally fought a duel with one of her slanderers, and was severely wounded. When he recovered at last after several dreary months of convalescence, he learned that the Föhren was married to a wealthy Russian."

" How detestable!" exclaims Stella.

" Good heavens! she had a practical mind," Stasy interposes. " I, to be sure, would on occasion have married a tinker for love, but the young women of the present day are not ashamed to declare that their choice in marriage is influenced by a box at the theatre, brilliant equipages, and toilets from Worth. Old Rohritz would have disinherited Edgar, or at all events allowed him a very inadequate income, while Prince Oblonsky——"

" Prince Oblonsky!" Stella hastily exclaims. "Did you say Oblonsky ?"

"Yes; that was her husband's name,—Boris Oblonsky. Now she is a widow, and still perfectly beautiful."

"Perfectly beautiful. I saw her in Venice at the Princess Giovanelli's ball," says Stella, "'with brilliant and far-gazing eyes.' So that was she!" And with a slight anxiety she wonders to herself, "A love-affair! What is the real meaning of a love-affair?"

CHAPTER IX.

FOUND.

A SLEEPY afternoon quiet broods over Erlach Court. Anastasia is sitting in the shade of an arbour, embroidering a strip of fine canvas with yellow sunflowers and red chrysanthemums. At a little distance the Baroness Meineck, who has volunteered to superintend Freddy's education during her stay at Erlach Court, is giving the boy a lesson in mathematics, making such stupendous demands upon his seven-year-old capacity that, ambitious and intelligent though the young student be, he is beginning to grow confused with his ineffectual attempts to follow the lofty flight of his teacher's intellect. Stella, with whom mental excitement is always combined with musical thirst,

is all alone in the drawing-room, playing from the
'Kreisleriana.' Her fingers glide languidly over
the keys. "A love-affair! What is the real meaning of a love-affair?" The question presents itself
repeatedly to her mind, and her veins thrill with
a mixture of curiosity, desire, and dread. Lacking all intimacy with girls of her own age or
older than herself, who might have enlightened
her on such points, she has the vaguest ideas as to
much that goes on in the world. A love-affair is
for her something connected with rope ladders and
peril to life, like the interviews of Romeo and
Juliet, something that she cannot fancy to herself
without moonlight and a balcony. Her innocent
curiosity flutters to and fro, spellbound, about the
Baden-Baden episode in Rohritz's youth, as a
butterfly flutters above a dull pool the pitiful mud-
diness of which is disguised by brilliant sunshine,
the blue reflection of the skies, and a net-work of
pale water-lilies.

She could not tear her thoughts from Baden-
Baden, which she knew partly from Tourganief's
'Smoke,' partly in its present shorn condition from
her own experience,—Baden-Baden, which when
the Föhren and Rohritz were together there might
have been described as a bit of Paradise rented to
the devil.

"I wonder if she called him Edgar when they
were alone?" the girl asked herself.

Her heart beat fast. It was as if she had by chance read a page of some forbidden book negligently left lying open. Not for the world would she have turned the leaf to read on, for, in common with every pure, young girl, when she approached the great mystery of love she was possessed by a sacred timidity almost amounting to awe.

"I wonder if he was very unhappy?" she asks herself. "Yes, he must have been;" Katrine had told her that he grew gray with suffering. A great wave of sympathy and pity wells up in her innocent heart. "Yes, she was very beautiful!" she says to herself.

She perfectly remembers her at the Giovanelli ball, leaning rather heavily on her partner's arm, her eyes half closed, her head inclined towards his shoulder, and again in a solitary little anteroom before a marble chimney-piece, below which a fire glowed and sparkled, lifting both hands to her head, an attitude that brought into strong relief the magnificent outline of her shoulders and bust. While thus busied with arranging her hair, she smiled over her shoulder at a young man who was leaning back in an arm-chair near, his legs crossed, holding his crush-hat in both hands, regarding her with languid looks of admiration.

This was Stella's friend, black-eyed Prince Zino Capito. All Venice was then talking of the Prince's adoration of the beautiful Livonian.

"What is it about her that makes every man fall in love with her?" Stella asks herself. And a sudden pang of something like envy assails her innocent heart. Ah, she would like just one taste of the wondrous poison of which all the poets sing. "Will any one ever be in love with me?" she asks herself. "Ah, it must be delicious,—delicious as music and the fragrance of flowers in spring; and I should so like to be happy for once in my life, even were it for only a single hour. But——" Her eyes fill with tears: what has she to do with happiness? it is not for her; of that she has been convinced from the moment when on that last melancholy journey with her father she found she had lost her little amulet. Poor papa! he would gladly have bestowed happiness upon her from heaven, and instead he had taken her happiness down with him into the grave. Poor, dear papa!

The breath of the roses outside steals in through the closed blinds, sweet and oppressive. Among the flowers below awakened to fresh beauty, the bees hum loudly, plunging into the honeysuckles, and gently as if with reverence touching the pale refined beauty of the Malmaison roses, while above the acacias and lindens they are swarming.

*   *   *   *   *   *   *

Rohritz has been occupied in writing his usual quarterly duty-letter to his married brother. As with all men of his stamp, a letter is for him a

great undertaking, accomplished wearily from a
strict sense of duty.

Seated at the writing-desk of carved rosewood
bestowed upon him long since by an aunt and provided with many secret drawers and with all kinds
of silver-gilt and ivory utensils of mysterious use-
lessness, he covers four pages of English writing-
paper with his formal, regular handwriting, and
then looks for his seal wherewith to seal his epistle.
Rummaging in the various drawers and receptacles
of the desk, he comes across a small bracelet,—a
delicate circlet to which is suspended a crystal
locket containing a four-leaved clover.

For a moment he cannot recall how he became
possessed of the trifle. Could it have been the gift
of some sentimental female friend? In vain he
taxes his memory: no, it certainly is no memento
of the kind. He swings it to and fro upon his
finger, letting the sunshine play upon it, and then
first perceives a cipher graven on the crystal, a
Roman S, surmounting a star. Involuntarily he
murmurs below his breath, " Stella !" and suddenly
remembers where he found the bracelet,—on the
red velvet seat of a first-class coupé, three years
before, towards the end of April.

He had advertised it in the Viennese and Grätz
newspapers, doing his best to restore the *porte-
bonheur* to its owner, but in vain.

" In fact——" In an instant he recalls what

Leskjewitsch had told him of Stella's sad journey with her father. He smiles, leaves his letter unsealed, goes to the window, looks down into the garden, sees Stasy busy with her chrysanthemums, hears, proceeding from a garden-tent at a little distance, decorated with red tassels, the contralto tones of the Baroness Meineck and the depressed and weeping replies of her pupil.

Through the languid summer air glide the harsh, forced modulations of the 'Kreisleriana.'

"Ah!" He wends his way to the drawing-room. There, in the romantic half-light that prevails, all the blinds and shades being closed to shut out the hot July sun, he sees a light figure seated at the piano. At his entrance she turns her golden head.

"Are you looking for any one?" she asks, in the midst of No. 6 of the 'Kreisleriana,' rather confused by his entrance, and trying furtively to brush away the tears that still show upon her cheeks.

"Yes; I was looking for you, Baroness Stella."

"For me?" she asks, in surprise.

"Yes; I wanted to ask you something."

"Well?" She takes her hand from the keys and turns round towards him, without rising.

"Three years ago I found a bracelet in a railway-coupé. Coming across it by chance to-day, I perceive that it is marked with your cipher. Does it belong——"

But Stella does not allow him to finish; deadly

pale, and trembling in every limb, she has sprung up and taken the bracelet from his hand.

"Oh, you cannot tell all you restore to me with this bracelet!" she exclaims, and in her inexpressible delight she holds out to him both her hands.

Are they so absorbed in each other as not to observe the apparition which presents itself for an instant at the drawing-room door, only to glide away immediately?

Meanwhile, in the garden a thrilling drama is being enacted. So thoroughly bewildered at last by the Baroness's system of instruction that his brain refuses to respond to even the small demands which her growing contempt for his capacity permits her to make upon it, poor Freddy feels so thoroughly ashamed of his inability that he lifts up his voice and weeps aloud. When his mother hastens to him to learn what has so distressed her son, he throws his arms around her waist and cries out, in a tone of heart-breaking despair, "Mamma, mamma, what will become of me? I am so stupid,—so very stupid!"

Katrine finds this beyond a jest. "I must entreat you not to trouble yourself further with my boy's education, if this is the only result you achieve, Lina," she says, provoked, whereupon the Baroness replies, angrily,—

"I certainly shall not insist upon continuing my lessons, especially as never in my life have I found any one so obtuse of comprehension in the simplest matters as your son."

"Ah, you insinuate that my boy is a blockhead. Let me assure you, however——"

In what mutual amenities the conversation of the sisters-in-law would have culminated must remain a subject of conjecture; for at this moment Stasy comes tripping along, saying, with an affected smile,—

"How wonderfully one can be mistaken as to character in others! Yes, yes, still waters—still waters. Ha! ha!"

"What do you mean with your still waters?" Katrine asks, contemptuously.

"Hush!" And Stasy archly lays her finger on her lip with a significant glance towards the boy, who with his arms still about his mother's waist is drying his tears upon her sleeve.

"Run into the house, Freddy, and bathe your eyes, and then we will take a walk," Katrine says to her little son. "What is the matter?" she then asks, coldly, turning to Stasy.

"Rohritz—aha!—we all thought him an extinct volcano. I, notoriously reserved as I am, permitted myself to tease him slightly now and then, thinking him entirely harmless. And now, now I find him in the yellow drawing-room, *tête-à-tête* with Stella, both her hands in his, gazing into her lifted eyes, deep in a flirtation,—a flirtation *à l'Américaine,*—quite beyond what is permissible. Really perilous!"

"If you thought the situation perilous for Stella, I really do not understand why you did not interrupt the *tête-à-tête,*" says Katrine, severely.

"It was no affair of mine," Stasy replies. "How was I to know that so sentimental an interview would not end in an offer of marriage? Improbable, to be sure, for Rohritz is too cautious for that,—even although he allows himself on a summer afternoon to be so far carried away as to kiss the hand of a pretty girl in a *tête-à-tête* with her."

Her eyes sparkling with anger, the Baroness hurries into the castle and up-stairs to the drawing-room.

"Stella, what are you about here? Have you nothing to do? Come with me!"

In terror Stella follows her mother as she strides on to their apartments. There the Baroness closes the door behind her, and, seizing her daughter by the arm, says,—

"Must I endure the disgrace of having my child conduct herself so shamelessly in a strange house that strangers inform me that she is flirting *à l'Américaine* with young men?"

"I, mother! I——" exclaims Stella, her eyes riveted upon her mother's angry face. "But I assure you—— Mother, mother, how can you say such dreadful things to me?" And the girl bursts out sobbing. "It is Stasy that has accused me. How can you attach any importance to what she says?"

"No matter what Stasy says. Your conduct is extraordinary."

"But, mother, mother——"

"What have you to do with *tête-à-têtes* with young men?" the Baroness asks, with dramatic effect,—the same Baroness who sent her child to a singing-teacher three times a week without an escort. "It is improper,—very improper. What must Rohritz think of you? You will come to be like your aunt Eugenie!"

CHAPTER X.

FREDDY'S BIRTHDAY.

IT is not to be denied that Stella's behaviour is always unconventional and sometimes very thoughtless. On the whole, however, her little indiscretions do not detract from her great natural charm. The Baroness, not having taken any pains with her education, never of herself notices these little indiscretions. But if a stranger alludes to them her maternal ambition is profoundly outraged, and the inevitable result is the bursting of a thunder-storm above Stella's innocent head, a storm always sure to culminate in the fearful words, "You will come to be like your aunt Eugenie!"

The real meaning of these words Stella never understands, since no one has ever told her what has become of her aunt Eugenie, but she knows that their significance must be terrible. Cowed and unhappy, she glides about after every such explosion as if guilty of some crime, until her bright animal spirits gain the upper hand and she begins afresh to talk and to be thoughtless.

Her mother's last indignant remonstrance puts an end to all the kindly freedom of her intercourse with Rohritz. She avoids him so evidently, is so stiff and monosyllabic with him, that he at last questions the captain as to the cause of this change, and receives from his friend a distinct explanation.

"It is indeed no great bliss to be my sister's daughter," the captain concludes. "Beneath her mother's intermittent care Stella seems to me like a noble, sensitive horse beneath a very bad rider. I hate to look on at such cruelty to animals, and I should be heartily glad to find a good husband for her before her mother entirely ruins her. He will have to be a good, noble-hearted fellow, clever and gentle at once, with a firm, light hand, and plenty of money, for the child has nothing,—more's the pity."

*   *   *   *   *   *   *

The time never flies faster than in summer: with no hurry, but with graceful celerity, the lovely July days glide past in their rich robes of dark green and sky-blue. The genii of summer play about us, fling roses at our feet, and strew the grass with diamonds. They offer us happiness, show it to us, whisper insinuatingly, "Take it,—ah, take it." And some of us would gladly obey, but their hands are bound, and others remember how they once, on just such enchanting summer days, stretched out their hands in eager longing for the roses, and at their touch the roses vanished, leaving only the thorns in their grasp, and they turn away with a mistrustful sigh. Others, again, examine the offered joy hesitatingly, critically, refuse to decide, linger and wait, and before they are aware the beneficent genii have vanished; autumnal blasts have driven them away with the roses and the foliage. The sun shines no longer, the skies are gray, and a cold wind sings a shrill song of scorn in their ears.

'Passing!—passing!' One week, two weeks have passed since the Meinecks arrived at Erlach Court. Each day Rohritz has found Stella more charming, each day he has paid her more attention, but his real intimacy with her has increased not one whit.

To-day is Freddy's birthday. Stella has presented him with a gorgeous paint-box; he has received all sorts of gifts and toys from his parents and relatives, and he has, of course, been more than usually petted and caressed by his father and mother. His delight is extreme when he learns that a picnic has been arranged for the day in his honour.

None of the older inmates of the castle take any special pleasure in picnics; least of all has Katrine any liking for these complicated undertakings. But Freddy adores them; and what would Katrine not do to give her darling a delight?

It is Sunday. A gentle wind murmurs melodiously through the dewy grass, and sighs among the thick foliage of the lindens like a dreamy echo of the sweet monotonous tolling of bells that comes from the gleaming white churches and chapels on the mountain-slopes on the other side of the Save. From the open windows of the dining-room can be seen across the low wall of the park the brown peasant-women, with pious, expressionless faces, and huge square white headkerchiefs knotted at the back of the neck, marching along the road to church. Above, in the dark-blue sky myriads of fleecy clouds are flying, and swarms of airy blue and yellow butterflies are fluttering about the Malmaison roses and over the beds of heliotrope and mignonette in front of the castle.

There has been rain during the previous night, but not much, and the whole earth seems decked in fresh and festal array. The sun shines bright and golden, but the barometer is falling,—a depressing fact which Baron Rohritz announces to all present at the birthday-breakfast.

Freddy's face grows long, and Katrine exclaims, hastily, "Your barometer is intolerable!" She has no idea of sacrificing her child's enjoyment to the whims of an impertinent barometer.

"Yes, Edgar, your barometer is a great bore," the captain remarks.

Whoever presumes to express an unpleasant or even inconvenient truth is sure to be regarded as a great bore.

Meanwhile, Katrine has stepped out upon the terrace and convinced herself that the weather is superb. Annihilating by a glance Rohritz and his warning, she orders the servant who has just brought in a plate of hot almond-cakes to have the horses harnessed immediately.

Rohritz placidly twirls his moustache, and re-marks, as he rises from table, that he will strap up his mackintosh. A few minutes afterwards the carriages, a light-built drag and a solid landau, are announced. To the drag are harnessed a couple of fiery young nags, while in default of the carriage-horses, which have been ailing for a few days, the landau is drawn by a pair of hacks, by no means spirited or prepossessing in appearance.

The guests stand laughing and talking on the sweep before the castle. Katrine's voice is heard giving orders; Stella is busy helping the captain

to pack away in the carriages the plentiful store
of provisions.

Swathed in airy clouds of muslin, sweetly suffering, but resisting the united entreaties of all the
rest that she will stay at home, Anastasia leans
against the vine-wreathed balustrade of the terrace,
a vinaigrette held to her nose.

Before Katrine has quite finished issuing her
commands, the captain with Stella mounts upon
the front seat of the drag, the general taking his
place beside Freddy on the back seat. Want of
room obliges the captain to act as driver himself.
He gathers up the reins, and his steeds start off
gaily. The rest of the company settle themselves
as best they can in the landau, the Baroness and
Fräulein von Gurlichingen on the back seat, Rohritz
with Katrine opposite them. A few anxious moments ensue, in which every one asks the rest if
they have not forgotten something. The servants
bring the due quantity of rugs, plaids, umbrellas, and
opera-glasses, and the coachman is bidden to drive
off. The hacks sadly stretch out their long, skinny
legs, and trot laboriously after the brisk drag.

In Reierstein, at the foot of a romantic ruin,—
no picnic is conceivable without a ruin,—a *déjeûner
à la fourchette* is to be spread in the open air.
Dinner, which has been postponed from six to
seven, is to be taken in Erlachhof on the return
of the party.

Katrine is right: the day is superb,—a fact of which she frequently reminds the possessor of the odious barometer.

"Wait until evening before declaring the day fine," Rohritz rejoins, sententiously. "The sun's rays sting like harvest-flies: that is a bad sign."

"Oh, you are always foreboding evil," Katrine says, with irritation.

Rohritz bows, and silence ensues. Katrine looks preoccupied, wondering whether the mayonnaise has not been forgotten at the last moment. Stasy flourishes her vinaigrette languishingly, and the Baroness, who has been hitherto absorbed in her own reflections, suddenly arouses sufficiently to utter in her deepest tones an astounding observation upon the imperfections of creation and the superfluity of human existence, whereupon Rohritz agrees with her, seconding her views with great ability in a Schopenhauer duet in which she maintains the principal part. She asserts that marriage, since it is a means for the continuance of the human species, should be avoided by all respectable people, while Rohritz suggests the invention of a tremendous dynamite machine which shall shatter the entire globe, as a fitting problem for the wits of future engineers.

Meanwhile, the sunbeams gleam warm and golden upon the luxuriant July foliage, and tremble upon the clear ripples of the trout-stream plashing

merrily along by the roadside. In the white cups
of the wild vines that drape with tender grace the
willows and elders on the banks of the little stream,
prismatic drops of dew are shining. The tall
grasses wave dreamily, and at their feet peep out
pink, yellow, and blue wild flowers, while the air is
filled with the melody of birds.

Our two pessimists, however, take no note whatever of these trifles.

The road grows stony and steep; the hacks drag
along more and more wearily and at last come to a
stand-still. Anastasia becomes greener and greener
of hue, and sinks back half fainting. " Ah, I feel
as if I should die!"

In hopes of lightening the carriage and of avoid-
ing the sight of Fräulein von Gurlichingen's distress,
Rohritz proposes to alight and pursue on foot the
shorter path to Reierstein, with which he is familiar.

CHAPTER XI.

CRABBING.

MEANWHILE, the captain's spirited steeds have long
since reached the appointed spot. Horses and carriage have been disposed of at the inn of a neigh-
bouring village. It is an excellent hostelry, and
would have been a very pleasant place in which to

take lunch, but, since the delight of a picnic culminates, as is well known, in preparing hot, unappe-
tizing viands at a smoky fire in the open air and
in partaking of excellent cold dishes in the most
uncomfortable position possible, the party immediately leave the village, and Stella, Freddy, and
the two gentlemen, with the help of a peasant-lad
hired for the purpose, drag out the provisions to
the ruin, where the table is to be spread, in the
shade of a romantic old oak.

Directly across the meadow flows the stream,
now widened to a considerable breadth, which had
rippled at intervals by the roadside.

While Leskjewitsch and the general, both resigned martyrs to picnic pleasure, set about collecting dry sticks for the fire, Freddy, who has
instantly divined crabs in the brook, having first
obtained his father's permission, pulls off his
shoes and stockings and wades about among the
stones and reeds in the water.

"You look, little one, as if you wanted to go
crabbing too," says the captain to Stella, noting
the longing looks which the girl is casting after
the boy.

"Indeed I should like to," she replies, nodding
gravely; "but would it be proper, uncle?"

"Whom need you regard?—me, or that old
fellow," indicating over his shoulder the general,
"who is half blind?"

Stella laughs merrily.

"I certainly should not mind him; but"—she colours a little—"suppose the rest were to come."

"Ah! you're thinking of Rohritz," says the captain. "Make your mind easy: if I know those steeds, it will take them one hour longer to drag the carriage up here, and by the time they arrive you can have caught thirty-six Laybrook crabs. As soon as I hear the carriage coming I will warn you by whistling our national hymn. So away with you to the water, only take care not to cut your feet."

A minute or two later, Stella, without gloves, the sleeves of her gray linen blouse rolled up above her elbows over her shapely white arms, and gathering up her skirts with her left hand, while with the right she feels for her prey, is wading in the sun-warmed water beside Freddy, moving with all the attractive awkwardness of a pretty young girl whose feet are cautiously seeking a resting-place among the sharp stones, and who, although extremely eager to capture a great many crabs, has a decided aversion to any spot that looks green and slimy.

The treacherous luck of all novices at any game is well known. Stella's success in her first essay at crabbing is marvellous. She goes on throwing more and more of the crawling, sprawling monsters into the basket which Freddy holds ready.

Her hat prevented her from seeing clearly, so she has tossed it on the bank, and her hair, instead of being neatly knotted up, hangs in a mass of tangled gold at the back of her neck, nearly upon her shoulders, the sunbeams bringing out all sorts of glittering reflections in its coils. She is just waving a giant crustacean triumphantly on high, with, "Look, Freddy, did you ever see such a big one!" when—the blood rushes to her cheeks, her brown eyes take on a tragic expression of dismay, and, utterly confused, she drops the crab and her skirts.

"Am I intruding?" asks the new arrival, Rohritz, smiling as he notices her confusion.

In her hurry to get out of the brook, she forgets to look where she is stepping, and suddenly an expression of pain appears in her face, and the water about her feet takes on a crimson tinge.

"You have cut your foot," Rohritz calls, seriously distressed, helping her to reach the shore, where she sits down on the stump of a tree. The captain and the general are both out of sight, and the blood runs faster and faster from a considerable cut in the girl's foot. "We must put a stop to that," says Rohritz, with anxiety that is almost paternal, as he dips his handkerchief in the brook. But with a deep blush Stella hides her foot beneath the hem of her dress, now, alas! soiled and muddy. "Be reasonable," he insists, adopting a sterner tone: "there should be no trifling with such things. Remember my gray hair: I might be your father." And he kneels down, takes her foot in his hands, and bandages the wound carefully and skilfully. In spite of his boasted gray hair, however, it must be confessed that he experiences odd sensations during this operation, the foot is so pretty, slender, but not bony, soft as a rose-leaf, and so small withal that it almost fits into the hollow of his hand.

Still more beautiful than her foot is her fair dishevelled head, so turned that he sees only a vague profile, just enough to show him how the blood has mounted to her temples, colouring cheek and neck crimson.

"Thanks!" she says, in a somewhat defiant tone, drawing the foot up beneath her dress after he has finished bandaging it. Then, looking at him with a lofty, rather mistrustful air, she asks, "How old are you, really?"

"Thirty-seven," he replies, so accustomed to her strange questions that they no longer surprise him.

"How could you say that you might be my father? You are at least five years too young!" she exclaims, angrily. "And why did you appear so suddenly?"

"I repent my intrusion with all my heart," Rohritz assures her. "The horses seemed so tired that I thought three people a sufficient burden for them, and so I alighted and came by the path across the fields."

At this moment shrill and clear across the meadow from the forest bordering it come the notes of 'God save our Emperor!' and immediately afterwards is heard the slow rumble of the approaching carriage.

"There, you see!" says Stella, still out of humour. "My uncle promised me to whistle that as soon as the carriage could be heard; but no one expected you on foot, and you came just twenty minutes too soon!"

CHAPTER XII.

DISASTER.

ALL that the Baroness says when she hears of Stella's mishap is, "I cannot lose sight of you for an instant that you are not in some mischief!"

Stella only sighs, "Poor mamma!" while Stasy, still livid as to complexion, finds herself strong enough to glance with great significance first at Stella and then at Rohritz. When she hears that it is Rohritz that bandaged Stella's foot she vibrates between fainting and a fit of laughter. She calls Rohritz nothing but ' my dear surgeon,' ac-

i

companying the exquisite jest with a sly glance from time to time.

His enjoyment of this brilliant wit may be imagined.

The general grins; the Baroness looks angry; the captain and Katrine are the only ones who observe nothing of Rohritz's annoyance or Anastasia's jest; they are entirely absorbed in reproaching each other for the absence of the corkscrew, which has been forgotten.

Yet, in spite of the double mischance thus attending the beginning of the *déjeûner sur l'herbe,* all turns out pleasantly enough. The general remembers that his pocket-knife is provided with a corkscrew; the married pair recover their serenity; the crabs, in spite of many obstacles, are half cooked at the fire, and—for Freddy's sake—pronounced excellent; the cold capon and the *pâté de foie gras* leave nothing to be desired; the mayonnaise has not been forgotten, and the champagne is capital.

Hilarity is so fully restored that when the carriages, ordered at five o'clock, make their appearance, the company is singing in unison 'Prince Eugene, that noble soldier,' to an exhilarating accompaniment played by the general with the back of a knife on a plate.

Baron Rohritz, who is not familiar with 'Prince Eugene,' and who consequently listens in silence to that inspiring song, glances critically at a small point of purple cloud creeping up from behind the mountains.

"My barometer——" he begins; but Katrine interrupts him irritably: "Ah, do spare us with your barometer!"

A foreign element suddenly mingles with the merry talk. A loud blast of wind howls through the mighty branches of the old oak, tearing away a handful of leaves to toss them as in scorn in the dismayed faces of the party; a tall champagne-bottle falls over, and breaks two glasses.

"It is late; we have far to go, and the hacks are scarcely trustworthy," the captain remarks. "I think we had better begin to pack up."

Preparations to return are made hurriedly. The general begs for a place in the landau, as his back-bone is sorely in need of some support, and Freddy also, who is apt to catch cold, is taken into the carriage from the open conveyance.

No one expresses any anxiety with regard to Stella; she slips into her brown water-proof and is helped up upon the box of the drag, where the captain takes his place beside her, while Rohritz gets into the seat behind them. They set off. Once more the sun breaks forth from among the rapidly-darkening masses of clouds, but the air is heavy and in the distance there is a faint mutter of thunder.

Wonderful to relate, the hired steeds follow the sorrels with the most praiseworthy rapidity, due perhaps to the fact that the coachman makes the whip whistle uninterruptedly about their long ears. Katrine, who is sitting with her back to the horses, sees nothing of this, but rejoices to find the pace of the hacks so much improved. Suddenly Stasy in a panic exclaims, " Katrine !"

" What is the matter ?"

" The driver—oh, look——"

Frau von Leskjewitsch turns, and sees the fat driver from the village swaying to and fro on his seat like a pendulum. The carriage bumps against a stone, the ladies scream, Freddy, who had fallen asleep between the Baroness and Anastasia, wakens and asks in a piteous voice what is the matter; the general springs up, tries to take the reins from the driver, and roars as loud as his old lungs will permit, " Leskjewitsch !"

The captain does not hear.

" Papa !" " Jack !" " Captain !" echo loud and shrill, until the captain, told by Rohritz to turn and look, gives the reins to his old comrade, jumps down from the drag, and runs to the assistance of his family. An angry scene ensues between him and the driver, who tries to withhold from him the reins,—is first violent, then maudlin, stammering in his peasant-patois asseverations of his entire sobriety, until the captain actually drags him down from the box and with a volley of abuse flings him into a ditch. Katrine is attacked by a cramp in the jaw from excitement. The Baroness ponders upon the etymological derivation of a word in the patois of the country which she has fished out of the captain's torrent of invective, and repeats it to herself in an undertone. The general folds his hands over his stomach with resignation, and sighs, "Dinner is ordered for seven o'clock." Freddy's blue eyes sparkle merrily in the general confusion, and Stasy, since there is positively no audience for her affectation, conducts herself in a perfectly sensible manner. In the midst of the excitement, one of the hacks deliberately lies down, and thus diverts the captain's attention from the driver.

"By Jove, our case is bad,—worse than might be supposed. These screws can scarcely stir," he exclaims: "that drunken scoundrel has beaten them half to death. How we are to get home God knows : these brutes cannot possibly drag this four-seated Noah's ark. We had better change horses. Ho! Rohritz?"

"What is the matter?"

"Unharness those horses!"

In a short time the exchange is effected. The sorrels in their gay trappings are harnessed to the heavy landau, the long-legged hacks to the drag.

It is beginning to rain, and to grow dark.

Freddy is nearly smothered in plaids by his anxious mamma. The captain mounts on the box of the four-seated vehicle, and calls to Rohritz,—

"Drive to Wolfsegg, the village across the ferry. We will await you with fresh horses, at the inn there. Adieu."

And the captain gives his steeds the rein, and trots gaily past the drag.

"*Tiens!* Stella is left *tête-à-tête* with Rohritz," Stasy whispers.

"And what of that?" Katrine says, rather crossly. "He will not kill her."

"No, no; but people might talk."

"Pshaw! because of an hour's drive!"

"Wait and see how punctual they are," Stasy giggles maliciously.

"Anastasia, you are outrageous!" Katrine declares.

"Wait and see," Anastasia repeats; "wait and see."

CHAPTER XIII.

IDYLLIC.

"Are you well protected, Fräulein Stella?" Rohritz asks his young companion, after a long silence.

"Oh, yes," says Stella, contentedly wrapping

herself in her shabby, thin, twenty-franc water-proof and pulling the hood over her fair head, " I am quite warm. It was a good thing that you gave us warning, or I should certainly have left my water-proof at home."

" You see an ' old bore,' as Les called my barom-eter, can be of use under certain circumstances."

" Indeed it can," Stella nods assent; " but it would have been a pity to give up the picnic at the bidding of your weather-prophet, for, on the whole, it was a great success."

" Are you serious ?" Rohritz asks, surprised.

" Why should you doubt it ?"

" Why, you have had less cause than any of us to enjoy the day. You have cut your foot, have spoiled a very pretty gown, and are in danger, if it goes on pouring thus, of being wet to the skin in spite of your water-proof."

" That is of no consequence," she declares from out the brown hood, her fair dripping face laugh-ing up at him through the rain and the gathering darkness. " Where is the harm in getting a little wet ? It is quite delightful."

He is silent. She is to be envied for her gay, happy temperament, and she looks wonderfully pretty in spite of her grotesque wrap.

Not the faintest breath of wind diverts from the perpendicular the downfall of rain. The road leads between two steep wooded heights, whence are wafted woodland odours both sweet and acrid. Intense peace—an unspeakably beneficent repose—reigns around; in grave harmonious accord blend the rushing of the brook, the falling of the rain, and the low whisper and murmur of the dripping leaves, informing the silence with a sense of enjoyment.

"How beautiful! how wonderfully beautiful!" Stella exclaims; her soft voice has a strange power to touch the heart, and in its gayest tones there always trembles something like suppressed tears.

"Yes, it is beautiful," Rohritz admits, "but"—with a glance of mistrust at the wretched hacks—"when we shall reach Wolfsegg heaven alone knows!"

Is he so very anxious to reach Wolfsegg? To be frank, no! He feels unreasonably comfortable in this rain-drenched solitude, beside this pretty fair-haired child; he cannot help rejoicing in this *tête-à-tête.* Since the day when Stella thanked him with perhaps exaggerated warmth for returning her locket, she has never seemed so much at her ease with him as now.

The desire assails him to probe her pure innocent nature without her knowledge,—to learn something of her short past, of her true self.

Meanwhile, he repeats, "But it is beautiful,—wonderfully beautiful!"

The wretched horses drag along more and more

laboriously. Rohritz has much ado to prevent their drooping their gray noses to the ground to crop the dripping grass that clothes each side of the road in emerald luxuriance.

"Delightful task, the driving of these lame hacks!" he exclaims. "I can imagine only one pleasure equal to it,—waltzing with a lame partner. This last I know, of course, only from hearsay."

"Did you never dance?" asks Stella.

"No, never since I left the Academy. Have you been to many balls?"

"Never but to one, in Venice, at the Princess Giovanelli's," Stella replies. "After the first waltz I became so ill that I would not run the risk of fainting and making myself and my partner ridiculous. My enjoyment then consisted in sitting for half an hour between two old ladies on a sofa, and eating an ice to restore me. At twelve o'clock punctually I hurried back, moreover, to the Britannia, for I knew that my poor sick father would sit up to be regaled with an account of my conquests. He was firmly convinced that I should make conquests. Poor papa! You must not laugh at his delusion! The next day the other girls in the hotel pitied me for not having had any partner for the cotillon; they displayed their bouquets to me, as the Indians after a battle show the scalps they have taken. They told me of their adorers, and of the *passions funestes* which they had inspired, and asked me what I had achieved in that direction. And I could only cast down my eyes, and reply, 'Nothing.' And to think that to-day, after all these years, I must give the same answer to the same question,—'Nothing!'"

"You have never danced, then!" Rohritz says, thoughtfully.

Strange, how this fact attracts him. Stella seems to him like a fruit not quite ripened by the sun, but gleaming among cool, overshadowing foliage in absolute, untouched freshness. Such dewy-fresh fruit is wonderfully inviting; he feels almost like stretching out his hand for it. But no, it would be folly,—ridiculous; he is an old man, she a child; it is impossible. And yet——

Both are so absorbed in their thoughts that they do not observe how very dark it has grown, how threatening is the aspect of the skies. Leaving the ravine, the road now leads along the bank of the Save. The pools on each side grow deeper, the mud splashes from the wheels on Stella's knees: she does not notice it.

"Your last remark was a little bold," Rohritz now says, bending towards her.

"Bold?" Stella repeats, in dismay: 'bold,' for her, means pert, aggressive,—in short, something terrible.

"Yes," he continues, smiling at her agitation; "you asserted something that seems to me incredible,—that you never have inspired any one with a——"

He hesitates.

A brilliant flash quivers in the sky; by its light they see the Save foaming along in its narrow bed, swollen to overflowing by the recent torrents of rain. Then all is dark as night; a loud peal of thunder shakes the air, and the blast of the storm comes hissing as if with repressed fury from the mountains.

The horses tremble, one of them stumbles and falls, the traces break, and down goes the carriage.

"Now we are done for!" Rohritz exclaims, as he jumps down to investigate the extent of the damage.

Further progress is out of the question. He succeeds by a violent effort in dragging to his feet the exhausted horse, then unharnesses both animals and ties them as well as he can to a picket-fence, the accident having occurred close to an isolated cottage with an adjacent garden. Rohritz knocks at its doors and windows in vain; no one appears. In the deep recess of one of the doors is a step affording a tolerable seat. He spreads a plaid over it, and then, going to Stella, he says, " Allow me to lift you down; I must drag the carriage aside from the road. There! you are not quite sheltered yet from the rain; move a little farther into the corner,—so."

"Oh, I don't in the least mind getting wet," Stella assures him; "but what shall we do? We cannot sit here all night long in hopes that some chance passers-by may fish us out of the wet."

"If you could walk, there would be no difficulty. The inn this side of the ferry is only a quarter of a mile off, and we could easily hire a couple of horses there. Can you stand on your foot?"

"It gives me a great deal of pain to stand, and, since Uncle Jack has my other shoe in his pocket, how am I to walk?"

"That is indeed unfortunate."

"You had better go for help to the inn of which you speak," Stella proposes.

"Then I should have to leave you here alone," says Rohritz, shaking his head.

"I am not afraid," she declares, with the hardihood of utter inexperience.

"But I am afraid for you; I cannot endure the thought of leaving you here alone on Sunday, when all the men about are intoxicated. One of the roughest of them might chance to pass by."

"In all probability no one will pass," says Stella. "Go as quickly as you can, that we may get away from here."

"In fact, she is right," Edgar says to himself. He turns to go, then returns once more, and, taking his mackintosh from his shoulders, wraps it about her.

He is gone. How slowly time passes when one is waiting in the dark! With monotonous force, in a kind of grand rhythmical cadence the rain pours down to the accompaniment of the swirling Save. No other sound is to be heard. Stella looks round at the horses, which she can dimly discern. One is lying, all four legs stretched out, in the mud, in the position in which artists are wont to portray horses killed on a battle-field; the other is nibbling with apparent relish at some greenery that has grown across the garden fence. From time to time a flash of lightning illumines the darkness. Stella takes out her watch to note the time by one of these momentary illuminations. It must have stopped, —no, it is actually only a quarter of an hour since Edgar's departure.

Hark! the rolling of wheels mingles with the rush of the Save and the plash of the rain. The sound of a human voice falls upon the girl's ear. She listens, delighted. Is it Rohritz? No, that is not his voice: there are several voices, suspiciously rough,—peasants rolling past in a small basket-wagon, trolling some monotonous Slav melody. By a red flash of lightning the rude company is revealed, the driver mercilessly plying his whip upon the back of a very small horse, that is galloping through the mire with distended nostrils and fluttering mane.

Stella's heart beats, her boasted courage shrivels

up to nothing.   A few more minutes pass, and now she hears steps.   Is he coming?   No; the steps approach from the opposite direction, stumbling, dragging steps,—those of a drunkard.

A nameless, unreasoning dread takes possession of her.   Ah! she hears the quick firm rhythm of an elastic tread.

"Baron Rohritz!" she screams, as loud as she can.   "Baron Rohritz!"

The step quickens into a run, and a moment later Rohritz is beside her.   "For God's sake, what is the matter?" he says, much distressed.

"Oh, nothing, nothing,—only a drunken man. My courage oozed away pitifully.   Heaven knows whether, if you had not appeared, I might not have plunged into the Save from sheer cowardice.   But all is well now.   Is a vehicle coming?"

"Unfortunately, there was none to be had.   I could only get a peasant-lad to take care of the horses.   If there was the slightest dependence to be placed upon these confounded brutes I could put you on the least broken-down of them and lead him slowly to the inn.   But, unfortunately, I am convinced that the beast could not carry you: he would fall with you in the first pool in the road. With all the desire in the world to help you, I cannot.   You must try to walk as far as the inn. I have brought you one of the ferryman's wife's shoes."

And while Stella is putting the huge patent-leather shoe on her bandaged foot, Rohritz directs the peasant-lad to fish his plaid and rugs out of the mud and to lead the horses slowly to the inn. As he walks away with Stella they hear the boy's loud drawling 'Hey!' 'Get up,' with which he seeks to inspirit the miserable brutes.

Leaning on the arm of her escort, Stella does her best to proceed without yielding to the pain which every minute increases, but her movements grow slower and more laboured, and finally a low moan escapes her lips.

"Let me rest just one moment," she entreats, piteously, ashamed of a helplessness of which a normally constituted woman would have made capital.

" Do not walk any farther," he rejoins, and, bending over her, he says, with decision, "I pray you put your right arm around my neck, clasp it well: treat me absolutely as a *porte-faix.*"

" But, Baron——"

" Do not oppose me, I entreat: at present *I* am in command." His tone is very kind, but also very authoritative.

She obeys, half mechanically. He carries her firmly and securely, without stumbling, without betraying the slightest fatigue. At first her sensations are distressing; then slowly, gradually, a pleasant sense of being shielded and cared for overcomes her: her thoughts stray far, far into the past,—back to the time when her father hid her against his breast beneath his cavalry cloak, and she looked out between its folds from the warm darkness upon the world outside. The minutes fly.

"We are here!" Rohritz says, very hoarsely.

She looks up. A reddish light is streaming out into the darkness from the windows of a low, clumsy building. He puts her down on the threshold of the inn.

"Thanks!" she murmurs, without looking at him. He is silent.

The inn parlour is empty. A bright fire is burning in the huge tiled stove; the fragrance of cedar-berries slowly scorching on its ledge neutralizes in part the odour of old cheese, beer, and cheap tobacco plainly to be perceived in spite of the open window. In a broad cabinet with glazed doors are to be seen among various monstrosities of glass and porcelain two battered sugar ships with paper pennons, and a bridal wreath with crumpled white muslin blossoms and arsenic-green leaves. The portraits of their Majesties, very youthful in appearance, dating from their coronation, hang on each side of this piece of furniture.

Among the various tables covered with black oil-cloth there is one of rustic neatness provided with a red-flowered cover, and set with greenish glasses, blue-rimmed plates, and iron knives and forks with wooden handles.

The hostess, a colossal dame, who looks like a meal-sack with a string tied around its middle, makes her appearance, to receive the unfortunates and to place her entire wardrobe at Stella's disposal.

" Can we not go on, then ?" Stella asks, in dismay.

" Unfortunately, no. I have sent to the nearest village for some sort of conveyance, and my messenger cannot possibly return in less than an hour. And I must prepare you for another unfortunate circumstance : we shall be forced to go by a very long and roundabout road ; the Gröblach bridge is carried away, and the Save is whirling along in its current the pillars and ruins, making the ferry impracticable for the present."

" Oh, good heavens !" sighs Stella, who has meanwhile taken off her dripping water-proof and wrapped about her shoulders a thick red shawl loaned her by the hostess. " Well, at least we are under shelter."

Thereupon the hostess brings in a grass-green waiter on which are placed a dish of ham and eggs and a can of beer.

" I ordered a little supper, but I cannot vouch for the excellence of the viands," Rohritz says, in French, to Stella. " I should be glad if you would consent to eat something warm. It is the best preventive against cold."

Stella shows no disposition to criticise what is thus set before her. "How pleasant!" she exclaims, gaily, taking her seat at the table. "I am terribly hungry, and I had not ventured to hope for anything to eat before midnight."

It is a pleasure to him to sit opposite to her, looking at her pretty, cheerful face,—a pleasure to laugh at her gay sallies.

Would it not be charming to sit opposite to her thus daily at his own table,—to lavish care and tenderness upon the poor child who had been so neglected and thrust out into the world,—to spoil and pet her to his heart's content? "Grasp your chance,—grasp it!" the heart in his bosom cries out: "her lot is hard, she is grateful for a little sympathy,—will she not smile on you in spite of your gray hair?" But reason admonishes: "Forbear! she is only a child. To be sure, if, as she has avowed, her heart be really untouched, why then——"

Whilst he, absorbed in such careful musings, grows more and more taciturn, she chatters away gaily upon every conceivable topic, devouring with an appetite to be envied the frugal refection he has provided.

"It is delightful, our improvised supper," she declares, "almost as charming as the little suppers at the Britannia which papa used to have ready for me when I came home from parties in Venice, as terribly hungry as one always is on returning from a Venetian soirée, where one is delightfully entertained but gets nothing to eat."

"It seems, then, that the Giovanelli ball was not your only glimpse of Venetian society?" Rohritz remarks, with a glance that is well-nigh indiscreetly searching.

"Before papa grew so much worse I very often went out: papa insisted upon it. The Countess L—— chaperoned me. And at Lady Stair's evenings in especial I enjoyed myself almost as much as I was bored at the Giovanelli ball. I cannot, 'tis true, dance; but talk,"—she laughs somewhat shyly, as if in ridicule of her talkativeness,—"I *can* talk."

"That there is nothing to eat at a Venetian soirée I know from experience," Rohritz says, rather ill-humouredly, "but how one can find any enjoyment there I am absolutely unable to understand. Venetian society is terrible: the men especially are intolerable."

"I did not find it so," Stella declares, shaking her head with her usual grave simplicity in asserting her opinion; "not at all."

"But you must confess that Italians are usually low-toned; that——"

"But I did not meet Italians exclusively; I met Austrians, English, Russians; although in fact" —she pauses reflectively, then says, with conviction—" the nicest of all, my very particular friend, was an Italian, Prince Zino Capito."

"He calls himself an Austrian," Rohritz interposes.

"He was born in Rome," Stella rejoins.

"I see you know all about him," Rohritz observes.

"We saw a great deal of each other," Stella chatters on easily. "We were in the same hotel, papa and I, and the Prince. His place at table was next to mine, and in fine weather he used to take us to sail in his cutter. He often came in the evenings to play bézique with papa. He was very kind to papa."

"Evidently," Rohritz observes.

"You seem to dislike him!" Stella says, in some surprise.

"Not at all. We always got along very well together," Rohritz coldly assures her. "I know him intimately; my oldest brother married his sister Thérèse."

"Ah! is she as handsome as he?" Stella asks, innocently.

"Very graceful and distinguished in appearance; she does not resemble him at all." And with a growing sharpness in his tone Rohritz adds,—

"Do you think him so very handsome?"

The hostess interrupts them by bringing in a dish of inviting strawberries. Stella thanks her kindly for her excellent supper, the woman says something to Rohritz in the peasant patois, which Stella does not understand, and he fastens his eyeglass in his eye, a sign with him of a momentary access of ill humour.

After the woman has withdrawn he remarks, with an odd twinkle of his eyes, "How many years too young did you say I was, Baroness Stella, to be your father?—four or five, was it not? *Eh bien*, our hostess thinks differently: she has just congratulated me upon my charming daughter."

But Stella has no time to make reply: her eyes are riveted in horror upon the clock against the wall. "Is it really half-past ten?" she exclaims. "No, thank heaven; the clock has stopped. What o'clock is it, Baron Rohritz?"

"A quarter after eleven," he says, startled himself, and rather uncomfortable. "I do not understand why the messenger is not here with the conveyance."

"Good heavens!" Stella cries, in utter dismay. "What will mamma say?"

"Be reasonable. Your mother cannot blame you in this case; she must be informed that it was impossible to cross the ferry," he says, anxious himself about the matter, however.

"Certainly; but while she does not know of our break-down she will think we have had plenty of time to reach Wolfsegg by the longest way round. You certainly acted for the best, but it would have been better, much better, if Uncle Jack had stayed with me. He knows all about the country, and he has a decided way of making these lazy peasants do as he pleases."

"I do not believe that with all his knowledge of the country, and his decision of character, he could have succeeded in procuring you a conveyance," Rohritz says, with growing irritation.

"If the ferry is useless, perhaps we might cross in a skiff," Stella says, almost in tears.

"I will see what is to be done," he rejoins. "At all events it shall not be my fault if your mother's anxiety is not fully appeased in the course of the next half-hour."

With this he leaves the room. Shortly afterwards the hostess makes her appearance.

"Where has the Herr Papa gone?" she asks.

"He has gone out to see if we cannot cross the Save in a boat."

"He cannot do it to-night," the woman asserts. "He would surely not think of——" Without finishing her sentence she puts down the plate of cheese she has just brought, and hurries away.

Stella is perplexed. What does he mean to do? What is the hostess so foolishly afraid of? She limps to the open window, and sees Rohritz on the bank of the stream, talking in the Slavonic dialect, which she does not understand, with a rough-looking man. The rain has ceased, the clouds are rent and flying, and from among them the moon shines with a bluish lustre, strewing silver gleams upon the quiet road with its net-work of pools and ruts, upon the wildly-rushing Save with its foaming billows, upon the black roof of the hut which serves as a shelter for the ferrymen, and upon a rocking skiff which is fastened to the shore. A sudden dread seizes upon Stella, a dread stronger by far than her childish fear of her mother's harsh words. The hostess enters.

"Not a bit will the gentleman heed,—stiff-necked he is,—the water boiling, and not a man will risk the rowing him: he be's to sail alone to Wolfsegg, and ne'er a one can hinder him."

Stella sees Rohritz get into the skiff, sees the fisherman take hold of the chain that fastens it to the shore. Not even conscious of· the pain in her wounded foot, she rushes out, and across the muddy road to the bank, where the fisherman has already unfastened the chain and is preparing to push the boat out of the swamp into the rushing current.

"Good heavens! are you mad?" she calls aloud to Rohritz. "What are you about?"

Rohritz turns hastily; their eyes meet in the moonlight. "After what you said to me there is nothing for me to do save to shield your reputation at all hazards.—Push off!" he orders the fisherman.

"No," she calls: "it never occurred to me to consider my reputation. I was only a coward, and afraid of mamma."

The fisherman hesitates. Rohritz takes the oars. "Push off!" he orders, angrily.

"Do so, if you choose," Stella cries, "but you will take me with you!" Whereupon she jumps into the boat, and, striking her poor wounded foot against a seat, utterly breaks down with the pain. "I was a coward; yes, yes, I was afraid of mamma; but I would rather have her refuse to speak to me than have you drowned," she sobs.

Her streaming eyes are riveted in great distress upon his face, and her soft, trembling hands try to clasp his arm. About the skiff the waves plash, "Grasp it, grasp it; your happiness lies at your feet!"

His whole frame is thrilled. He stoops and lifts her up. " But, Stella, my poor foolish angel——" he begins.

At this moment there is a rattle of wheels, and then the captain's voice: " Rohritz! Rohritz!"

" All's right now!" says Rohritz, drawing a deep breath.

As it now appears, the captain has come by the long roundabout road, with a borrowed vehicle, to the relief of the unfortunates. The general, who, whatever disagreeable qualities he may possess, is a 'gentleman coachman' of renown, has declared himself quite ready to conduct the landau with its spirited span of horses to Erlach Court.

"What have you been about? What has happened to you?" the captain repeats, and he shakes his head, claps his hands, and laughs by turns, as with mutual interruptions and explanations the tale of disaster is unfolded to him.

Then Stella is packed inside the little vehicle, Rohritz takes his place beside her, and the captain is squeezed up on the front seat.

Before fifteen minutes are over Stella is sound asleep. Rohritz wraps his plaid about her shoulders without her knowledge.

"She is tired out," he whispers. "I only hope her foot is not going to give her trouble. Were you very anxious?"

"My wife was almost beside herself. My sister took the matter, on the contrary, very quietly, until finally Stasy put some ridiculous ideas of impropriety into her head, and then she talked nonsense, alternately scolding you and the child, marching up and down the common room at the Wolfsegg inn like a bear in a cage, until I could bear it no longer, but left the entire party on the general's shoulders to be driven home, and set out in search of you. How did Stella behave herself? Did she give you any trouble?"

"No; she was very quiet."

"She is a dear girl, is she not? Poor child! she

really has had too much to bear.   Of course I would not confess it to Stasy, but it is a fact that if any other man had been in your place I should have been excessively annoyed."

"My gray hair has been of immense advantage to your niece," Rohritz assured him.   "The hostess at the ferry persisted in taking me for her father."

"Nonsense!"

"Nonsense which at least showed me at the right moment precisely where I stood," Rohritz murmured.   "And, between ourselves,—never allude to it again,—it was necessary."

*　　*　　*　　*　　*　　*　　*

The captain, who naturally enough sees nothing in his friend's words but an allusion to his altered circumstances, sighs, and thinks, "What a pity!"

CHAPTER XIV.

A DEPARTURE.

When the three wanderers arrive at Erlach Court a little after midnight, they find the rest in the dining-room, still sitting around the remains of a very much over-cooked dinner. Stasy, in a pink peignoir, hails Rohritz upon his entrance with, "I have won my bet,—six pair of Jouvin's gloves

from Katrine. I wagered you would be late—
ha! ha!"

"A fact easy to foresee, in view of the condition of the horses and the roads," Rohritz rejoins,
frowning.

The affair, so far as it concerns Stella, who approaches her mother with fear and trembling,
turns out fairly well. As the Baroness's natural
feeling of maternal anxiety for her daughter's
safety has only been temporarily disturbed by
Stasy's insinuations, she forgets to scold Stella, in
her joy at seeing her safe and sound. That she
may not give way to an outburst of anger upon
further consideration, and that an end may be put
to Stasy's jests, the captain instantly plunges into
a detailed account of all the mishaps that have
befallen Stella and her escort.

Katrine meanwhile searches for a telegram that
has arrived for Rohritz, finally discovering it under
an old-fashioned decanter on the sideboard.

"What is the matter?" she asks, kindly, seeing
him change colour upon reading it.

"Moritz, an apoplectic stroke, come immediately.
ERNESTINE."

he reads aloud. "'Tis from my eldest sister. Poor
Tina!" he murmurs. "I must leave to-morrow
by the seven-o'clock train from Gradcnik. Can
you let me have a pair of horses, Les?"

The captain sends instantly to have everything in readiness.

Shortly afterwards Rohritz takes leave of the ladies; he does not, of course, venture to expect that after the fatigues of the day they will rise before six in the morning for his sake. Stella's hand he retains a few seconds longer than he ought, and he notices that it trembles in his own.

So summary is his mode of preparation that his belongings are all packed in little more than half an hour, and he then disposes himself to spend the rest of the night in refreshing slumber. But sleep is denied him: a strange unrest possesses him. Happiness knocks at the door of his heart and entreats, 'Ah, let me in, let me in!' But Reason stands sentinel there and refuses to admit her.

He tossed to and fro for hours, unable to compose himself. Towards morning he had a strange dream. He seemed to be walking in a lovely summer night: the moon shone bright through the branches of an old linden, and lay in arabesque patterns of light on the dark ground beneath. Suddenly he perceived a small dark object lying at his feet, and when he stooped to see what it was he found it was a little bird that had fallen out of the nest and now looked up at him sadly and helplessly from large dark eyes. He picked it up and warmed it against his breast. It nestled delightedly into his hand. He pressed his lips to the warm little head; an electric thrill shot through his veins. "Stella, my poor, dear, foolish child!" he murmured.

Rat-tat-tat—rat-tat-tat! He started and awoke. The servant was knocking at his door to arouse him. "The Herr Baron's hot shaving-water."

When, half an hour later, he appears, dressed with his usual fastidious care, in the dining-room, he finds both the master and the mistress of the house already there to do the honours of what he calls, with courteous exaggeration, 'the last meal of the condemned.' Shortly afterwards Stasy appears. The general, through a servant, makes a back-ache a plea for not rising at so early an hour.

The carriage is announced; Rohritz kisses Katrine's hand and thanks her for some delightful weeks. She and the captain accompany him to the carriage, while Stasy contents herself with kissing her hand to him from the terrace. At the last moment Rohritz discovers that he has no matches, and a servant is sent into the house to get him some.

"It is settled between us, now," Katrine begins, "that whenever you are fairly tired out with mankind in general——"

"I shall come to Erlach Court to learn to prize it in particular; most certainly, madame," Rohritz replies, his glance roving restlessly among the upper windows of the castle. "*Au revoir* at Christmas!"

The morning is cool; the cloudless skies are pale blue, the turf silver gray with dew; the carriage makes deep ruts in the moist gravel of the sweep; the blossoms have fallen from the linden and are lying by thousands shrivelled and faded at its feet, while the rustle of the dripping dew among its mighty branches can be distinctly heard.

The servant brings the matches. Rohritz still lingers.

"Do not forget, madame, to bid the Baroness Meineck——" he begins, when the sound of a limping foot-fall strikes his ear. He turns hastily: it is Stella,—Stella in a white morning gown, her hair loosely twisted up, very pale, very charming, her eyes gazing large and grave from out her mobile countenance.

"Have you, too, made your appearance at last, you lazy little person? 'Tis very good of you,—highly praiseworthy," the captain says, with a laugh to annul the effect of Stella's innocent eagerness.

A burst of laughter comes from the terrace.

"I hope you are duly gratified, Baron," a discordant voice calls out. "When our little girl gets up at six o'clock it must be for a very grand occasion!"

Blushing painfully, Stella with difficulty restrains her tears; she says not a word, but stands there absolutely paralyzed with embarrassment.

"I thank you from my heart for your kindness,"

Rohritz says, hastily approaching her. "I should have regretted infinitely not seeing you to say good-bye."

"You had a great deal of trouble with me yesterday, and were very patient," she manages to stammer. "Except Uncle Jack, no one has been so kind to me as you, since papa died, and I wanted to thank you for it."

He takes her soft, warm little hand in his and carries it to his lips.

"God guard you!" he murmurs.

"Hurry, or you will be too late!" the captain calls to him. He is going to accompany him to the station, and he fairly drags him away to the carriage.

The driver cracks his whip, the horses start off, Rohritz waves his hat for a last farewell, and the carriage vanishes behind the iron gates of the park.

"Poor Stella! poor Stella!" Stasy screams from the terrace, fairly convulsed with laughter. "Delightful fellow, Rohritz: he knows what he's about!"

But Stella covers her burning face with her hands. "I will go into a convent," she says; "there at least I shall be able to conduct myself properly."

Meanwhile, Rohritz and the captain roll on towards the station. They are both silent.

"He is desperately in love with her," thinks

the captain. " Is he really too poor to marry, I wonder?"

Yes, it is true Rohritz is desperately in love with her; she hovers before his eyes in all her loveliness like a vision. He would fain stretch out his arms to her, but he is perpetually tormented by the persistent question, " Whom does she resemble ?" Suddenly he knows. The knowledge almost paralyzes him !

Beside the pure, fresh vision of Stella he sees leaning over a black-haired, vagabond-looking man at the roulette-table at Baden-Baden the hectic ruin of a woman who has been magnificently beautiful, a woman with painted cheeks and with deep lines about her eyes and mouth,—otherwise the very image of Stella.

Twelve years since he had seen her thus, and upon asking who she was had been told that she was the mistress of the Spanish violinist Corrèze, and that she was little by little sacrificing her entire fortune to gratify the artist's love of gaming. His informant added that she was a woman of birth and position, and that she had left her husband and child in obedience to the promptings of passion. He did not know her husband's name: she called herself then Madame Corrèze.

Why do all Stasy's malicious remarks about Stella's unpleasant connections, and about the Meineck temperament, crowd into his mind?

There is no denying that Stella is lacking in a certain kind of reserve.

While he is waiting with the captain beneath the vine-wreathed shed of the station for the train which has just been signalled, these hateful thoughts refuse to be banished. He suddenly asks his friend, who stands smoking in silence beside him,—

"What is the story about your sister's sister-in-law to which Fräulein von Gurlichingen so often alludes? Was she the same Eugenie Meineck to whom you were once devoted?"

"Yes," the captain makes reply, half closing his eyes, "and she was a charming, enchanting creature; Stella reminds me of her. No one has a good word for her now, but there was a time when it was impossible to pet and praise her enough."

"What became of her?"

"She fell into bad—or rather into incapable—hands. She married an elderly man who did not know how to manage her. Good heavens! the best horse stumbles under a bad rider, and——"

"Well, and——?"

"She had not been married long when she ran off with a Spanish musician, a coarse fellow, who beat her, and ran through her property. He was quite famous. His name was—was——" The captain snaps his fingers impatiently.

"Corrèze?" Rohritz interposes.

"Yes, that is it,—Corrèze!"

At this moment the train arrives.

"All kind messages to the ladies at Erlach Court, and many thanks for your hospitality, Jack!" Rohritz says, jumping into the coupé.

"I hope we shall see you soon again, old fellow; but—hm!—have you no message for my foolish little Stella?" asks the captain.

"I hope with all my heart that she may soon fall into good hands!" Rohritz says, with emphasis, in a hard vibrant voice.

And the train whizzes away.

"The deuce!" thinks the captain; "there's but a slim chance for the poor girl. Good heavens! if I loved Stella and my circumstances did not allow of my marrying, I'd take up some profession. But Rohritz is too fine a gentleman for that."

Meanwhile, Rohritz leans back discontentedly in the corner of an empty coupé.

"A charming, bewitching creature,—Stella resembles her," he murmurs to himself. "She married an elderly man from pique, and so on." He lights a cigar and puffs forth thick clouds of smoke. "She might not have married me from pique, but from loneliness, from gratitude for a little sympathy. And if Zino had come across her later on—— I was on the point of losing my head. Thank God it is over!"

He sat still for a while, his head propped upon his hand, and then found that his cigar had gone out. With an impatient gesture he tossed it out of the window.

"I could not have believed I should have had such an attack at my years," he muttered. He set his teeth, and his face took on a resolute expression. "It must be," he said to himself.

Outside the wind sighed among the trees and in the tall meadow-grass.

It sounded to him like the sobbing of his rejected happiness.

CHAPTER XV.

SCATTERED.

SUMMER has gone. The birds are silent; brown leaves cover the green grass, falling thicker and thicker from the weary trees; long, white gossamers float in the damp, oppressive air: the autumn is weaving a shroud for the dying year.

Scared by the whistling blasts and the floods of rain, the swallows have assembled in dark flocks; they are seen in long rows on the telegraph-wires in eager twittering discussion of their approaching flight, and then, the next morning, early, before the lingering autumn sun has opened its drowsy eyes, the heavens are black with their flying squadrons.

But the final death-struggle is not yet over, the warmth in all vegetation is not yet chilled; bright flowers still bloom at the feet of the fast-thinning trees, and, shaking the falling leaves from their cups, laugh up at the blue skies.

The little company which at the beginning of this simple story we found assembled at Erlach Court is now dispersed to all quarters of the world: the general is ' grazing,' as Jack Leskjewitsch expresses it, with somebody in Southern Hungary; Stasy is fluttering, with sweet smiles and covert malice, from friend to friend, seeming at present on the lookout for a fixed engagement for the winter; Rohritz is off on his wonted autumnal hunting-expedition, and more than usually bored by it; and the Leskjewitsches are still at Erlach Court, where Freddy is in perpetual conflict with his new tutor, a spare, lank philosopher lately imported for him from Bohemia, and Katrine quaffs full draughts of her beloved solitude, without experiencing the great degree of rapture she had anticipated from it; there is a cloud upon her brow, and her annoyance is principally due to the fact that the captain begins to show unmistakable signs of a lapse from his former manly energy of character; he scarcely holds himself as erect as was his wont, and the only occupation which he pursues with any notable degree of self-sacrifice and devotion is the breaking of a pair of very young and very fiery horses.　This praiseworthy pursuit, however, absorbs only a few hours at most of each day, and he kills the rest of the time as best he can, irritating by his idleness his wife, who is always occupied with most interesting matters. In addition he reads silly novels, and greatly admires the ' Maître de Forges.'

"How can any man admire the ' Maître de Forges' ?" Katrine asks, indignantly.

The Baroness and Stella have been back in their mill-cottage at Zalow for many weeks, and Stella is, as usual, left entirely to herself.

In addition to the daily scribbling over of various sheets of foolscap, the Baroness, instead of bestowing any attention upon her daughter, is mainly occupied with superintending the carrying out of all the governmental prophylactic measures which are to secure to Zalow entire immunity from the cholera. She has come off victorious in many a battle with the culpably negligent village authority, and, to the immense edification of the inmates of the various villas, already somewhat accustomed to the vagaries of the Baroness Meineck, she now goes from one manure-heap to another of the place, at the head of a battalion of barefooted village children provided with watering-pots filled with a disinfectant, the due apportionment of which she thus oversees herself.

It was long an undecided question whether this winter, like the last, should be spent in Zalow.

Finally the Baroness decided that it was absolutely necessary for herself as well as for Stella that the cold season of the year should be passed in Paris, for herself that she might have access to much information needed for the completion of her 'work,' for Stella that a final polish might be given to her singing and that she might be definitively prepared for the stage.

Every one who has ever had anything to do with Lina Meineck knows that if she once takes any scheme into her head it is sure to be carried out: therefore, having made-up her mind to go to Paris, she will go, although no one among all her relatives has an idea of where the requisite funds are to come from.

It does not occur to any one that she could lay hands upon the small fortune belonging to Stella, who has lately been declared of age.

CHAPTER XVI.

ZALOW.

It is a mild autumn afternoon; Stella, just returned from a visit to her sister, who has lately been blessed by the arrival of a little daughter, has taken a seat with some trifling piece of work in her mother's study to tell her about the pretty child and Franzi's household, but at her first word her mother calls out to her from her writing-table,—

" Not now,—not now, I beg; do not disturb me."

And the girl, silenced and mortified, bends over the tiny shirt which she has begun to crochet for her little niece, and keeps all that she had hoped to tell to herself.

The autumn sun shines in at the window, and its crimson light gleams upon a large tin box standing on the floor in a corner, the box in which the deceased colonel had kept all the letters he ever received from his wife. Tied up with ribbon, and methodically arranged according to their dates, they are packed away here just as they were sent to his wife from his old quarters at Enns. She has never looked at them, has not even taken the trouble to destroy them, but has simply pushed them aside as useless rubbish.

Stella had rummaged among them, with indescribable sensations in deciphering these yellow documents with their faint odour of lavender and decay, for here were letters full of ardour and passion, letters in which Lina Meineck wrote to her husband, for instance, when he was away during the Schleswig campaign,—

" The weather is fine to-day, and every one is praising the lovely spring; but it is always winter for me in your absence; with you away my thermometer always stands at ten degrees below zero!"

With a shudder Stella put back these relics of a dead love in their little coffin. It was as if she had heard a corpse speak.

Since then she has often wished to burn the letters, out of affectionate reverence for the dead who held them sacred, but she has never summoned up sufficient courage to ask her mother's permission.

The little shirt is finished; with a sigh Stella folds it together, and is just wondering what she shall do next to occupy the rest of the afternoon, when the Baroness says,—

"Have you nothing to do, Stella?"

"No, mamma."

"Well, then, you can run over to Schwarz's and buy me a couple of quires of paper; my supply is exhausted, and I will, meanwhile, have tea brought up."

Donning her hat and gloves, Stella sets forth. Herr Schwarz is the only shopkeeper in the village, and his shop contains a more heterogeneous collection of articles than the biggest shop in Paris. He often boasts that he has everything for sale, from poison for rats, and dynamite bombs, to paper collars and scented soap. His shop is at the other end of the village from the mill, and to reach it Stella must pass the most ornate of the villas.

Most of the summer residents have left Zalow; only a few special enthusiasts for country air have been induced by the exceptionally fine autumn weather to prolong their stay. In the garden of the tailor who built himself a hunting-lodge in the style of Francis the First a group of people are disputing around a croquet-hoop in the centre of a very small lawn, and in the Giroflé Villa some one is practising Schumann's 'Études symphoniques' with frantic ardour. Stella smiles; the last sound that fell upon her ears before she went to Erlach Court with her mother was the 'Études symphoniques,' the first that greeted her upon her return in the middle of August was the 'Études symphoniques.' She knows precisely who is so persistently given over to these rhapsodies,—an odd creature, a woman named Fuhrwesen, who has been a teacher of the piano for some years in Russia, and who, now over forty, still hopes for a career as an artist.

Stella's little commission is soon attended to. As she hands her mother the paper on her return, their only servant, a barefooted girl from the village, with a red-and-black checked kerchief tied about her head, brings the tea into the room.

"A letter has come for you," the Baroness says to her daughter,—"a letter from Grätz. I do not know the hand. Who can be writing to you from Grätz? Where did I put it?"

And while her mother is rummaging among her papers for the letter, Stella repeats, with a throbbing heart, "From Grätz. Who can be writing to me from Grätz?" and she covertly kisses the four-leaved clover on her bracelet which is to bring her good fortune, and proceeds instantly to build a charming castle in the air.

Her uncle has told her of Edgar's loss of property and his consequent inability to think of marriage at present. Perhaps Uncle Jack told her this to comfort her. That Edgar loves her she has, with the unerring instinct of total inexperience of the world, read, not once, but hundreds of times, in his eyes, and consequently she has spent many a long autumn evening in wondering whether he is looking for a position—some lucrative employment—to enable him to marry. He is not lacking in attainments; he could work if he would. "And he will for my sake," the heart of this foolish, fantastic young person exults in thinking.

From day to day she has been hoping that he would send her—perhaps through Jack or Katrine—some message, hitherto in vain. But now at last he has written himself; for from whom else could this letter from Grätz be? She knew no human being there save himself.

"Here is the letter," her mother says, at last.

Stella opens it hastily, and starts.

"Whom is it from?" asks the Baroness. She uses the hour for afternoon tea to rest from her literary labours; with her feet upon the round of a chair in front of her, a volume of Buckle in her lap, a pile of books beside her, a number of the 'Revue des deux Mondes' in her left hand, and her teacup in her right, she partakes alternately of the refreshing beverage and of an article upon Henry the Eighth. "Whom is the letter from?" she asks, absently, laying her cup aside to take up a volume of Froude.

"From Stasy," Stella replies.

"Ah! what does she want?"

"She asks me to send her from Rumberger's, in Prague, three hundred napkins or so, upon approbation, that she may oblige some friend of hers whom I do not know, and for whom I do not care."

"Positively insolent!" remarks the Baroness. "And does she say nothing else?"

"Nothing of any consequence," says Stella, reading on and suddenly changing colour.

"Ah!" The Baroness marks the Revue with her pencil. When she looks up again, Stella has left the room. Without wasting another thought upon her, the student goes on with her reading.

Stella, meanwhile, is lying on the bed in her little room, into which the moon shines marking the floor with the outlines of the window-panes.

Her face is buried among the pillows, and she is crying as if her heart would break.

'Nothing of any consequence'! True enough, of no consequence for the Baroness, that second sheet of Stasy's, but for Stella of great, of immense consequence.

"Guess whom I encountered lately at Steinbach?" writes the Gurlichingen. "Edgar Rohritz. Of course we talked of our dear Erlach Court, and consequently of you. He spoke very kindly of you, only regretting that in consequence of your odd education, or of a certain exaggeration of temperament, you lacked reserve, *tenue*, a defect which might be unfortunate for you in life. Of course I defended you. They say everywhere that he is betrothed to Emmy Strahlenheim.

"Have you heard the news,—the very latest? Rohritz *is* a sly fellow indeed. All that loss of property of which we heard so much was only a fraud. The report originated in some trifling depreciation of certain bank-stock. He did not contradict the report, allowing himself to be thought impoverished that he might escape the persecutions of the mothers and daughters of Grätz. Max Steinbach let out the secret a while ago. Is it not the best joke in the world? I am glad no one can accuse me of ever making the slightest advances to him."

CHAPTER XVII.

WINTER.

The death-struggle of the year is over,—past are the treacherous gleams of sunlight among falling leaves and smiling flowers,—past, past! Cold and grave like a hired executioner, mute and secret like a midnight assassin, the first hard frost has fallen upon the earth in the previous night and completed its great work of destruction.

It is All Souls'; the Meinecks leave for Paris in the evening, and in the morning Stella goes to mass in the little church on the mountain-side at the foot of which is the churchyard,—the churchyard in which the colonel lies buried. The flames of the thick wax candles on the altar, the flames of the candles thick and thin lighted everywhere in memory of the dead, flicker dull and red in the gray daylight.

In one of the carved seats beside the altar sits the priest's sister, her prayer-book bound in red velvet, and a large yellow rose in her new winter hat. She nods kindly to Stella when she enters, and gathers her skirts aside to make room for her.

In the body of the long narrow church are cowering on the benches all kinds of dilapidated figures, men and women, almost all old, frail, and crippled,—those able to work have no time to pray. It is very cold; their breath comes as vapour from their lips; the outlines of their blue wrinkled faces show vaguely behind clouds of yellowish-gray smoke; the odour of damp stone and damp clothes mingles with the smell of incense and wax; the sputter of the candles, the dripping of the wax, the rattle of beads, mingle with the monotonous chant of the priest at the altar.

When mass is over, and she has taken leave of the priest's kindly sister, Stella goes out into the churchyard,—a miserable place, with neglected graves, scarcely elevated in mounds above the ground, with iron crosses upon which rust has eaten away the inscriptions, or wooden ones which the wind has blown down to lie rotting on the ground. The colonel's grave is beneath a weeping-willow at the extreme end of the churchyard, whence one can look directly down upon the broad shining stream. Tended like a garden-bed by Stella, cherished as the very apple of her eye, it yet looks dreary enough to-day: the leaves are hanging black and withered from the stalks of the chrysanthemums which Stella planted with her own hands only a few weeks ago, their pretty flowers, which but yesterday stood forth red and yellow against the blue of the sky, now colourless and faded beyond recognition. A wreath of fresh flowers

lies among the chrysanthemums, but these too are
. beginning to fade. Stella kneels down on the gray
rimy grass beside the grave and kisses fervently
the hard frozen ground.

"Adieu, papa," she murmurs, and then adds,
"But why say adieu to you? You are always with
me everywhere I go; you are beside me, a loving
guardian angel seeking for happiness for me. Do
not grieve too much that you cannot find it: open
your arms and take me to you; I am all ready."

*   *   *   *   *   *   *

Then the mill is closed; the keys are left with
the pastor, and the Meinecks go to Prague, which
on the same evening they leave by the train for the
west. As far as Furth they are alone, but when they
change coupés after the examination of their luggage they are unable, in spite of bribing the officials,
to exclude strangers. At the last moment, just as
the train is about to start, a lady with two hand-
bags, a travelling-case, a shawl-strap, and a band-
box steps into their compartment and hopes she
does not disturb them. Much vexed, Stella scans
the lady, who wears a water-proof adorned with as
many tassels as bedeck the trappings of an Anda-
lusian mule, and with a red pompon in her hat,
fastened in its place with a bird's claw four inches
long. Stella instantly recognizes her as Fräulein
Bertha Fuhrwesen, the same pianist who has been
spending her holidays upon the 'Études sympho-

niques;' she recognizes Stella at the same moment,
and, although until now she never has exchanged
four words with her, hails her as an old acquaintance and enters into conversation; that is, without
waiting for replies from the young girl she imparts
to her the story of her entire life.

In the course of her experience as teacher of
the piano in Russia, of which mention has already
been made, she has learned much of the rude
nature of Russian social life and the amiability
of young Russian princes; at present she is on
her way to Paris, whence she is to make a tour
with an impresario through South America and
Australia, by the way of Uruguay and Tasmania.
Apart from the artistic laurels she expects to win,
she anticipates furthering greatly the advance of
civilization among the savage aborigines by her
musical efforts.

She asks Stella several times why she is so silent,
and when the girl excuses herself on the plea of
a headache she says she had better eat something,
and produces from her travelling-case, embroidered
with red and white roses, and from between a
flannel dressing-sacque and various toilet articles, a
bulky brown package containing the remains of a
cold capon.

Stella thanks her, and declines the tempting deli-
cacy, saying that she will try to sleep.

Fräulein Fuhrwesen of course attributes Stella's

reserve to the notorious arrogance of the Meinecks, who will have nothing to say to a poor pianist, and, mortally offended, she likewise takes refuge in silence

Stella dozes.

The conductor opens the door to tell the ladies that the next station is Nuremberg, whereupon the artiste takes a comb and a tangled braid of false hair out of her travelling-case and begins to dress her hair.

The train puffs and whizzes through the grayish light of the late autumn morning and stops with a shrill whistle at Nuremberg.

Stella and her mother through the pillars of the railway-station catch a glimpse, among the picturesque gables and roofs of the old town, of ugly new houses pretentious in style, looking as if built of pasteboard; they partake of a miserable breakfast, buy a package of gingerbread and a volume of Tauchnitz, get into another train, and are whirled away, on—on—through yellow and brown harvest-fields, through small bristling forests of pines and barren meadows, past villages, churchyards, and little towns that look positively dead. Late in the afternoon the Rhine comes in sight: gray, shrouded in mist, not at all like itself, without sunshine, without merriment, without Englishmen, almost without steamers, it grumbles and groans as if vexed by some evil, melancholy dream, while a

m

thousand sad sighs tremble through the red-and-yellow vineyards on its shores,—the shores where folly grows.

Away—on—on! More dead towns, with dreamy old names that fall upon the ear like echoes of ancient legends. Everything is drowsy; gray shadows cover the earth; the night falls; green and red lanterns gleam through the darkness.

Cologne!

Cologne, where one can sup, and dress, and at all events see the cathedral in the dark.

CHAPTER XVIII.

SOPHIE OBLONSKY.

STELLA and her mother have finished their supper. The Baroness, who has exhausted her entire stock of literary food provided for the journey, is at the book-stall, looking for more reading-matter; she examines the counterfeit presentments on exhibition there of the great German heroes, the Emperor Wilhelm, Bismarck, and Von Moltke, among which distinguished personages chance has slipped in the portrait of Mademoiselle Zampa. Suddenly, under a pile of books that seem to have been pushed out of the way, she discovers a green pamphlet which she instantly recognizes as a child of her own, an essay entitled 'Is Woman to be Independent?' Of course she buys the book, and, betaking herself to the small 'ladies' parlour' adjoining the spacious waiting-room, takes a seat opposite Stella, and, her eyes sparkling with enthusiasm, is soon absorbed in the study of her work.

Meanwhile, Stella has vainly tried to become interested in the English novel purchased at Nuremberg; she leaves the lovers, after their twenty-second reconciliation, beneath a blossoming hawthorn, and, closing the book with a slight yawn, sits up and looks about her. At the other end of the room, as far as possible from Stella, sits the pianist, writing a letter: from time to time she looks up to bestow upon Stella a hostile glance. On the other side of the same table two ladies are engaged in partaking of the best supper that the restaurant of the railway-hotel can afford,—a supper with *foie gras*, mayonnaise of lobster, and a bottle of champagne. One of them, with the figure and face of a Juno, her costly furs falling gracefully from her full shoulders, is so perfumed that even the atmosphere about Stella reeks with *peau d'Espagne.* Eyebrows, lips—her entire face is painted; and yet she does not look in the least like a travelling prima donna.

" Can that be the Princess Oblonsky?" Stella

says to herself, with a start. "No doubt of it: it is."

And there beside the Princess, on Stella's side of the table, but with her back to her,—who is that?

Jack Leskjewitsch always used to declare that Stasy's shoulders were shaped like a champagne-bottle. Stella wonders whether anywhere in the world can be found a pair of more sloping shoulders than those which that fur-trimmed circular fails to conceal. Both ladies devote their entire attention for a time to their supper; at last the Princess pushes away her plate with a certain impatience, and with an odd smile says, "Where did you first know him?"

"Whom?" asks the other.

It is Stasy, of course; there may be another woman in the world with those same sloping shoulders, but there can be none with such a thin, affected voice.

"Why, him, my chevalier *sans peur et sans reproche*," says the Princess.

"Edgar? Oh, I spent a long time in the same house with him last summer," Stasy declares. "He is still one of the most interesting men I have ever met. Such a profile! such eyes! and so attractive in manner!"

The ladies speak French, the Princess with perfect fluency but a rather hard accent, Stasy somewhat stumblingly.

"Strange!" the Oblonsky murmurs.

"What is strange?" asks Stasy.

"Why, that you have seen him," the Princess replies; "that he is yet alive; in fact, that he ever did live, and that we loved each other. I was wont for so many years to regard that episode at Baden-Baden as a dream that at last I forgot that the dream had any connection with reality." The words fall from the beautiful woman's lips slowly, softly, with veiled richness and intense melancholy. After a pause she goes on: "I seem to have read there in Baden-Baden a romance which enthralled my entire being! It was on a lovely summer day, and the roses were in bloom all about me, while delicious music in the distance fell dreamily and softly on my ear, and the fragrance of roses and the charm of melody mingled with the poem I was reading. Suddenly, and before I had read to the end, the romance slipped from my hands, and since then I have sought it in vain! But it still seems to me more charming than all the romances in the world; and I cannot cease from searching for it, that I may read the last chapter." Then, suddenly changing her tone, she shrugs her shoulders and says, "Who can tell what disappointment awaits me?—how Edgar may have changed? How does he seem? Is he gay, contented with his lot?"

"No, Sonja, that he is not," Stasy assures her, sentimentally. "To be sure, he is too proud to parade his grief; in society he bears himself coldly, indifferently; but there is an inexpressible melancholy in his look. Oh, he has not forgotten!"

Stella's eyes flash angrily.

"She lies!" the heart in her breast cries out; "she lies!"

Meanwhile, the friends clasp each other's hands sympathetically.

"He never knew how I suffered," the Princess sighs. "Does he suppose that I accepted Oblonsky's hand with any thought of self? No,—a thousand times no! I determined to free Edgar from the martyrdom he was enduring from his family because of me. I took upon myself the burden of a joyless, loveless marriage, I had myself nailed to the cross, for his sake!"

"She lies!" Stella's heart cries out again; "she lies!"

But Stasy sighs, "I always understood you, Sonja." After a pause she adds, "You know, I suppose, that he grew gray immediately after that sad affair,—after your marriage,—almost in a single night?"

"Gray!" murmurs the Princess; "gray! And he had such beautiful dark-brown hair. He must have heard much evil of me; perhaps he believed it: it pleases men to think evil of the women who have caused them suffering. Well, you know how innocent were all the little flirtations with which I tried in vain to fill the dreary vacuum of my existence, from the artists whom I patronized, to Zino Capito, with whom I trifled. If only some one could explain it all to him!—or if "—the Princess's eyes gleam with conscious power,—"if I could only meet him myself, then——"

"Then what?" says Stasy, threatening her friend archly with her forefinger; "then you would turn his head again, only to leave him to drag out a still drearier existence than before."

"You are mistaken," the Princess whispers. "There is many a strain of music that beginning in a minor key changes to major only to close softly and sweetly in minor tones. Anastasia, my first marriage was a tomb in which I was buried alive——"

"And would you be buried alive for the second time?" Stasy asks.

"No; I long for a resurrection."

A cold shiver of dread thrills Stella from head to foot. The Baroness looks up from her pamphlet and exclaims, "I really must read you this, Stella. I do not understand how this brochure did not attract more notice. To be sure, when one lives so entirely withdrawn from all intercourse with the literary world, and has no connection at all with the journals, one may expect——"

Stasy turns around. "My dear Baroness!" she exclaims, with effusion. "And you too, Stella! What a delightful surprise! I must introduce you: Baroness Meineck and her daughter,—Princess Oblonsky."

With the extreme graciousness which all great ladies whose social position is partly compromised testify towards their thoroughly respectable sisters, the Princess rises and offers her hand to both Stella and her mother. The Baroness smiles absently; Stella does not smile, and barely touches with her finger-tips the hand extended to her. Meanwhile, Stasy has recognized in Fräulein Fuhrwesen an old acquaintance from Zalow.

"Good-day, Fräulein Bertha!"—"Fräulein Bertha Fuhrwesen, a very fine pianist,"—to the Princess; then to the Meinecks, "You are already acquainted with her." And while the Princess talks with much condescension to the pianist of her adoration for music, Stasy whispers to Stella, "Don't be so stiff towards Sonja: you might almost be supposed to be jealous of her."

"Ridiculous!" Stella says angrily through her set teeth, and blushing to the roots of her hair.

Stasy taps her on the cheek with her forefinger, with a pitying glance that takes in her entire person, from her delicate—almost too delicate—pale face to her shabby travelling-dress, the identical brown army-cloak which she had worn on the journey to Venice three years before, and rejoins,—

"Ridiculous indeed—most ridiculous—to dream

of rivalling Sonja. Wherever she appears, we ordinary women are nowhere."

" Verviers—Paris—Brussels !" the porter shouts into the room.

All rise, and pick up plaids and travelling-bags; the porters hurry in ; a lanky footman and a sleepy-looking maid wait upon the Princess Oblonsky, who nods graciously as they all crowd out upon the railway-platform. The Meinecks enter a coupé where an American whose trousers are too short, and his wife whose hat is too large, have already taken their seats. The pianist looks in at the door, but as soon as she perceives Stella starts back with horror in her face.

" I seem to have made an enemy of that woman," Stella thinks, negligently. What does it matter to her? Poor Stella! Could she but look into the future !

The train starts; while the Baroness, neglectful of the simplest precautions with regard to her eyes, continues to peruse her masterpiece by the yellow light of the coupé lamp, the American goes to sleep, hat and all, upon her companion's shoulder, and Stella sits bolt upright in the cool draught of night air by the window, repeating to herself alternately, " I long for a resurrection !" and " Wherever Sonja appears, we ordinary women are nowhere !"

She, then, is the enchantress who has ruined the happiness of his life,—she the—— She is indeed

beautiful; but how hollow,—how false! Everything about her—soul, heart, and all—is painted,
like her face. Could he possibly be her dupe a
second time? Suddenly the girl feels the blood
rush to her cheeks.

"What affair is it of mine? What do I care?"
she asks herself, angrily. "He too is false, vain,
and heartless; he too can act a part."

CHAPTER XIX.

PARIS.

STELLA has scarcely closed her eyes, when the
train reaches Paris, about six o'clock. The morning is cold and damp, the usual darkness of the
-time of day disagreeably enhanced by the white
gloom of an autumn fog,—a gloom which the
street-lamps are powerless to counteract, and in
which they show like lustreless red specks.

Through this depressing white gloom, Stella and
her mother are driven in a rattling little omnibus,
with a couple of other travellers, through a Paris as
silent as the grave, to the Hôtel Bedford, Rue Pasquier. An Englishwoman at Nice once recommended it to the Baroness as that wonder of wonders,
a first-class hotel with second-class prices, and it is
under English patronage. English lords and ladies

now and then occupy the first story, and consequently the garret-rooms are continually inhabited by impoverished but highly distinguished scions of English "county families." In the reading-room, between 'Burke's Peerage' and Lodge's 'Vicissitudes of Families' is placed an album containing the photographs of two peeresses. The *clientèle* is as aristocratic as it is economical: each despises all the rest, and one and all dispute the weekly bills. Stella and her mother are by no means enchanted with this hotel, and they sally forth as soon as they are somewhat rested, in search of furnished lodgings.

But the funds are scanty: their expenses ought to be paid out of a hundred and fifty francs a month!

The first day passes, and our Austrians have as yet found nothing suitable. The cheapest lodgings are confined and dark, and smell, as the ladies express it, of English people; that is, of a mixture of camphor, patchouli, and old nut-shells. The bedrooms in these cheap lodgings consist of a sort of windowless closets, entirely dependent for ventilation upon a door into the drawing-room which can be left open at night.

Meanwhile, the living at the Bedford is dear. The Baroness arrives at the conclusion that private quarters at three hundred francs a month would be more economical, and finally decides to spend this sum upon her winter residence.

For three hundred francs very much better lodgings are to be had; the bedrooms have windows, but there are still all kinds of discomforts to be endured, the worst of which consists perhaps in the fact that none of the proprietors of these rooms, which are mostly intended for bachelors, is willing to undertake to provide food for the two ladies.

At last in the Rue de Lêze an *appartement* is found which answers their really moderate requirements; but just at the last moment the Baroness discovers that the concierge is a very suspicious-looking individual, and remembers that the previous year a horrible murder was committed in the Rue de Lêze; wherefore negotiations are at once broken off.

A pretty *appartement* in the Rue de l'Arcade pleases Stella particularly, perhaps because the drawing-room is furnished with buhl cabinets. The Baroness is just about to close with the concierge, who does the honours of the place,—there is merely a question of five francs to be settled,— when with a suspicious sniff she remarks, " 'Tis strange how strongly the atmosphere of this room is impregnated with musk!"

Whereupon the concierge explains that the rooms have lately been occupied by Mexican gentlemen, who shared the reprehensible Southern habit of indulging too freely in perfumes; and when the Baroness glances doubtfully at a dressing-table which scarcely presents a masculine appearance, and which boasts a sky-blue pincushion stuck full of different kinds of pins, he hastens to add, without waiting to be questioned, that the Mexican gentlemen had chiefly occupied themselves in collecting and arranging butterflies.

" Mexican men would seem to have long fair hair, mamma," Stella here interposes, having just pulled a golden hair at least a yard long out of the crochetted antimacassar of a low chair.

The face of the Baroness, who always suspects French immorality everywhere, turns to marble; tossing her head, she grasps Stella by the hand and hurries out with her, passing the astounded concierge without so much as deigning to bid him good-bye.

She refuses to take a lodging in the Rue Pasquier, because it seems to her ' too reasonable;' she is convinced that some one must have died of cholera in a certain big bed with red curtains, else the rent never would have been so low.

At last, after a four days' pilgrimage, the ladies find what answers their requirements in a little hotel called ' At the Three Negroes,' kept by a kindly, light-hearted Irishwoman.

At the Baroness's first words, " We are looking for lodgings for two quiet, respectable ladies," she instantly rejoins, " My house will suit you exactly; the quietest house in all Paris. I never receive any—hm !—a certain kind of ladies, and never

more than one Deputy; two always quarrel."
Whereupon the Irishwoman and the Austrian lady
come to terms immediately, and the Meinecks
move into the second story of 'The Three Negroes'
that very day, the Irishwoman being quite ready
also to provide them with food. · The price for a
salon and two bedrooms—with very large windows,
'tis true, as Stella observes—is three hundred and
twenty francs a month.

*   *   *   *   *   *   *

After the lodgings are thus fortunately secured the
Baroness sets about finding a singing-teacher for
Stella.   Always decided and to the point, she goes
directly to the man in authority at the Grand Opera
to inquire for a 'first-class Professor.'   Oddly
enough, it appears that this authority has no time
to attend to matters so important.   Dismissed with
but slight encouragement, the Baroness tries her
fortune at the office of one of the smaller operas;
but since she presents herself here with her daughter without introduction of any kind, the official
seated behind a dusty writing-table has no time to
devote to her, all that he has being absorbed in
a quarrel with two ladies who have just applied to
him for the ninth time,—"yes," he exclaims, with
a despairing flourish of his hands, "for the ninth
time this month, for free tickets!"
Whilst the Baroness and Stella linger hesitatingly
on the threshold, a slender, sallow young man with

sharply-cut features, and with a picturesque Astrachan collar and a very long surtout, enters the place by an opposite door. He scans Stella's face and figure keenly, and, approaching her, asks what she desires. The Baroness informs him of their business, whereupon ensues an exchange of civilities and mutual introductions.

The gentleman in the fur collar is none other than the famous impresario Morinski, now on the lookout for a new Patti.

With a pleasant glance towards Stella, he asks who has been the young lady's teacher hitherto.

Of whom has she not taken lessons! The list of her teachers embraces Carelli at Naples, Lamperti at Milan, Garcia in London, and Tosti in Rome.

Here Morinski shakes his black curly head, says, "Too many cooks spoil the broth," and asks, "Why did you not stay longer with one teacher?"

The Baroness takes it upon herself to reply, and explains at considerable length how her historical schemes and researches have hitherto rendered a wandering life for herself and her daughter imperatively necessary.

Morinski, who seems to take more interest in Stella's fine eyes than in her mother's historical studies, interrupts the elder lady with some rudeness, and, turning to Stella, asks, "Do you intend to go upon the stage?"

"Yes," Stella meekly replies.

"Only upon condition of her capacity to become a star of the first magnitude should I consent to my daughter's going upon the stage," the Baroness declares, in her magnificent manner.

"It is a little difficult to prognosticate with certainty in such a case," Herr Morinski observes, with an odd smile. "Hm! hm! You may sometimes see a brilliant meteor flash across the skies, larger apparently than any of the stars; you fix your eyes upon it, but hardly have you begun to admire so exquisite a natural phenomenon when it has vanished. Another time you scarcely perceive a small red spark lying on the pavement, but before you are aware of it, it has set fire to half the town. Just so it is with our artistic *débuts*."

At the close of this tirade, which Herr Morinski has enunciated in very harsh French with a strong Jewish accent, he turns again to Stella and asks, "Will you sing me something? It would interest me very much to hear you."

Stella's heart beats fast. How many other singers have had to engage in an interminable correspondence and to entreat for infinite patronage before gaining admission to the famous Morinski and inducing him to listen to them, while he has asked her to sing, unsolicited, after scarcely ten minutes' conversation!

She gratefully accedes to his proposal.

"I should greatly prefer your making the trial

on the stage itself, rather than in the foyer," says Morinski. "I could decide far better as to the strength of your voice. Have the kindness to follow me."

And, leading the way, he precedes them through an endless labyrinth of ill-lighted corridors to the stage, which, illuminated at this hour by only a couple of foot-lights, shows gray and colourless against the pitch-dark auditorium.

The boards of the stage are marked with various lines in chalk, cabalistic signs of mysterious significance to Stella; in front of the prompter's box stands a prima donna with her bonnet-strings untied and her fur cloak hanging loosely about her shoulders, singing in an undertone a duet with a tenor in a tall silk hat who is kneeling at her feet; at the piano, just below, sits the leader of the orchestra, a little Italian, with long, straight, white hair, and dark eyebrows that protrude for at least an inch over his fierce black eyes, pounding away at the accompaniment, evidently more to accentuate the rhythm than with any desire to accompany harmoniously the duet of the pair.

"The rehearsal will be over immediately," Morinski assures the two ladies.

In fact, the duo between the prima donna and the tenor shortly comes to an end. A short discussion ensues, during which the prima donna alternately scolds the leader, whom she accuses of paying no

attention to the *ritardandos*, and the tenor for his
"lamentable want of all passion."

Morinski throws himself metaphorically between
the disputants and kisses the prima donna's hand.
Without paying him much attention, she scans
Stella from head to foot, says, with an ironical de-
pression of the corners of her mouth, "Ah! a new
star, Morinski!" and withdraws, with an intensely
theatrical stride, her loose fur dolman trailing behind her.

"Hm! a new star, Morinski!" the leader repeats also ironically, stuffing an immense pinch of
snuff the while into his nose.

"Let us hope so," Morinski replies, with re-
proving courtesy.

"Is the signorina to sing us something? It is
twelve o'clock, Morinski; I am hungry. If it
must be, let us be quick. What shall I accompany
for you, mademoiselle?"

"*Ah fors' è lui che l'anima!*" Stella says, in a shy
whisper, "from——"

"I know, I know,—from Traviata," the leader
replies. "You sing it in the original key?"

"Yes."

Almost before Stella has time to take breath, the
little man has struck the chords of the prelude. In
the midst of the aria he takes his hands from the
keys, and shakes his head disapprovingly, so that
his long hair flutters about his ears.

" *Eh bien?*" Morinski calls, with some irritation.

"I have heard enough," the other declares, decidedly. "Haven't you, Morinski? It is a perfectly impossible way to sing,—a perfectly impossible way!"

"Do not be discouraged, Fräulein," says Morinski, reassuringly. "Your voice is superb, full, soft, —one of the finest that I have heard for a long time."

"I do not say no, Morinski," the leader interposes, with the croak of a raven, "but she is absolutely lacking in rhythm, routine, and aplomb."

"She needs a good teacher," says Morinski.

"The teacher has nothing to do with it!" shouts the leader, and with an annihilating stare at Stella he sums up his judgment of her in the words, " *C'est une femme du monde.* You will never make a singer of her!" Then, with the energy that characterizes his every movement, he sets about trying to repair the injury he has just done to his silk hat by brushing it the wrong way.

Poor Stella's eyes fill with tears. Morinski takes both her hands:

"Do not be discouraged, I beg of you, my dear mademoiselle, I entreat;" and with an ardent glance at her delicate face he assures her, "Believe me, you have great qualifications for success on the stage."

"Trust to my experience,—the experience of

forty years; you never will succeed on the stage!"
shouts the Italian.

"Never mind what he says," Morinski whispers.
"I will do all I can for you. I shall take great
pleasure in superintending your lessons personally."

But the leader has sharp ears: "*Pas de bêtises*,
Morinski!" He has put on his hat, and is searching with characteristic eagerness in all his pockets.
"There is my card," he says, at last, drawing it
forth and handing it to the Baroness. "If you
want your daughter taught to sing, take her to
della Seggiola, Rue Lamartine, No ——, the singing-teacher of the Faubourg Saint-Germain and
the Faubourg Saint-Honoré, precisely what you
want. Refer to me if you like; he will make his
charges reasonable for you. *Dio mio*, how hungry
I am! *Allons*, Morinski!"

This is the exact history of Stella Meineck's trial
of her voice at the lyric opera in Paris.

The Baroness has just enough sense and prudence left not to allow Stella to take lessons of
Morinski.

Following the advice of the energetic Italian, she
takes her daughter to Signor della Seggiola.

CHAPTER XX.

THÉRÈSE DE ROHRITZ.

WINTER—such winter as Paris is familiar with —has set in, to make itself at home. The gardeners have stripped the squares and public gardens of their last flowers; the trees and the grass and the bare sod are powdered with snow. When one says 'as white' or 'as pure' as snow, one must never think of Paris snow, for it is brown, black, gray,—everything except white; and, as if ashamed of its characterless existence, it creeps as soon as possible into the earth.

Full six weeks have passed since the Meinecks took up their abode in 'The Three Negroes.' In order to increase their means, the Baroness has generously determined to write newspaper articles, although she has a supreme contempt for all journalistic effort, and she has also completed two shorter essays, for which the Berlin 'Tribune' paid her twenty-five marks.

With a view to making her descriptions of the world's capital vividly real, she pursues her study of Paris with all the thoroughness that characterizes her study of history. She has visited the Morgue, as well as Valentino's, note-book in hand, but escorted by an old carpenter, who once mended a trunk for her and won her heart by his sensible way of talking politics. She paid him five francs for his companionship, and maintains that he was far less tiresome at Valentino's than a fine gentleman. She has devised a most interesting visit shortly to be paid to the Parisian sewers. Meanwhile, in order to make herself perfectly familiar with the life of the streets, she spends three hours daily, two in the forenoon and one in the afternoon, upon the top of various omnibuses.

And Stella,—how does she pass her time? Four times a week she takes a singing-lesson,—two private lessons, and two in della Seggiola's ' class,' besides which she practises daily for about two hours at home. She is at liberty to spend the rest of her time in any mode of self-culture that pleases her. She can go, if she is so inclined, to the Rue Richelieu with her mother, or visit the Louvre alone, can attend to little matters at home, or read learned works and write extracts from them in the book bound in antique leather which her mother gave her upon her birthday.

What wealth of various and interesting occupations and pleasures for a girl of twenty-one! It is quite inconceivable, but nevertheless it is true, that in spite of them she feels lonely and unhappy,— grows daily more nervous and restless, and, without being able to define exactly the cause of her sadness, more melancholy. Her energetic mother, to whom such a vague discontent is absolutely inconceivable, reproaches her with a want of earnestness in her studies and induces a physician to prescribe iron for her.

What is there that iron is not expected to cure?

To-day Stella is again alone at home; her mother has gone out after lunch to take her bird's-eye view of Paris from the top of an omnibus. She has graciously offered to take Stella with her, but Stella thanks her and declines; she detests riding in omnibuses, on the top she grows dizzy, and inside she becomes ill.

"Well, I suppose the only thing that would really please you would be to drive in a barouche-and-pair in the Bois," her mother remarks. "Unfortunately, that I cannot afford." With which she hurries away.

Stella's throat aches; she often has a throat-ache, —the specific throat-ache of a poor child of mortality who has learned to sing with seven different professors, and whose voice has been treated at different times as a soprano, a mezzo-soprano, and a deep contralto. She has been obliged to stop practising in consequence, to-day, and has taken up a volume of Gibbon, but is too *distraite* to comprehend what she reads. It really is strange how slight an interest she takes in the decline of the Roman Empire.

" And if I should not succeed upon the stage, if my voice should not turn out well," she constantly asks herself, " what then ? what then ?"

Why, for a moment—oh, how her cheeks burn as she recalls her delusion !—she absolutely allowed herself to imagine that—— How bitterly she has learned to sneer at her fantastic dreams !

" Has Edmund Rohritz's wife not yet been to see you ?" Leskjewitsch had asked her mother in a letter shortly before. " You do not know her, but I begged Edgar awhile ago to send her to you,— she would be so advantageous an acquaintance for Stella."

"She would indeed," the poor child thinks; " but not even his old friend's request has induced him to do me a kindness."

Her sad, weary glance wanders absently over the various lithographs that adorn the walls, portraits of famous singers, Tamberlik, Rubini, Mario, all with the signature of those celebrities. Apparently the hotel must formerly have enjoyed an extensive artistic patronage.

She takes up Gibbon once more, and does her best to become absorbed in the destinies of the tribunes of the people. In vain.

" Good heavens !" she exclaims, irritably, " who could read a serious book in all this noise ? And ' The Negroes' was recommended to us as a quiet hotel !"

The Deputy from the south of France is pacing
the room above her to and fro, now repeating in a
murmur and anon declaiming with grotesque pathos
to the empty air the speech which he is learning
by heart.

In the room next to him an amateur performer is
piping 'The Last Rose of Summer' on a very hoarse
flute,—an English bagman, who is suffering from
an inflammation of the eyes, wherefore we must not
grudge him his musical distractions. He is piping
'The Last Rose' for the eighteenth time; Stella
has counted.

"'Tis beyond endurance!" the girl exclaims,
closing her Gibbon. "Ah, heavens, how dreary
life is!" she groans. "I wish I were dead!"

Just then there comes a ring at the door. Stella
opens it. A tall, smooth-shaven lackey stands in
the corridor and hands her a card:

"*La Baronne Edmond de Rohritz, née Princesse
Capito.*"

"Madame la Baronne wishes to know if the
Frau Baroness is receiving?" the man asks, van-
ishing when Stella assents.

"He probably takes me for a waiting-maid,"
Stella thinks, childishly, not without some petty
annoyance that she was forced to open the door herself for the servant, and she hurries into the salon,
to put away a piece of mending which is by no
means ornamental. Scarcely has she done so when

a light foot-fall comes tripping up the stairs. There is another ring, and again Stella opens the door. A lady enters, slender, very pale, with delicately-cut features, and large, black, rather restless eyes, which she slightly closes as she looks at Stella, and then pleasantly holds out her hand:

"Mademoiselle Meineck, *n'est-ce pas?*"

Not for one moment is she in doubt whether this tall girl in a plain stuff dress be a soubrette or not.

"My brother-in-law Rohritz wrote me some time ago telling me to call upon your mother and yourself and to ask if I could be of any service to you. I have promised myself the pleasure of doing so every day since; my very critical brother's letter inspired me with eager curiosity; but one never has time for anything in Paris,—nothing pleasant, that is. Well, here I am at last. Is your mother at home?"

"My mother has gone out, but will shortly return; she would greatly regret missing you, madame. If you could be content with my society for a while——" Stella rejoins.

"I should be delighted to have a little talk with you," the lady assures her; "but do you suppose I have time to stay? What an idea in Paris! I had to fairly steal a quarter of an hour of time already appropriated to come to see you. We must postpone our talk. I trust I shall see a great deal of you; I am always at leisure in the evening,—that is, when I do not have to go to bed from sheer fatigue! And how have you passed the time since you came to Paris?"

Madame de Rohritz has installed herself in an arm-chair by the fireplace, has put up her veil and thrown back her furs from her shoulders.

A delicate fragrance exhales from her robes; all Parisian women use perfumes, but how refined, how exquisite, is this fragrance compared with the overpowering odour of *Peau d'Espagne* which surrounds the Princess Oblonsky!

Thérèse Rohritz does not possess her brother's beauty, but everything about her is graceful and attractive,—her veiled glance,—a glance which can be half impertinent sometimes, but which rests upon Stella with evident liking,—her beaming and yet slightly weary smile,—yes, even her hurried articulation and her high-pitched but soft and melodious voice.

"How have you passed the time since you came to Paris?" she asks again.

"We live very quietly," Stella stammers. "Mamma is studying that she may finish her book, and of course has no time to go out with me."

"Yes, yes, I know; my brother-in-law told me," Madame de Rohritz replies. "And you——"

"I? I take singing-lessons four times a week."

"My brother-in-law wrote me that you intend to go upon the stage." Madame de Rohritz laughs. "If I were a Frenchwoman I should be horrified at the idea, but I am half an Austrian. I know those whims: a cousin of mine, a Russian, Natalie Lipinski——"

"Natalie Lipinski! Ah!" Stella exclaims; "my fellow-student. We take lessons together twice a week in Signor della Seggiola's class."

"Indeed! Well, she is thinking of going upon the stage,—and with a fortune of ten million roubles. In Austria and Russia such ideas will take possession of the brains of the best-born and best-bred girls; *cela ne tire pas à conséquence!* I never oppose Natalie, but I mean to have her married before she knows what she is about. And what shall I do with you, my fair one with the golden locks? Do you know I like you exceedingly? *Le coup de foudre en plein,*—love at first sight."

The clock on the chimney-piece—a clock apparently dating from the days when 'L'Africaine' was the rage, for the face is adorned with a manchineel-tree in miniature and a barbaric maiden in a head-dress of feathers dying beneath it—strikes three.

The lady starts up, takes out her watch, and compares it with the clock.

"Positively three o'clock, and my poor little boy is waiting for me in the carriage! I was to take him to his solfeggio class at three. Adieu, adieu; my compliments to your mother, and *au revoir, n'est-ce pas?*" She turns once again in the door-way, and, taking both Stella's hands, says, "You will come to dine with us once this week with your mother quite *en famille* the first time, that we may learn to know one another. I will excuse a formal call: you can pay that later: it is silly to lose time with formalities when one is *simpatica*. Adieu, adieu. What beautiful eyes you have! *Je me sauve!*"

The lively young madame kisses Stella's forehead, and then goes—or rather flies—away.

Stella's heart beats fast and loud.

"After all, he sent her: he has not quite forgotten me."

CHAPTER XXI.

AN AUSTRIAN HOST.

"Hm! indeed! Now I can no longer be shabby at my ease." These were the words with which the Baroness on her return home greeted Stella's joyous announcement of Madame de Rohritz's visit. "I took such pleasure in living in a place where nobody knew me."

However problematical in some respects the creative power of the Baroness may be, she is certainly thoroughly saturated with what the English call 'the sublime egotism of genius.'

When on the morning after her visit a note redolent of violets arrives from Madame de Rohritz, inviting in the kindest manner the two ladies to dinner at half-past seven the next evening but one, the Baroness makes a wry face, and remarks that really Madame de Rohritz might have waited until her call had been returned,—that such a degree of eagerness on the part of a woman of the world betokens a degree of exaggeration,—but, despite her grumbling, permits herself to accede to the entreaty in her daughter's eyes, and to accept the invitation.

"Upon condition that you attend to my dress," she says; to which Stella of course makes no objection.

The evening wardrobe of the Baroness consists of a black velvet gown which is now precisely seventeen years old, and which underwent renovation at the time of her eldest daughter's marriage. The number of Stella's evening dresses is limited to two very charming gowns which the colonel had made for her in Venice, regardless of expense, by the best dress-maker there, but which are at present slightly old-fashioned.

But, neglectful as the Baroness is about her per-

sonal appearance, she has an air of great distinction when she makes up her mind to be pre-
sentable, and covers her short gray hair, usually
flying loose about her ears, with a black lace cap;
while Stella is always charming. She would be
lovely in the brown robe of a monk; in her pale-
blue cachemire, with a bunch of yellow roses on her
left shoulder, directly below her ear, she is bewitching. Her heart throbs not a little as she drives
with her mother in a draughty, rattling fiacre across
Paris to the Avenue Villiers.

She is not at all tired of life to-day, but, entirely
forgetting how quickly her air-built castles fall to
ruin, she is eagerly engaged again in similar architecture.

Madame de Rohritz occupies a rather small hôtel
with a court-yard and garden. The entire household conveys the impression of distinguished comfort without ostentation. In the vestibule—a gem
of a vestibule, with two ancient Japanese monsters on either side of the door of entrance, with
Flanders tapestries embroidered in gold on the
walls, and Oriental rugs under-foot—a servant re-
lieves the ladies of their wraps.

Stella immediately perceives by the way in which
her mother arranges her hair before the mirror
that, whether it be the monsters at the door, or
the Arazzi on the wall, something has had a beneficial effect upon her mood,—that to-night, as is

sometimes the case, her ambition is roused to prove that a learned woman under certain circumstances can be more amiable and amusing than any woman with nothing in her head save 'dress and the men.'

In the salon, whither they are conducted by the maître-d'hôtel, a familiar spirit who is half a head shorter but half a head more dignified than the footman, they find only the master of the house. Not introduced, and quite unacquainted, he nevertheless advances with both hands extended, saying,—

"It rejoices me exceedingly to welcome two of my compatriots!"

"It rejoices us also," the Baroness amiably assures him.

Baron Rohritz scans her with discreetly-veiled curiosity. "Why did my brother write that I should find the Baroness rather extraordinary at first? She is a charming, distinguished old lady." Aloud he says, "My wife made promises loud and earnest to be here in time to present me to the ladies; but it seems she was mistaken."

"Perhaps we were too punctual," the Baroness replies, smiling.

"Not at all," the Baron declares; "but my poor wife is proverbially unpunctual. No one has ever been able to convince her that there are but sixty minutes in an hour, and consequently she always tries to do in an afternoon that for which an entire week would hardly suffice. Pray warm yourselves meanwhile, ladies: here, these are the most comfortable places,—not too near the blaze. I have had an Austrian fire made for you, and have actually nearly succeeded in warming the entire salon. We Austrians require a higher degree of heat than these crazy Frenchmen; they always maintain they are never cold; they are quite satisfied if they can see a little picturesque blaze in the chimney, and they sit down close to it and thrust their hands and feet and heads into it, thereby giving themselves chilblains, neuralgia, rheumatism, and heaven knows what else; but they are never cold."

Although the fire is large enough, Baron Rohritz throws on another log, so eager is he to bear his testimony to the affectation and self-conceit of the Parisians.

" How wonderfully cosey and comfortable you have contrived to make your home here! As I entered I seemed to be breathing the air of Austria. Since we came to Paris I have not felt so comfortable as at present," says the Baroness. If Baron Rohritz knew that since her arrival in Paris her time has been spent either on the top of an omnibus or in rather comfortless furnished lodgings, the worth of this compliment might be less: in happy ignorance, however, he feels extremely flattered, and, with a bow, rejoins,—

"I am very glad our nest pleases you. The chief credit for its arrangement belongs to my wife. You cannot imagine how she runs herself out of breath to pick up pretty things. But it is like Austria here, is it not?"

"Entirely," the Baroness assures him.

"My wife is incomprehensible to me," the master of the house remarks, after the above interchange of civilities, glancing uneasily at the clock on the chimney-piece. "It is now just half an hour since I helped her half dead out of a fiacre, with I cannot tell how many packages. I trust she is not——"

The portière rustles apart. Extremely slender, bringing with her the odour of violets, and shrouded in a mass of black crêpe de Chine and black lace, dying with fatigue and sparkling with vivacity, the Baroness Rohritz enters, fastening the clasp of a bracelet as she does so.

"Good-evening. I beg a thousand pardons! I am excessively glad to make your acquaintance, Baroness Meineck. Can you forgive my ill-breeding in keeping you waiting on this the first evening that you have given me the pleasure of seeing you here? It is terrible!"

"Ah, don't mention it," the Baroness replies, and, although the younger lady speaks German in her honour, answering in French: she is very proud of her French.

" *Mais si, mais si,* I am most unfortunate, but innocent,—quite innocent. It is positively impossible to be in time in Paris. Well, and how do you do?" turning to Stella and lightly passing her hand over the girl's cheek. "You are always twitting me with my enthusiasm, Edmund: did I exaggerate this time?"

"No, not in the least," her husband affirms: it would have been difficult, however, for him to make any other reply without infringing upon the rules of politeness.

"Who made your dress for you? It is charming. And how beautifully you have put in your roses!—but violet suits light blue better than yellow. Shall we change?" And, unfastening the roses from Stella's shoulder, Thérèse Rohritz takes a bunch of dark Russian violets from her girdle and arranges them on Stella's gown, all with the same graceful, laughing, breathless amiability.

To conquer all hearts, to make everybody happy, to give every one advice, to attend to every one's commissions, to oblige all the world,—this is the mania of Edgar's sister-in-law. He once declared that she went whirling through existence, a perfect hurricane of over-excellent qualities.

"What are we waiting for, Thérèse?" the master of the house interrupts the flow of his wife's eloquence, in a rather impatient tone.

"For Zino."

"He excused himself. I put his note on your dressing-table. When he received your invitation he was unfortunately—*very unfortunately*, underscored—engaged; but he hopes to be here soon after ten," Rohritz explains, having rung the bell meanwhile, whereupon the maître-d'hotel, throwing open the folding-doors, announces,—

" *Madame la Baronne est Servie.*"

CHAPTER XXII.

FRENCH INFERIORITY.

ONE observation Stella makes during the dinner, —namely, that married people apparently living happily together in Paris suffer quite as much from a chronic difference of opinion as those in Austria. Baron Rohritz and Thérèse do not quarrel one iota less than Jack Leskjewitsch and his wife.

Although Rohritz, as a former diplomatist,—a career which he abandoned five years ago on account of a difference with his chief and an absolute lack of ambition,—and from long residence in Paris, speaks perfect French, the conversation at his special request is carried on in German.

During dinner he incessantly makes all kinds of comparisons between Austria and France, of course to the disadvantage of the latter country. Nothing suits him in Paris; he abuses everything, from the perfect cooking, as it appears at his own table, to the exquisite troop of actors at the Français.

"I have no objection to make to the fish," he says, condescendingly. "I am entirely without prejudice; and when there is anything to be praised in France I always do it justice. But look at the game: French game is deplorable,—marshy, tasteless, without flavour. Even the Strasburg pie can be had better in Vienna. Do you not think so?"

"You will be thought an actual ogre, Edmund," Thérèse remonstrates, half laughing, half vexed. "You talk of nothing to-day but food."

"Perhaps so; but, as you will have observed, only from a lofty, strictly patriotic point of view," her husband remarks, composedly.

"Of course," Thérèse replies. "I can, however, assure you," she says, turning to her guests, "that although I cannot defend the Parisians in all respects, in one thing they are far beyond the Viennese: although they do not fall behind them in cookery, they think much less of things to eat."

"True," Edmund agrees, "and very naturally; they think less of their eating because they can't eat; they have no digestion. They certainly are a weak, degenerate race. Did you ever watch a regiment of French soldiers march past, ladies,

either cavalry or infantry? It is quite pitiable,
their military. Do you not think so?"

The Baroness cannot help admitting that he is
measurably right this time, and as the widow of
a soldier she indulges in a hymn of praise of the
Austrian army, thus enchanting the Baron, who
before entering the diplomatic corps served, to
complete his education, in a cavalry regiment.

"I should really like to know why these people
are in such a hurry," he begins again, after a while,
calling attention to the speed with which dinner
is being served. "I suppose the rascals intend to
go to Valentino's after dinner."

"Their hurry will do them no good then,"
Thérèse remarks, shrugging her shoulders; "they
will have to serve tea later in the evening. I
simply suppose that they take it as a personal af-
front that we should converse in a language which
they do not understand."

"Possibly," sighs Rohritz. "These Parisian
lackeys are intolerable; their pretensions far out-
strip our modest Austrian means. You may read
plainly in their faces, 'I serve, 'tis true, but I ad-
here to the immortal principles of '89.' Every
fellow is convinced that his period of servitude
is only an intermezzo in his life, and that some fine
day he shall be Duke of Persigny or Malakoff,—in
short, a far grander gentleman than I. Am I not
right, Thérèse?"

" Perfectly," his wife asserts. " But let me ask you one question, my dear: if you find Paris so inferior in everything, from Strasburg pie to the domestics, why did you not stay in Vienna?"

" Oh, that is another question,—quite a different question," Rohritz replies.

" Ah, yes," Thérèse says, triumphantly. " You must know, ladies, that my husband's patriotism is not so ardent as would seem, but rather of a platonic character; he loves his country at a distance. When, five years ago, after we had been here some time, he gave up his career and wanted to go back to Vienna, I made no objections whatever, and we established ourselves in his beloved native city, at first only provisionally. At the end of six months he was so frightfully bored that he actually longed for Paris."

Edmund dips his fingers in his finger-glass with a slightly embarrassed air.

"That is true," he admits. "Paris is the Manon Lescaut of European capitals: worthless thing that she is, we can never be rid of her if she has once bewitched us."

And as Thérèse prepares to rise from table he asks, " Do you object to a cigarette, ladies, and are you fond of children? Then, Thérèse, let us take coffee in the smoking-room, where I am sure the children are waiting for me."

CHAPTER XXIII.

PRINCE ZINO CAPITO.

The smoking-room is a somewhat narrow apartment, with a large Oriental rug before the broad double windows, with very beautiful old weapons in a couple of stands against the wall, and with heavy antique carved oaken chests. The broad low arm-chairs and divans are covered with Oriental rugs and carpets which Rohritz, as he informs Stella, brought from Cairo himself.

The two children, a little boy twelve years old, with tight red stockings and very short breeches, and a little girl hardly three, in a white gown, with bare legs and arms, help their mamma to serve the coffee. Momond takes the ladies their cups, and Baby is steady enough on her legs to trip after him with a face of great solemnity, carrying the silver sugar-bowl tightly hugged up in her arms. After she has happily completed her round she puts the sugar-bowl down before her mother, with a sigh of relief as over a difficult duty fulfilled, and smooths down her short, stiff skirts with a very decorous air. But when her father, from the other side of the room, where he is talking with Stella, smiles at her, she runs to him with a glad cry, forgetting all decorum springs into his lap, and is petted and caressed by him to his heart's content.

"Do you know whom that picture represents, Baroness Stella?" the host now asks, pointing to a life-size photograph hanging beneath the portrait in oil of a beautiful, fair woman. Although Stella had noticed the photograph as soon as she entered the smoking-room, she pretends to have her attention attracted by it for the first time.

"Yes, the likeness can still be recognized," she replies, bestowing a critical glance upon the picture, "although if it ever looked really like Baron Edgar Rohritz he must have altered very much."

"Of course," says Rohritz: "the picture was taken twelve years ago. Edgar had it taken for our mother, just before he went to Mexico. When he returned to Europe, three years later, our mother was dead, and he was gray,—gray at twenty-seven! As he was always our mother's favourite, I have hung his picture below hers."

"I maintain that photograph to be the handsomest head of a man which I know," Thérèse interrupts her conversation with the Baroness to declare. "We often dispute about it with my brother Zino, who always cites the Apollo Belvedere as the highest type of manly beauty——"

"Because he himself resembles that arrogant fellow in the Vatican," her husband interposes, dryly.

It is strange how constantly the elder brother recalls Baron Edgar, although considerably older, and by no means so distinguished in looks.

Meanwhile, Thérèse runs on with her usual fluency:

"It is an immense pity that my brother-in-law cannot make up his mind to marry. You really cannot imagine, ladies, the pains I have taken to throw the lasso over his head. Quite in vain! And such superb matches as I have made for him, —Marguerite de Lusignan, who has just married the Duke Cesarini, and the charming Marie de Gallière,—in short, the loveliest, wealthiest girls, —*tout ce qu'il y a de mieux.* Oddly enough, the mothers liked him as well as the daughters. In vain! I never have seen a man with so decided a distaste for matrimony as Edgar's. Did you chance to hear of the scheme by which he contrived in Grätz to rid himself of manœuvring mammas?"

"Yes," says Stella, very coldly: "he spread abroad a report that he had suddenly lost his property."

"A delicious idea," Thérèse laughs. "Do you not think so?"

Stella is silent.

"It never occurred to him to originate the report," Edmund interposes now, rather irritably; "he was merely too lazy to contradict it. To hear you talk, Thérèse, one would suppose Edgar to be the most self-conceited coxcomb under the sun,—a man who spent his life in defending himself from the attacks of matrimonially-inclined ladies. But I assure you, Baroness Stella, that Edgar has not a trace of such nonsensical coxcombry. Perhaps you know him well enough to make your own estimate of his character."

"I know him very superficially," Stella replies, with a shrug.

"Why, I thought you spent several weeks last summer with him at Leskjewitsch's," says Rohritz, looking at her in surprise.

Without making any reply to this remark, Stella opens and shuts her fan, and says, with a slight curl of her lip, "His heroic opposition seems overcome at last; for, as I learned lately from a letter from Grätz, he has just been betrothed to a certain little Countess Strahlheim."

"Who wrote you so?" Thérèse cries. "That interests me immensely! Oh, the Machiavelli!"

"I had the intelligence from a Fräulein von Gurlichingen," says Stella.

"Gurlichingen? Anastasia Gurlichingen?" asks the Baron.

"You know the Gurlichingen?" Stella asks, in her turn.

"Know her! Who does not know the Gurlichingen?" says Rohritz. "She is the most restless phantom I have ever encountered, continually fluttering to and fro through the world, always in the train of some wealthy friend who pays her expenses. It has been her specialty hitherto to sacrifice herself for consumptive ladies: she has haunted Meran, Cairo, Corfu. There was no taint of legacy-hunting in her conduct,—heaven forbid such a suspicion! Hm! my brother-in-law Zino christened her the turkey-buzzard. If you owe your piece of news to no more trustworthy source of information, Baroness Stella, I must take the liberty of doubting its correctness."

"You know she is in Paris? She called upon me a little while ago, but I was not at home," said Thérèse, turning to Stella. "Have you any idea whom she is with now?"

"With the Princess Oblonsky," Stella replies.

"With the Oblonsky? Not with the former von Föhren?" husband and wife exclaim simultaneously.

"Certainly!"

"What a joke!—with the Oblonsky!"

Thérèse almost chokes with laughter.

It is ten o'clock. The children have long since disappeared with their *bonne;* the servant has brought in the tea-equipage. There is a pause in the conversation, such as is apt to ensue when people have laughed until they are tired. The Baron puts a fresh log on the fire and rakes the embers together. The blaze flames and crackles; little hovering lights and shadows dance over the old golden-brown leather tapestries. Suddenly the door opens, and unannounced, with the *sans gêne* of close relationship, a young man enters the room, tall, slender, with a certain attractive audacity expressed in the lines about his mouth and in his eyes which puts beyond question his resemblance to the Olympian dandy. It is the Apollo of modern drawing-room dimensions, the Apollo forty-four years old, already a little gray about the temples, with a wrinkle or two at the corners of his eyes, in a coat of Poole's, a gardenia in his button-hole, his crush hat under his arm,—Prince Zino Capito!

"Pray present me," he says, after he has greeted his sister, and Stella also, turning towards the Baroness.

"And you already know my new star?" Thérèse exclaims, in surprise, after she has fulfilled his request.

The Prince looks full at Stella, with a look peculiar to himself,—a look in which admiration reaches the boundary of impertinence without crossing it,—then says, smiling,—

"*Cà*, Sasa!" when he is in a good humour he calls his sister thus, by the name which he gave her when he was a lisping baby in the nursery,— "*çà*, Sasa, do you really suppose that I would have rushed back from Lyons simply on the strength of

the enthusiastic description of your latest *trouvaille*
that you sent me in your note of invitation? No,
my little sister, I am too well aware of your liability
to acute attacks of enthusiasm not to receive your
brilliant perorations with a justifiable mistrust. I
once had·the pleasure of seeing Mademoiselle very
often, for a while," he continues, speaking French.

"Where?—when?" asks Thérèse.

"Three years ago, in Venice. Baron Meineck
lived at the Britannia, where I also lodged, and
Fräulein Stella came to Venice to take care of him.
—They were sad days for you," he says, turning to
Stella, very gravely, and with a degree of cordiality
which he can impart to his voice when he chooses.

"And yet they were delightful days for me in
spite of all," Stella replies, her eyes full of tears,
and turning away her head.

"Most certainly you can look back to that time
with a contented heart," he continues, in the same
sympathetic tone. "I never have seen a daughter——" Suddenly he notices how the Baroness's
glance rests upon him, and, becoming aware of the
delicate nature of the situation, he finishes his sentence as best he can and tries to change the subject.
But the Baroness has lost her equanimity: it is
always intensely painful to her to know that she
recalls to strangers the fact that her husband in
his last illness was obliged to forego her care;
Capito's words are like a reproof to her.

"Will you have the kindness to have a fiacre called for us?" she says, turning to the host.

Resisting all entreaties to prolong her stay, and to take another cup of tea, she pleads fatigue, the necessity of rising early, and so forth. When Capito takes leave of her he asks permission to pay his respects to the ladies.

But the Baroness begs him to give himself no further trouble with regard to them, as she is scarcely ever at home,—whereupon she vanishes on the arm of the host, and the Prince twirls his moustache with a comical grimace.

"What annoys you, Zino?" Edmund asks on his return to the smoking-room; and when the Prince enlightens him as to the extent of his lack of tact, and the unfortunate family history of the Meinecks, he says,—

"I really do not see why Edgar considered it necessary to prepare us so carefully for the absurdities of the old Baroness. It is quite possible that she drove her husband distracted with her learning: nevertheless in ordinary intercourse she is very agreeable, and a very handsome old lady: she must have been handsomer in her time than her daughter."

"Do you think so?" asks Thérèse. "To me Stella seems charming."

"*Elle est tout bêtement adorable,*" says Zino Capito, drinking his tea out of the Japanese cup his sister has just handed him. "How good your tea is, Sasa! in all Paris no one has such good tea as yours."

"You are very suspiciously complimentary," Thérèse rejoins. "What do you want me to do for you?"

"Ask me to dine soon, and ask the Meinecks," Zino replies, with his attractively audacious smile.

"No, I will not," Thérèse says, resolutely.

"And why not?"

"Because, as I now see, you would do all that you could to turn Stella's brain. I thought you had outgrown such foolish tricks."

"Hm!" says Capito.

"I am going to do all that I can to marry her well," Thérèse declares.

"Hm!" Capito says again, but in a different tone.

"If you like, I will invite you to meet the Gurlichingen; she is in Paris at present."

"Indeed! With whom is she travelling?"

"With——" Thérèse looks full at him, with mirth in her eyes,—" with the Oblonsky!"

"Ah! Have her lungs become affected lately?" Zino asks, indifferently.

"Not that I know of; but she probably covets respectability," says Thérèse.

"*Ah, tiens! cela doit être drôle.* An entire change of system on Stasy's part, then," says Zino, putting down his teacup, and rising.

"She seems to have abandoned the lucrative calling of a turkey-buzzard," Rohritz remarks.

"Yes, and instead to have opened a laundry for the purification of—caps which have fallen among—among nettles, in the vicinity of mills.* Not a bad trade,—hm !"

"Going already, Zino ?"

"Of course," says Zino, stretching himself and yawning as spoiled brothers allow themselves to do in presence of their sisters. "If you suppose I tore myself away from Lyons to drink tea with you, you are mistaken. Be good, Sasa : when will you invite the Meinecks and myself to dine ?"

Thérèse, moving her forefinger to and fro before her face, makes the Roman gesture of refusal.

"Oh, very well; as you please," Zino mutters in an ill-humour. "Good-evening." "I wonder where I could meet her," he says, musingly, before lighting his cigar in the coupé that awaits him.

"Strange !" Rohritz remarks to his wife; "Edgar described the young Meineck to me as particularly gay and amusing."

"Indeed ?"

"Now, for so young a creature, she seems to me particularly quiet."

"What would you have? Punchinello himself would grow melancholy with such a life as hers."

---

* A play upon the French proverb, '*jeter son bonnet par-dessus le moulin,*' as much as to say ' to lose one's reputation.'

p

Her husband reflects for a few moments. After a while he says, "I wonder whether, after all, she was not a little smitten with Edgar?"

"Upon what do you base your conjecture?" Thérèse asks, in astonishment.

"She put on so extraordinarily indifferent an expression whenever he was mentioned."

Thérèse laughs aloud.

"What is there to laugh at?" her husband asks, rather crossly.

"Forgive me, but you remind me of the Frenchman who proposed to a young lady through her mother, and when he was asked by her what reason he had to suppose that her daughter liked him, replied, 'I am quite sure of it, for she always leaves the room as soon as I enter it.'"

"Laugh away; we shall soon see who is right. Moreover, Edgar must take some interest in her, or he would not have recommended her to us so warmly," replies Rohritz.

"Bah! he recommended her to us at the express request of our common friend Leskjewitsch," his wife rejoins.

"True; but——"

"She is a child in comparison with him. He might be her father."

Edmund is silent for a while, and then says, "That is true; she is a child,—and he is very sensible."

CHAPTER XXIV.

A MUSIC-LESSON.

FOLLOWING the advice of the little Italian conductor of the orchestra, Stella refers to him in order to procure more reasonable terms from Signor della Seggiola for her singing-lessons.

These 'more reasonable terms' are twenty-five francs for an hour abbreviated at both ends, and sixty francs a month for a share in the singing-class,—that is, in the musical dissertations which Signor della Seggiola holds three times a week for six or seven pupils in a small room in the Gérard piano-building.

For the sake of those who consider twenty-five francs an hour a tolerably high price for lessons, and who are inclined to regard the leader's recommendation as a humbug, it may be well to state that twenty-five francs is really a lowered price, and that dilettanti usually pay from thirty to thirty-five francs for a private lesson from della Seggiola.

It is with the maestro's wife that Stella makes the business arrangement, since della Seggiola himself—an artist, an idealist, a child—understands nothing about money. He evidently labours under the delusion that he gives the lessons for nothing,

since he does not take the slightest pains to give
his scholars an honest equivalent in valuable instruction for their twenty-five, thirty, or thirty-five
francs.

As we already know, Stella is tolerably familiar with the singing-teachers of many lands: she
knows that, as is the case also with dentists, they
all abuse one another and testify the same horror at
the misdeeds of their predecessors, declaring with
the same tragic shake of the head that it will be
necessary to begin with the A, B, C,—that is, with
Concone's solfeggi,—and that it is indispensable for
the scholar that she should procure the work upon
the art of singing with which the new teacher, as
well as his predecessor, has enriched musical literature. Stella already possesses five exhaustive
works upon the 'Bel Canto,' 'L'Art lyrique,' 'L'Art
du Chant,' and so forth; each cost twenty francs
and contains a more or less valuable collection of
solfeggi. Some of these volumes are adorned with
the portrait of the author, others have prefaces in
which some famous man, such as Rossini, for example, recommends the work to the public as
something extraordinary, something destined by its
intrinsic merit to outlast the Pyramids.

Della Seggiola's work differs from all these
clumsy compositions. Adorned neither with the
portrait of the author nor with a preface by a de-
lebrity, it displays upon its first page the profile of

a human being cut in half,—an imposing proof of
the maestro's anatomical knowledge, as well as of
his close study of the physical conditions of a true
training of the voice.

The large and magnificently-bound volume contains no series of solfeggi, but simply some scanty,
musically impossible fiorituri, or musical examples
borrowed from other works, which swim like little
islands in an ocean of text. As Signora della
Seggiola expresses herself, her husband's volume is
no compilation of senseless solfeggi, but a Bible for
the lovers of song.

A Bible for those who believe in della Seggiola's
infallibility.

At the private lessons—the maestro gives these,
of course, only at his own home—the accompaniments are played by an ambitious young musician
who has once been with Strakosch on a tour; in
the class, Fräulein Fuhrwesen accompanies, her
impresario having postponed for the present the
concert tour in South America.

Della Seggiola never touches the piano himself.
He is a broad-shouldered, jolly Italian, with a big,
kindly, smiling face, and a black velvet cap.

Without ever having possessed even a tolerably
good voice, he ranked for a time among the distinguished singers of the world. His fine singing
is, however, of little use to his pupils.

He passes the time of the lessons chiefly in reading aloud chapters from his 'Bible,' while the accompanist, with unflagging enthusiasm, praises the wisdom of the work; then the pupil sings some trifle, della Seggiola meanwhile gazing at her with a solemn air, sometimes grimacing to show the position of the lips, or tapping alternately her throat and her chest, exclaiming, " *Ne serrez pas!*" or " *Soutenez! soutenez!*" Then he directs the pupil to rest, tells something funny, clicks with his tongue, throws his velvet cap into the air, and— kling-a-ling-ling—Signora della Seggiola gives the signal that the lesson is over.

The class is a rather more serious and artistic affair than the private lessons, from the fact that there are no different prices to be paid here, but that every one—with the exception of a *protégé* of Signora della Seggiola's, a barytone from Florence, who pays nothing—pays as in an omnibus the same sixty francs a month, whether the class consist of thirty or only three persons.

And the company reminds one somewhat of an omnibus. Against the background of usual shabbiness one or two brilliant social stars stand forth, making one wonder how they came there. It can hardly be asserted that even here among the disciples of della Seggiola, the only true prophet of his art, any great progress in singing is made. During the six weeks for which Stella has now belonged to the class it has been singing the same

.thing, only with less and less voice; that is all the difference.

Condemned by the formation of his throat, which is extraordinarily ill adapted to song, to spare the organ, della Seggiola never allows one of his faithful disciples to sing one natural, healthy note, but condemns them also to a constant mezzo-voce which cannot but contract the throat.

Thus artificially restrained, Stella's warm rich voice diminishes with extraordinary rapidity. When she complains to the maestro that this is so, he remarks that it is a very good sign, her great fault being that she has too much voice, and only when she has lost it entirely can the cultivation of a really *bel canto* begin.

This astounding assertion gives Stella food for reflection, and it occurs to her to-day as she sits at the piano preparing for the class-lesson and finds that two of her notes break as she sings the scale.

"Della Seggiola ought to be pleased with my progress," she says to herself, with some bitterness, and her heart beats hard as the constantly-recurring question arises in her mind, "If I should really lose my voice——? But where is the use of thinking of it?" she answers herself, with a shrug. The clock on the chimney-piece, the one with the manchineel-tree, strikes a quarter of ten. "It is high time to go," the girl says aloud. Slipping

on the still handsome scalskin jacket which her
father had given her five years before for a Christmas-present, she hurries along the various thronged
streets, broad and narrow, through the pale-yellow
January sunshine, to her destination.

The 'hall' in the Gérard piano-warehouse, Rue
du Mail, where della Seggiola holds his classes, is
hardly more spacious than an ordinary room in Berlin or Vienna, and, being partly filled with pianos
sewed up in linen, leaves something to be desired
from an acoustic point of view. The lesson has
already begun when Stella enters. Fräulein Fuhrwesen, in her tassel-bedecked water-proof, is seated
at the piano, upon the lid of which the 'Bible'
lies open. Della Seggiola, resting his right hand
upon its pages, and gesticulating with his left, is
delivering an inspiring discourse upon the art of
song, while a tall, sallow young man, with very little
hair upon his head, but all the more upon his face,
is awaiting with ill-disguised impatience the moment when he can burst into song.

This young man's name is Meyer (pronounced
Meyare): he is clerk in a banking-house, and is
studying for the stage.

A second barytone, a young Italian, is also waiting with longing for his turn. He is the star of
the class, a Florentine, who has wandered to Paris
with his two sisters, who regularly come to the class
with him. They are sallow and elderly, wear very

large Rembrandt hats, which, as they privately inform Stella, they purchased in the Temple, sit on
each side of their brother, and keep up a constant
nod of encouragement.

In strict seclusion from the young men, and
guarded by a gray-haired duenna, across whose
threadbare brown sacque she gaily ogles the barytone from Florence, sits a dishevelled little soprano,
the daughter of a diva and a journalist.

Of course she has no idea of going on the stage;
she speaks with horror of the theatre, and thinks a
dramatic career not at all *comme il faut.*

An elderly Englishwoman, quite copper-coloured,
with very long teeth and the figure of a tallow dip,
seems to be of a different opinion. She is just
confessing in very problematical French to the
barytone from Florence how much she repents not
having voice enough '*pour remplir un opéra,*' and
her eyes fill with tears.

Natalie Lipinski has not yet arrived.

With a pleasant greeting to the two sisters of
the barytone, and to the crazy Miss Frazer, Stella
passes as quietly as possible to her place.

After della Seggiola has ended his discourse,
and Monsieur Meyare has finished his '*Dolcessi
perduti,*' Miss Frazer sings the waltz from 'Traviata' transposed a fifth lower than the original key,
breathing very loud, and singing very low. In
the middle of it she stops short, lays her red hand,

covered to the knuckles with a knitted wristlet, upon her heart, and sighs.

"What is it?" asks della Seggiola, not without a certain impatience. "What is the matter?"

"This aria is so deeply affecting," sighs the Englishwoman; "it always gives me palpitation of the heart."

"That is very unfortunate," says della Seggiola, taking a pinch of snuff. "Pray consult a physician; he will prescribe digitalis."

"Oh, the doctor could not help me," Miss Frazer asserts, wagging her head to and fro with enthusiasm. "My nervous system is too highly strung. If my voice were only stronger I should certainly have a *succès* upon the stage,—*parce que je suis très-passionnée.*"

Della Seggiola bites his lip. At this moment the door opens, Natalie Lipinski enters, and behind her —Stella can hardly believe her eyes—Zino Capito!

"Permit me to present to you my cousin, Prince Capito, Signor della Seggiola," says Natalie, in her fluent but hard-sounding Russian-French. "He hopes to be allowed to profit by your instructions."

Of course the lesson is interrupted. Miss Frazer's eyes, which always remind one more or less of a melancholy-minded rabbit, and which now wear a very sympathetic air, rest with benevolence upon the Prince, who offers della Seggiola his hand with the *aplomb* for which he is justly celebrated throughout Europe, hurriedly thanks him for the great pleasure he has given him by his art, and prays beforehand for indulgence and patience, since he is, as he maintains, a beginner,—only a beginner.

Natalie conscientiously presents him to the class, blundering, of course, with all the names.

He bows stiffly, looks directly over the gentlemen's heads, scans the ladies with a curious glance, and then goes directly to Stella, beside whom he takes his place, after bowing to her with the most attractive mixture of courtesy and deference. Without being deterred by Miss Frazer's starting off with her transposed song and getting through as much of it as asthma and palpitation of the heart will permit, he begins:

"I made an attempt to see you the day after meeting you at my sister's, but, unfortunately, in vain. Did you get my card?"

"Yes."

"I was so very sorry not to find the ladies at home. Might I be admitted some evening?"

"I will ask mamma; but——"

"And how have you amused yourself meanwhile?"

"Oh, I have been very gay this week; Madame de Rohritz took me with her once to the theatre and once to the Bois de Boulogne."

"And when Thérèse does not take you out a

little do you devote your entire time to historical studies and to your singing?"

"Sometimes I sit about in the Tuileries,—I have made the acquaintance of an old governess, who chaperons me,—and sometimes I go to the Louvre, which I know as perfectly as ever a guide in Paris."

Is it by mere chance that just at this point of the conversation, which is carried on in an undertone, Fräulein Fuhrwesen turns and stares at the Prince and Stella?

Meanwhile, it is Natalie's turn to sing. Her song is the grand cavatina from 'I Puritani,' '*Qui la voce sua soave!*'

Natalie is an odd little person, short, slender, undeveloped as to figure, with a face rather too sallow, but with regular delicate features and dazzling teeth. With a fanatical enthusiasm for art and a determination to go upon the stage she combines a fortune of some millions of roubles, and, what is in still more comical contrast with her proposed career, a strict unbending sense of propriety, far transcending the prudery of the most English of Englishwomen,—not that shy sense of propriety which is always on the defensive, but that which is quick to look down with aggressive contempt upon any infringement of the rules of decorum.

Too well bred to speak when a lady whom he knows, were she a hundred times his cousin, is singing, Zino listens with exemplary attention to the Bellini cavatina, not indeed without a merry twinkle of the eye now and then.

Natalie's voice is rather shrill, her Italian accent harsh; her rendering of the impassioned aria is strictly confined to following the musical directions, *p.p.*, *cresc.*, *ritard.*, and so forth; even at the point where the inspiration of the love-stricken Elvira culminates in the words '*Vien' ti posa—vien' ti posa sul mio cor!*' she never ceases to beat the time with her right hand.

After this brilliant outburst della Seggiola interrupts her. The Fuhrwesen lifts her hands from the keys, and Natalie looks inquiringly at the maestro, who takes a pinch of snuff and shakes his head.

" *Très-bien, mon enfant,*"—it is needless to say that this familiar address is very little to the taste of the haughty Russian,—"*très-bien, mon enfant;* you sing in excellent time, but you must try to infuse animation into your style. Fancy the situation,— half crazy with love and longing, you are calling out into the night, ' Ah, come—come to my heart !' You must sing that with—how shall I express it ?— with more conviction, thus :"

The Fuhrwesen drums the accompaniment, and della Seggiola, stretching out his arms like angels' wings, throws back his head a little, and warbles, ' *Qui la voce !*'

Estimate as you please his method of instruction,

all who still find delight in the old Italian traditions must admit his art in singing.

And Prince Zino—a musical Epicurean to his finger-tips, rejecting everything clumsy and indigestible in music,—Prince Zino, for whom Mozart is the only god of music and Rossini is his prophet—strokes his moustache, delighted, and calls "Bravo!" and della Seggiola bows.

The lesson continues to be quite interesting.

Signor Trevisiani, the barytone from Florence, sings something very depressing, with the refrain,—

> ' Maladetto sulla terra,
> Condannato nel ceil sarò.'

The little soprano sings, ' *Plaisir d'amour*,' and Zino perfectly, gravely, goes through a scale, swelling the notes, during which two sad facts are brought to light,—first, that he is the third barytone in the class,—della Seggiola had hoped for a tenor,—and, secondly, that he cannot read by note. Della Seggiola, however, praises the charming timbre of his voice, and asks if he may not send him a teacher to correct his defective reading; whereupon Fräulein Fuhrwesen declares herself ready to give the Prince lessons. He pretends not to hear this heroic proposition, seeming not even to perceive her; whereby he makes a mortal enemy of that extremely sensitive and irritable person.

The glory of the class is the closing performance,

—the famous duet between Don Giovanni and Zerlina, rendered by Signor Trevisiani and Natalie Lipinski.

It would be difficult to imagine a more lugubrious Don Giovanni than the young man from Florence. He is freshly shaven, perhaps in honour of his part; his cheeks are covered with red scratches, like those of a German youth who bears about in his face the record of his bravery; his hair, artistically dishevelled about his forehead and ears, falls over his coat-collar at the back of his neck. Except for a grass-green cravat, he is dressed entirely in black, like the page in 'Marlbrook;' his costume, evidently provincial, comes from the same quarter of Paris that has produced his sisters' hats,—the Temple.

Much intimidated by his haughty Zerlina, his throat contracts so that his voice, naturally fine and resonant, comes from his dry lips hoarse and miserably thready. Although Natalie sings, as ever, in faultless time, the notes that should be in unison are far from sounding so, whereupon della Seggiola advises the singers to take each other's hands. Mademoiselle Lipinski edges away still farther from her Don Giovanni, and extends to him her finger-tips.

Della Seggiola makes them repeat the duo three times, does his best to make it go smoothly, gently entreats Zerlina to be more coquettish, orders Don

Giovanni to be more seductive. In vain. Zerlina draws down the corners of her mouth and looks at the wall; Don Giovanni scratches his ear. The duo sounds worse and worse. Much irritated at this melancholy result, which she ascribes entirely to Signor Trevisiani's awkwardness, Natalie at last says crossly to the young Florentine, "I beg you not to torment me any more: it will never do!" Then across her shoulder to her cousin she explains, impatiently, "Zino, Signor Trevisiani is hoarse; you and I used to sing the duo together. Come, try it."

"If there is time," Zino says, with amiable readiness, taking his place beside his cousin.

There is really no time for it, as della Seggiola would have informed any one save the Prince. Twelve o'clock has struck, but he does not mention that fact to Zino. Hungry and resigned, he sits down beside the piano, his hands clasped upon his stomach, his eyes fixed upon the tips of his boots stretched out before him, prepared to endure the blessed duo for the fourth time. But what is this? He listens eagerly, all present listen, all eyes are riveted upon the Prince, from whose lips there flows such melody as we expect only from the greatest Italian singers.

Without paying any further attention to Zerlina, della Seggiola inquires at the close of the duo,—

"Do you sing the serenade also?"

" *À peu près*," says Zino, whereupon the Fuhr-wesen strikes the first notes of the accompaniment, and he sings it.

The singers of the new high-art school, the interpreters of Wagner, curse out the notes at their auditors; Prince Zino smiles them at his hearers, and the strong infusion of irony in his smile only heightens the effect of his style.

Erect but unstudied in attitude, his hands in the pockets of his jacket, his head slightly thrown back, he is the veritable personification of the gay, thoughtless *bon-vivant*, Mozart's Don Giovanni as the master created him.

As he ends, Miss Frazer, bathed in tears, rushes up to him with both hands held out, exclaiming, " *Merci! merci!* "

Stella, laughing, claps applause, and Signor Trevisiani gazes at him as if he longed to learn his art.   But della Seggiola asks,—

" Where did you learn to sing, mon Prince ? "

" Everywhere. "

" From whom ? "

" From no one. "

" That's right ! " exclaims Seggiola, forgetting all humbug in genuine artistic enthusiasm. " For, between ourselves be it said, singing is never taught. "

And when the Prince laughs, and hopes on the contrary to profit much from the art of the maestro, the latter replies, with the inborn courtesy of his nation,—

"If you will kindly help me to reveal to my class here the beauty of song, you shall always be welcome, mon Prince.   I can teach you nothing."

*   *   *   *   *   *   *

The lesson is over.   Zino helps Stella and his cousin to put on their wraps, takes leave of della Seggiola with his brilliant smile and cordial press-ure of the hand, of the rest with a very brief nod, and leaves the room with his two special ladies.

"A charming man, that Principe Capito," says della Seggiola, rubbing his hands delightedly. "And he can sing like Mario in his best days. I used to give his sister lessons."

"I have met him before in Vienna," Fräulein Fuhrwesen mutters. "He is an Italian, to be sure, but his arrogance he learned in Austria."

CHAPTER XXV.

A NEW ACQUAINTANCE?

THE lesson at an end, the members of della Seggiola's class have no more acquaintance with one another than have people who have travelled together by railway after they have left the train. The soprano with her slovenly duenna in a long

French cachemire shawl, the Italian with his two sisters, one on each arm, all fly apart like bits of lead from an exploding shell.

A saucy smile about his mouth, Capito walks beside the two girls; he softly hums to himself '*La ci darem la mano!*'

"You sang well, Zino," Natalie remarks, after a while. "Della Seggiola was absolutely enthusiastic."

"What good did it do me?" says Zino, shrugging his shoulders. "It gave him a reason for politely turning me away."

"He was afraid you might agitate Miss Frazer: she suffers already from her heart," Stella says, with her usual audacity in alluding to uncomfortable topics.

"On the whole, della Seggiola was right," Natalie declares: "it would not have been becoming for you to join the class."

"'Tis odd how often the pleasantest things in this world are unbecoming," Zino murmurs.

"Do you really think it would have been so very pleasant to hear us practising away at the same things twice a week?" Stella asks, gaily.

Without giving him time to reply, Natalie begins to cross-examine him upon his impressions of della Seggiola's method of instruction.

"What do you think of him as a teacher?" she asks.

"He sings delightfully," Zino replies, somewhat vaguely.

"Yes, but he is too lax as a teacher; he is not strict enough,—does not suit to their capacity the tasks he imposes upon his pupils."

"Do you think so?" says Zino. "On the contrary, I thought he exacted far too much of his scholars' capacity."

"How so?" Natalie asks, rather offended.

"He required you to be coquettish, and that fellow—what was his name?—Trappenti—to be seductive. Rather too difficult a task for both of you, I should think," says the Prince.

Natalie frowns:

"I thought della Seggiola's remarks to-day highly unbecoming."

"Of course, when you were singing a love-song, to require you to imagine yourself in the place of the singer,—*c'est de la dernière inconvenance.* Moreover, it was exacting more than you were capable of performing,—that is, so far as I know." And, with a quick turn of the conversation which would be quite inexcusable in any one else, he looks her in the face, and asks with a light laugh, as if the question concerned something infinitely comical, "Do tell us,—it will interest Baroness Stella too, I am sure,—you are twenty-five years old——"

"Twenty-six," Natalie corrects him.

"Twenty-six, then. Were you ever in love?"

To the Prince's no small surprise, Natalie turns away her head at this question, and, blushing to the very roots of her hair, mutters angrily between her set teeth, "You are intolerable to-day!"

"Ah, indeed!" says Prince Zino, with a merry twinkle of his eyes. "It must be with one of the lithographic portraits hanging in the corridor in your home at Jekaterinovskoe,—Orlow, or Potemkin. By the way, 'tis a great pity you blush so seldom, Natalie: it becomes you charmingly."

At the next street-corner Stella's and Natalie's ways separate, to the great vexation of the Prince, seeing that he too must of course take his leave of the beautiful Austrian. But, if he can no longer enjoy the pleasure of talking with Stella, he resolves to please himself by still keeping her in sight. Instead of remaining with his cousin and quietly going his own way, he decides to walk along the same street with Stella, on the other side of the way.

Natalie, who understands his little manœuvre perfectly, looks after him before turning her corner, and shakes her head. "I wonder how many times he has been in love before?" she thinks. "Poor little star! she is very pretty. I trust she may be more sensible than I."

Meanwhile, Zino and Stella walk leisurely along on opposite sides of the Rue des Petits-Champs.

"How well she walks! what a fine carriage she

has!" he murmurs, never losing sight of her. "Her movements have such an easy grace, and now and then a dreamy, gliding rhythm about them; 'tis music for the eyes. And then such colour,—the fair face with its black eyes and red lips, the gold of the hair setting off the exquisite glow of the complexion,—she is enchanting!"

Zino is one of those men whose sensuality is refined and idealized by the admixture of a purely artistic and æsthetic appreciation of the beautiful. The worship of the beautiful is, as he is fond of declaring, his own special, private religion; the paroxysms of enthusiasm which this worship was apt to cause in him in former years have long since grown rarer and rarer. But to-day he is distinctly conscious of the slow approach of an attack.

"Bah! it will pass away," he says to himself, "as all such attacks do; it can lead to nothing. But all the same she is bewitching!"

Thus both go their ways,—he with his eyes, quite intoxicated with beauty, riveted upon her face and figure,—she, as he is rather annoyed to perceive, so absorbed in her own thoughts as to be utterly oblivious of his vicinity. Between them, around them, swarms Parisian life, with its bustle and noise; on the pavements pass neat grisettes by twos and threes, their smooth hair uncovered, either coming from or going to breakfast, men with dirty grayish-white blouses, servant-girls in white caps, Englishwomen with long teeth, and Parisians of all kinds, recklessly pressing on towards some aim known to themselves only; in the middle of the street there is a hurly-burly of every kind of vehicle, from little hand-carts, laden with fish, flowers, oranges, or vegetables, and pushed by women with bent backs, to omnibuses as big as small houses, their tops reaching above the shop-windows, and dragged with difficulty by the strongest horses. Here and there some one is running after one or other of these conveyances, a breathless day-governess, helped up by both hands to the back platform by the conductor, or a notary with a leather wallet under his arm, who climbs to the top with the agility of a monkey.

These tops are crowded. Beside respectable business-men with clean-shaved cheeks and thick sausage-like moustaches are seated all sorts of Bohemians, half-students, half-artists, pale and thin, with melancholy eyes in faces weary with cheap pleasures, a strange and genuinely Parisian species of human being, always eager for any variety, be it a ball at Bulliers or the overthrow of a government, a restless, excitable, shallow, sparkling crowd, which might be called the oxygen of Paris in contrast with its hydrogen. And beside the huge city omnibus there toil, slowly, heavily-laden carts to which are harnessed long trains of huge white Norman steeds, with blue sheepskins upon their

backs and bells around their necks, bells which
have a rustic simple sound amid all the demoniac
clatter of Paris, like the clear voices of children
heard in some Bacchanalian revel. Tall, sturdy
Normans in white, flapping broad-brimmed hats
walk beside them, shaking their heads as they look
down upon the wealthy degradation and the sordid
misery of the filigree population of Paris.

The January sun shines above it all. There in
the fresh cold air is an odour of oranges, fish, and
flowers. Stella stops beside a flower-cart to buy a
bunch of violets. Zino pauses to watch her.
Amid the noise of the street he cannot understand what she says, but through the roar of the
mid-day crowd, the loud pulsation of the great
city stronger at this hour than at any other, he
distinguishes brief detached notes of her gentle
bird-like voice. How cordial the smile she has
just bestowed upon the flower-girl!

"If she smiled at me like that I should give her
the entire cart-full of flowers. I wonder if I might
send her a bouquet to the 'Negroes?'"

Stella, with a charming shake of the head, has
just taken out her purse, when a lumbering omnibus interposes between her and Zino's admiring
gaze. The omnibus is followed by a cart, then by
another, and another. At last the view is once
more uninterrupted; but where is Stella? There
she stands, pale, agitated, her eyes cast down, be-

side a tall, thin, consumptive-looking woman in shabby black, leading by the hand a little girl,—a woman with golden hair, and features in which, pinched and worn though they be by many a bitter experience, a striking likeness may be traced to Stella's beautiful profile.

"Where did she pick up that acquaintance?" the Prince asks himself; but before he can decide where and when he has seen that woman before, Stella and the stranger have vanished in a little confectioner's shop.

CHAPTER XXVI.

FIVE-O'CLOCK TEA.

HOWEVER recklessly a woman may have trifled with her reputation in her youth, tossing it about as a thing of naught, there is sure to come a time in the progress of years when the first wrinkle appears, and instantly a careful search is made for the lost article. Then she needs a friend who shall smooth it out and polish it up and return it to her, —a friend who believes in its inherent spotlessness and will do her best to convince others of the same.

This office Stasy has undertaken to perform for

the Princess Oblonsky. And what is to be her
reward for her efforts? Delicious food, exquisite
lodgings and service in apartments fairy-like in
their appointments, numerous presents, and altogether very considerate treatment, with the exception of a few outbreaks of temper, unavoidable with
such women as the Princess.

From all which it may be clearly perceived that
the position of the Oblonsky is far from being as
good as it was upon her husband's death, three
years ago, or she would scarcely covet at so high a
price the support of such a person as Anastasia.

She certainly has been most unfortunate,—poor
Princess Sophie. When, three years ago, she returned from Petersburg a widow and possessed of
a colossal fortune, she hoped to obliterate all memo-
ries of former irregularities by a marriage with
Prince Zino Capito. But Zino did not second her
views. Two months after the death of the Prince
he scarcely spoke to her.

It was during the following winter that Sophie
Oblonsky committed the serious 'imprudence' by
which she lost forever her social position. At
the roulette-table in San Carlo she made the acquaintance of a young Hungarian who was presented to her as a Comte de Bethenyi. He was
young, ardent, wore picturesque fur collars and
jackets which well became his handsome gypsy
face, flung his money about everywhere, and played

the piano. Sophie Oblonsky was always sensitive to music. The picturesque Hungarian inspired her with an interest such as none but a disappointed woman of forty can experience. In dread of compromising herself, she consented to marry him, and they were betrothed, whereupon suddenly various Esterhazys and Zichys of her acquaintance appeared at San Carlo, and in the casino of the place met the Princess upon her lover's arm, bowed to her, and honoured her companion with a very odd stare. After they had passed, Sophie heard them laugh.

In an hour all Monaco knew that the Princess Oblonsky had betrothed herself to a fencing-master from Klausenburg, who shortly before had won a prize of ten thousand marks in the Saxon lottery. That same evening Caspar Bethenyi risked his last thousand francs on number twenty-nine,—perhaps because the twenty-ninth of January was his birthday,—and lost. The following night he put a bullet through his brains.

The correspondent of ' Figaro' wrote an amusing article upon the episode, and the Princess Oblonsky was henceforth impossible : she had made herself ridiculous.

The world found the affair extremely comical,— so comical that there was a strong admixture of contempt even in the compassion accorded to the poor fencing-master, who had signed his name simply

Caspar Bethenyi in the strangers' book, and who, it was afterwards discovered, had accepted rather unwillingly the rank bestowed upon him by waiters and journalists.

Since this had occurred, two years before, the Oblonsky had tried in vain to regain a footing in society. Considerable surprise was expressed that when thus exiled from the 'world' of western Europe she did not retire to Petersburg; but she probably had her own reasons for not doing so.

Another woman in her place, with her immense means, might have let go all she had lost and lived gaily from day to day. But she was naturally slow, and with the luxurious tendencies of her temperament were mingled sentimentality and a certain liability to sporadic attacks of a sense of propriety. She grasped at everything that could make her at one with the world.

She had set her heart upon a respectable marriage, becoming her rank. In the far distance Edgar von Rohritz hovered before her as the St. George who was destined to slay for her the dragon of prejudice.

Certain people, especially women, understand how to touch up their reminiscences with the same artistic skill that a photographer expends upon his pictures, so that very little remains of the fact as it was originally projected upon the memory.

Sophie Oblonsky erased, in this touching up of

her reminiscences, everything that she disliked. She talked so much of her virtue that she finally came to believe in it.

Meanwhile, she behaved with perfect propriety and was fearfully bored.

It is five o'clock, and the heavy curtains before the windows of her drawing-room are already drawn close. The lamps shed a mild, agreeable light. A lackey has just brought in the tea. Upon a pretty Japanese stand, beside the silver samovar, sparkle the glass decanters of cordial and all the modern accompaniments of afternoon tea.

It is the Princess's reception-day.

That she entirely ignores in her intercourse with Stasy her own loss of position, that she ascribes her seclusion solely to a voluntary retirement from a hollow world which disgusts her, there is as little need of saying as that Stasy, without a word from the Princess to induce her to do so, feels herself under obligations to introduce Sophie to a new social circle.

This 'circle' consists as yet but of a few wealthy Americans, just arrived in Paris, and of—artists.

The Princess has a special liking for artists; they are, she maintains, so much fresher, so much quicker and pleasanter as companions, than her equals in rank, of whose wearisome shallowness she has many a story to tell. And her special favourite among these is the pianist Fuhrwesen.

Why, good heavens, the only occupation which really interests the Princess at this time is the search for some private irregularity in the lives of women of extreme apparent respectability; and in these investigations the pianist is always ready to assist her.

Dressed with great taste but with severe simplicity, holding a small Japanese hand-screen between her face and the glow from the fire, the Princess is leaning back in a low chair near the hearth, complaining of headache, and hoping that there will not be as many people here to-day as on her last reception-day.

A quarter of an hour—yes, half an hour—passes, and no one appears. Stasy is hungry; the *foie gras* sandwiches are very tempting, but to partake of one would be a tacit admission that there is no hope of a visitor, and she must not be the first to confess the fact.

"Poor Boissy!"—this is a painter whom the Oblonsky has taken under her protection,—"poor Boissy! probably he cannot summon up the courage to come; he is ashamed of his wife. Ah, he really cannot dream how considerate I am for artists' wives. It is a theory of mine that it is our duty, as ladies, to educate artists' wives for their husbands. I know it is not usual to receive them; but that seems to me very petty, and I hate all pettiness."

Another quarter of an hour passes. Stasy is faint with hunger.

"One of the Fanes must be ill," she observes, " or they would certainly be here. I must find out what——" But Sophie interrupts her impatiently.

"Pour me out a cup of tea," she orders her.

The tea is cold and bitter from waiting so long for guests who do not arrive. Sophie finds it detestable, and reproaches Stasy therefor.

Stasy consoles herself for her friend's capricious injustice by taking two glasses of cordial, three sandwiches, and half a dozen little cakes.

Meanwhile, Sophie observes, with a yawn, "I cannot tell you how glad I am that no one came. People bore me so. I revel in my solitude. And to think that I must shortly resign it! I must call upon our ambassadress shortly."

In spite of her wonderful degree of *aplomb*, Anastasia at this point of the conversation is silent and looks rather confused.

" You saw her in the Bois lately," the Oblonsky continues, in a somewhat irritated tone.

" Yes; you pointed her out to me."

" Well, you must have noticed how stiffly she bowed. No wonder. She must have known how long I have been in Paris without calling upon her."

" I have always told you that you carry to excess your passion for solitude," Stasy chirps. " It is easy to go too far in such a preference."

"Ah, the world is odious to me," Sophie declares.

The bell outside is heard to ring at this moment.

"Insufferable!" Sonja exclaims. "I trust no one is coming to disturb us now!" And, glancing at the mirror over the chimney-piece, she adjusts her *jabot* and a curl above her forehead.

The lackey flings wide the folding doors and announces, "Mademoiselle Urwèse,"—the French abbreviation, apparently, for Fuhrwesen; for, even more copper-coloured than usual, in consequence of the biting north wind outside, with her hair blowing about her eyes, a kind of reddish-yellow turban upon her head, and wearing her tassel-bedecked water-proof, the pianist enters.

"How nice of you! This is really charming, my dear Fuhrwesen!" exclaims Sophie, hastily concealing her disappointment. "This is my day, but I closed my doors for all strangers,—absolutely for all," the imaginative Princess asseverates; then, pausing suddenly, she glances uneasily at Stasy. But Stasy has long since learned to let such rhapsodies pass her by without so much as the quiver of an eyelash: her face is motionless, and the Oblonsky goes on fluently: "You were the only one whom Baptiste had orders to admit. Take off your wraps: you will stay and dine, of course, dear, will you not?"

"With your kind permission," Fräulein Fuhrwesen says, submissively, kissing the Oblonsky's hand.

"And now sit here by the fire and warm yourself. Anastasia,"—this is drawled over her shoulder,— "pour out a glass of cordial for her.—You can have nothing more, my dear; I cannot permit you to spoil your appetite. We are going to have an extremely fine dinner."

"Your Highness is really too kind," says the pianist. "Ah, how intensely becoming that green gown is to you! Did you hear Prince Oláry's description of you?—'The Venus of Milo, dressed by Worth.' Was it not capital?" And the pianist gazes at the Oblonsky with enthusiastic admiration.

"Yes, yes, you are in love with me, my dear: 'tis an old story," the Princess says, with a laugh. "But now tell us something new: you always have a budget of news. Any fresh scandal in the Faubourg?"

"Let me think," Fräulein Fuhrwesen says, reflectively. "What news have I heard? *À propos* —yes, I remember; but it will shock your Highness terribly. I really had no idea of such depravity in girls of what is called the best standing."

"Oh, tell us, tell us!" the Princess urges her.

"I must first be sure that I shall not wound Fräulein Anastasia," the pianist remarks, discreetly. "Are you not in some way related, or a very near

friend, to the little Meineck, Fräulein vou Gurlichingen ?"

"Not at all," Anastasia assures her. "I spent a
couple of weeks in the same house with her last
summer, but I had very little to say to her. I
never liked her."

" Meineck ? Meineck ?" says the Oblonsky, with
lifted eyebrows. "Is not she the young person
who you told me fell so desperately in love with
Rohritz ?"

Anastasia nods.

" The young lady apparently possesses an inflam-
mable heart," Fräulein Fuhrwesen remarks, contemptuously : "it already throbs for another,—for
Prince Lorenzino Capito."

The Princess becomes absorbed in contemplation of her nails; Anastasia observes, " That would
seem to be rather an aimless enthusiasm. Pray how
did you learn anything about this affair ?"

Fräulein Fuhrwesen draws a deep breath : " You
know I play the accompaniments at della Seggiola's class. Stella Meineck has attended it for
two months. The company is rather mixed, especially so far as the men are concerned. Who
do you suppose made his appearance to join the
class the day before yesterday ? It really is too
ridiculous,—pretending to want to learn to sing!
Prince Lorenzo Capito."

" You don't say so !" Stasy ejaculates.

"Yes, Prince Capito," the narrator repeats. "He stares past all the others, takes a seat beside little Meineck, and talks with her during the entire lesson. What do you think of that, ladies?"

Stasy sighs, and the Oblonsky says,—

"*C'est bien extraordinaire!* I certainly should not have thought that so insignificant a person could have inspired Capito with the sligtest interest."

"I know Prince Capito," the visitor goes on: "I met him in Vienna at the Countess Thierstein's. His reputation, so far as women are concerned, is disgraceful. Any girl is good enough to help him while away an hour or two."

"Yes, he is a terrible creature," the Princess sighs. "I really had no idea of it. He used to be a good deal at our house while my husband was alive. Of course he never presumed with me."

"*Cela va sans dire,*" exclaims Stasy.

"Of course, you know me: to friendly intercourse—yes, I do not pretend to more reserve than I possess—even to a slight flirtation with an interesting man—I have no objection; but anything beyond that absolutely passes my comprehension."

"The little Meineck, however," Fräulein Fuhrwesen continues, with a malicious smile, "does not appear to be so strict in her ideas. I distinctly heard her during the singing-lesson arranging a rendezvous in the Louvre with the Prince."

"A rendezvous?" Sophie repeats, with horror.

"That is indeed—— And do you know whether Capito kept the appointment?"

"Certainly. I made sure of it," continues her informant. "The morning after the singing-class I had a lesson to give near the Louvre, and after it was over I had a little time to spare. I am perfectly familiar with the museum, as I often go there to visit an acquaintance of mine. I never look at the pictures any more, they tire me to death, but the Louvre is always a nice place to get warm. So I mounted the staircase, and lingered for a while beside the register in the Salle La Caze, exchanging a word or two with an Englishman who is copying a Ribera. Suddenly the man turned, as every man turns to look after a pretty girl. I turned also, and whom should I see but Mademoiselle Stella, with her yellow hair and her sealskin jacket! Please tell me, ladies, how a person so miserably poor as she is—I know all about the Meinecks' pecuniary circumstances, coming as I do from Zalow—can buy a sealskin jacket,—and a beautiful one? Why, one has to save for three years to get a respectable water-proof."

"Probably it was given to her," the Princess says, with a shrug. "But go on."

"She went directly through the room, without looking at the pictures, precisely like some one who had come simply to meet some one else. I went up to her, and, though I cannot endure the haughty creature, I spoke to her: 'Ah, Baronne, how are you?' She replied curtly, looking past me to the right and left, and finally, observing that she could not stay, for she had promised to meet some one,—oh, a lady, of course!—walked quickly away. My time was up. I looked after her, and was leaving, when whom should I encounter in the Galerie d'Apollon but Prince Capito! I suppose any one who knows of his devotion to art can readily imagine why he should be in the Louvre! What do you say to such conduct?"

"Absolutely depraved!" exclaims the Princess.

"We all know whither these 'innocent meetings' in the picture-galleries lead," the Fuhrwesen continues. "The next thing she will pay him a visit in his lodgings."

"Oh, my dear!" the Oblonsky laughs affectedly.

"Bah! I live opposite the Prince in the Rue d'Anjou; I should not be at all surprised if I were to see that young lady walk into No. —— some fine day."

"If you do you must come and tell us instantly!" exclaims the Princess, taking her visitor's hand. "Oh, how cold you are! Is it possible you are not warm yet? Indeed, you are not sufficiently clothed——"

"My cloak is a little thin, but I cannot help that. Your Highness will readily understand that I am not able to buy a sealskin jacket."

"You—— Anastasia, be kind enough to tell Justine to bring down my two winter cloaks."

Anastasia obligingly brings the cloaks herself, and the Princess requests Fräulein Fuhrwesen to try them on. Although the little pianist is shorter by almost a head and shoulders than the majestic Princess, and consequently the garments trail behind her like coronation-robes, the Oblonsky assures her that they fit her as though they had been made for her, and immediately bestows upon her one of the two, a magnificent wrap of dark-green velvet, trimmed with fur.

The pianist kisses both hands of the donor, and kneels before her; the Princess says, laughing, "Don't be absurd, my dear. You see that giving—making others happy—is a passion with me. Stasy has one of my cloaks, you have another, I keep the simplest for myself. I have always lived for others only."

CHAPTER XXVII.

A CHANGE AT ERLACH COURT.

"There is something rotten in the state of Denmark," Edgar von Rohritz says to himself, looking out of his window at Erlach Court upon the snow-covered garden below.

Six days ago he arrived at the castle to spend Christmas, as had been agreed upon. The Christmas festivities are at an end. The children from the three villages upon whom Katrine had showered gifts have all, as well as Freddy, become accustomed to their new possessions, but the giant Christmas-tree, robbed, it is true, of its sugar-plums, still stands with its candle-stumps and gilt ornaments in the corridor, and from the brown frames of the engravings in the dining-room a few evergreen boughs are still hanging, remnants of the Christmas decorations.

Rohritz has enjoyed celebrating the lovely festival in the country,—everything was bright and gay; but there is a change of atmosphere at Erlach Court; the social charm for which it used to be renowned is lacking.

Edgar's reception both by husband and by wife was most cordial: the captain is gay, talkative,—almost gayer and more talkative than in summer; but there is a cloud on Katrine's brow.

Instead of the frank but thoroughly good-humoured tone in which she was wont to deride the captain's exaggerated outbreaks, she now passes them by in silence. She never quarrels with him, she is decidedly displeased with him, and—what surprises Rohritz more than all else—the captain seems to care very little for her displeasure.

To-day Rohritz asked Katrine if it was quite

decided that the captain was to leave the army and retire once for all to the country. Whereupon Katrine's fine eyes sparkle angrily, and with a slight quiver of her delicate nostril she replies, " So it seems. He will not listen to any suggestion of resuming the hard duties of the service, but has accustomed himself entirely to the lazy life of a landed proprietor." And when Rohritz remains silent, she exclaims, angrily, " I know what you are thinking : that I gave him no choice save to resign his career or his domestic life,—which is no choice at all with men of his stamp, whose love of domesticity is very pronounced, and who have no ambition ! But when I acted so I thought he would lead a country life, without deteriorating ; I thought he would occupy himself,—would devote his energies to politics, to Slavonic agricultural interests——"

" Indeed ?" Rohritz asks. " Did you really expect that of Les ?"

" Yes," Katrine exclaims, " I did expect that of Jack ; and I had a right to expect it, for he lacks neither energy nor sense."

" He was always considered one of the keenest and most gifted officers in the army," says Rohritz.

" And with justice," Katrine confirms his words. " You have no idea of the energy with which he devoted himself to the service. Were you ever in Hungary ?"

"Yes, madame, I served as captain for two years in W——."

"Then you are familiar with the fearful heat of the Hungarian summers. To order dinner and to sit upright at table exhausted my capacity; whilst he, although he rose at four that he might get through riding-school before the terrible heat of the day, scarcely ever lay down for half an hour. He continually had something to arrange, to decide, to command; he occupied himself with the individual concerns of every soldier in his squadron; he never took a moment's rest from morning until night; while now—now he does nothing, nothing but sleigh, mend a toy for the boy now and then, and read silly novels."

Rohritz is spared the necessity of replying, for at this moment the quiet drawing-room where this conversation is going on is invaded by the sharp clear tinkle of large sleigh-bells. Katrine turns her head hastily and walks to the window.

"So soon again!" she exclaims, as a fair, stout, pretty woman, wrapped in furs, allows herself, with much loud talking, to be helped out of the sleigh by the captain. Whilst Katrine, with a very gloomy face, takes her seat in an arm-chair to await the stranger's appearance, Rohritz withdraws, under the pretext of an obligation to answer immediately an important letter.

But he writes no letter; he does not even sit

down at his writing-desk, but stands at his window looking out at the snow. In town he had quite forgotten how pure and white snow originally is. He gazes at it as at some curiosity which he is beholding for the first time. On the rose-beds, the bushes, the old linden,—everywhere it lies thick,—thick!

Here and there some branch thrusts forth a black point from the white covering, and the trunks of the trees are all divided in halves, a black half and a white one.

He reflects upon the domestic drama about to be enacted close at hand.

He is sorry for Katrine, although he lays at her door the blame for all the annoyances of which she has spoken to him, petty, provoking annoyances, which under certain circumstances may be the fore-runners of actual misfortune.

"One more who has thrust aside happiness," he murmurs, bitterly, adding on the instant, "If we could only recognize our happiness at the right time! If it could only say to us, 'Here I am,—clasp me close!' But the truest, finest happiness is never self-asserting: it walks beside us mute and modest, warming and rejoicing our hearts, while we know not whence come the warmth and the delight."

*   *   *   *   *   *   *

As the stout blonde whom Leskjewitsch helped

out of the sleigh not only remains to lunch, but also takes afternoon tea and dinner at Erlach Court, Rohritz has abundant opportunity to observe her. That, like all sirens who disturb domestic serenity, she should be inferior in every respect to the wife whose peace of mind she threatens, was to have been expected; but that she should be so immeasurably inferior to Katrine,—for that Rohritz was not prepared.

Anywhere else save in the country, and moreover in a world-forgotten corner of Ukrania, where the foxes bid one another good-night, and human beings are consequently easier to be induced than in civilized countries to bid one another good-day in spite of stupid social prejudices, any intercourse between this lady and the family at Erlach Court would have been impossible.

The daughter of a lucifer-match manufacturer in P——, with a moderate degree of education and a strong passion for hunting, three years ago she had married the son of a riding-teacher, a certain Herr Ruprecht, who had been first a cavalry-officer, then a circus manager in America, and finally a newspaper-man in Vienna. After these various experiences with her promising husband, they had shortly before taken up their abode in a villa not far from Erlach Court, on the opposite bank of the Save. As the husband spent most of his time with a pretty actress, the young wife passed

her days in dreary solitude. The country-people
called her the grass-widow.

"I need not assure you that I am not in the least
jealous," Katrine remarks to Rohritz in the drawing-room, while the grass-widow with Freddy and
the captain is playing billiards in the library, "but
I frankly confess that I find the pleasure which Jack
takes in the society of that common creature—
that fat goose—incomprehensible. It irritates me.
Moreover, she is ugly!"

Rohritz receives this outburst of Katrine's precisely as he receives all her outbursts,—in thoughtful, courteous silence. Frau Ruprecht certainly is
common and silly; ugly she is not. She has a dazzling complexion, a magnificent bust, and a regular
profile, although with lips that are too thick, a
double chin, and light eyelashes. She speaks in a
common, Viennese dialect, has never read a sensible
book in her life, uses perfumes in excess, and has
no taste whatever in dress.

But she drives like a Viennese hackman, she rides
like a jockey, and her knowledge of sporting-mat-
ters would do honour to a professional trainer. She
allows Leskjewitsch the utmost freedom of speech,
and is ready to laugh at his worst jokes.

She disgusts Edgar Rohritz quite as much as
she disgusts Katrine; nevertheless he understands
what there is about her to attract Leskjewitsch.

CHAPTER XXVIII.

A PARIS LETTER.

A few days after the appearance at Erlach Court of the grass-widow, the mail brings Rohritz a letter with the Paris post-mark. Edgar recognizes his sister-in-law's hand, opens it not without haste, and reads it not without interest. It runs thus:

"*Eh bien*, my dear Edgar, *j'espère que vous serez content de moi*,"—Thérèse always writes to her brother in a jargon of French, Italian, German, and English, which, out of regard for the pedantry of modern purists, we translate into as good English as we are able to command: "I hope you will be pleased with me. I frankly confess to you, what you probably guessed from my last postal card, that your request to me to try to brighten their life in Paris for two of your countrywomen did not afford me much pleasure. As a rule, compatriots so recommended are an unmitigated bore, from the pianists whose three hundred—no, that's too few—five hundred tickets we must dispose of, and who then, when you ask them to a soirée, are too grand to play the smallest mazourka of Chopin, to the Baronesses Wolnitzka, who request you to introduce them to

Parisian society because they never have an opportunity to see any one at home. The pianists are bad enough, but the Wolnitzkas—oh! In one respect they are precisely alike : they are always offended. If you invite them *en famille* they are offended because they suppose you are ashamed of them ; if you invite them to a ball they are offended because you pay them no particular attention. The upshot is that you always have to refuse them something,—to lend a thousand francs to the genius when he already owes you five hundred,—to procure for the Wolnitzkas an invitation to some ball at the embassy ; then ensues a quarrel, and they draw down the corners of their mouths and look the other way when they meet you in the street.

"Only at the repeated request of your brother, who wherever anything Austrian is concerned is the personification of self-sacrificing devotion, did I make up my mind to call upon your acquaintance at the 'Negroes.'

"The hôtel is—very plain, but I believe very respectable,—which is more than one has a right to expect of just such furnished lodgings in Paris. The staircase, a narrow crooked flight of steps with slippery sloping stairs, creaked beneath my feet ; I was afraid it would break down as I mounted to the Meinecks' *appartement.* One final, depressing, menacing memory of the Wolnitzkas assailed me. Justin rings, the door opens, and all my prejudices vanish like snow before the sun. The daughter alone was at home. I fell in love with her on the instant,—so deeply in love that before I left I called her Stella and kissed her cheek. She is enchanting.

"It is not only that she is exquisitely beautiful; she combines the most innocent simplicity with the greatest distinction, a combination never found except in Austrian women. You see I know how to value your countrywomen when they are really worth it.

"Her face, her entire air, seemed created to banish all sadness from her presence; and yet there was a pathos in her look, in her smile, that went to my heart. But she must be happy. I mean to search for happiness for her; and I shall find it.

"*Ce que femme le veut, Dieu le veut!* When I do anything I do it thoroughly. What do you think? It took me three weeks to resolve to call upon the Meinecks. I invited them to dine without waiting for them to return my visit. You know my way. We passed a charming evening together, strictly informal, to become acquainted with one another. The mother was as little eccentric as is possible for a blue-stocking to be, and in the course of four hours had only two attacks of absence of mind, which does her honour. What a handsome face! Edmund, who is a connoisseur in such matters, maintains that she must have been more beautiful than her daughter,—high praise, since the daughter, by the way, pleases him as much as she does me. And then what wealth of learning behind that brow with its white hair! Wells of knowledge! a walking encyclopædia!

" Although the fashion of her gown was that of twenty years ago, she is still a thorough *grande dame ;* and that is saying much in consideration of the evident dilapidation of their finances.

" As a mother she may have her disagreeable side; she is too original,—too egotistic. She neglects her lovely daughter frightfully. All the time not absorbed by her literary labours she devotes to the study of Paris; and what mode of pursuing this study with the due amount of thoroughness do you suppose she has invented? She drives about for a certain number of hours daily on the tops of the various omnibuses.

" Fancy!—on the top of an omnibus! A day or two ago, coming home from the Bon-Marché, as I was detained by a crowd of vehicles in the Rue du Bac I saw her comfortably installed upon the dizzy height of an omnibus-top. She wore a short black velvet cloak frayed at all the seams, the fur trimming eaten away by moths, pearl-gray gloves (her hands are ridiculously small), such as were worn twenty years ago upon state occasions, a black straw bonnet, and no muff. She sat between two vagabonds in white blouses, with whom she was talking earnestly, and looked like—well, like a queen dowager in disguise. As it was just beginning to rain, I sent my servant to beg her to alight, and took her home in my carriage.

" A lady on the top of an omnibus! It is frightful; it is impossible. But still more impossible is a young girl who wishes to go upon the stage; and Stella wishes to go upon the stage.

"Nevertheless my relations with the Meinecks grow daily more intimate. Heroic conduct on my part, is it not?

"Poor little Stella! I feel an infinite pity for her. I have no faith in her career. Pshaw! Stella Meineck on the stage! 'Tis ridiculous! She does not know what she is talking about.

"Meanwhile, I have impressed upon her that she is to tell no one of her artistic plans, which may come to naught. It might do her an injury. And I have a scheme! Ah, leave it to me. What I do I do well. Before the season is over Stella will be married. To establish a young girl with no money is difficult nowadays, particularly in Paris, where every man has a fixed price; but there are bargains to be had occasionally.

" She is beautiful, she is lovely, and if the Meinecks do not date precisely from the Crusades the name sounds fine enough to impress some wealthy citizen who writes on his card the name of his estate in the country after his own, in hopes of thus manufacturing a title for himself.

"I see you curl your haughty Austrian lip; you regard all these pseudo-aristocrats with sovereign contempt. You are wrong. Good heavens! why should not a man call himself after his castle if it has a prettier name than his own? Do we not find it more agreeable to present him to our acquaintances as Monsieur de Hauterive than as Monsieur Cabouat? Now 'tis out! There is a certain Monsieur Cabouat de Hauterive whom I have in my eye for Stella. He is very rich, has frequented the society of gentlemen from childhood, and has been received during the last few years by everybody; he loves music, has one of the finest private picture-galleries in Paris, and is in the prime of life,—barely forty-two,—quite young for a man : in short, he seems made for Stella. Last summer he laughingly challenged me to find a wife for him, expressly stating that he desired no dowry. At that time he was longing for repose and a home. I heard lately, however, that he had become entangled in a *liaison* with S——, of the Opéra-Bouffe. That would be frightful.

"Moreover, I have two other men in view for Stella,—an Englishman, forty-five years old, rather shy in consequence of deafness, of very good family, an income of six thousand pounds sterling, and of good trustworthy character; and a Dutchman whose ears were cut off in Turkey, wherefore he is compelled to wear his hair after the fashion of the youthful Bonaparte; but these are trifles.

"Poor melancholy little Stella will be glad to shelter her weary head beneath any respectable roof. The only thing that troubles me is that Zino knew her three years ago in Venice, and is perfectly bewitched by her. Can I prevent him from making love to her? It would be dreadful. Not that it would ever occur to him to be wanting in respect for her, but he might turn her head, and that would ruin all my plans. She might then conceive the idea of marrying only a man with whom she is in love, —perfect nonsense in her position: there is none such for her. Love is an article of supreme luxury in marriage, and exists for wealthy people and day-labourers only.

" Yes, when I do anything I do it well! I do not write to you for two years, but then I give you twenty pages at once. Have you had the patience to read all this? If you have, let me entreat you to take to heart what follows.

" Give us the pleasure of a visit from you. You do not know our new home, and I am burning with desire to show it to you. In the first story of our little house there is a room all ready for you, very comfortable, and, I give you my word, the chimney does not smoke. If you cannot be induced to come to us, let Edmund take rooms for you wherever you please. Only come! I shall else fancy that you have never forgiven me for once being bold enough to want to marry you off. Adieu! I promise you faithfully not to try to lasso you again. With kindest messages from us all,

"Your affectionate sister,

"THÉRÈSE."

An extra slip of paper accompanied this succinct document. Its contents were as follows:

"PARIS, 27th December.

"How forgetful I am! The enclosed letter has been lying for a week in my portfolio. Although it is an old story now, I send it, because it will inform you of all that has been going on.

"Two words more. Since I wrote it I have invited Stella and Hauterive to dinner once, and have had them another evening in our box at the opera. They both dislike Wagner: that is something. Moreover, he thinks her enchanting, and she does not think him very disagreeable,—which is about all that can be expected in a *mariage de convenance*. Everything is working along smoothly; the betrothal is a mere question of time. What do you say now to my energy and capacity?"

*   *   *   .*   *   *   *

He says nothing. He is very pale, and his hands tremble as he folds the letter and puts it away in his desk. A distressing, paralyzing sensation over-powers him. For a moment he sits motionless at his writing-table, his elbows resting upon it, his head in his hands. Suddenly he springs to his feet.

"'Tis a crime! I must prevent it!" The next moment he slays his zeal with a smile. He prevent? And how? Shall he, like his namesake in the opera, rush in at the moment when the betrothal is going on and shout out his veto? And what is it to him if Stella chooses to lead a wealthy, brilliant existence beside an unloved husband? No one forces her to do so.

Meanwhile, the door of his room opens, and with the familiarity of an old comrade the captain enters.

"Will you not play a game of billiards with me, Edgar, before I drive out?" he asks.

Rohritz declares himself ready for a game.

CHAPTER XXIX.

A STORM AND ITS CONSEQUENCES.

The billiard-table is in the library, a long, narrow room, with a vast deal of old-fashioned learning enclosed in tall, glazed bookcases. In a metal cage between the windows swings a gray parrot with a red head, screaming monotonously, 'Rascal! rascal!" The afternoon sun gleams upon the glass of the bookcases; the whole room is filled with blue-gray smoke, and looks very comfortable. The gentlemen are both excellent billiard-players, only Edgar is a little out of practice. Leaning on his cue, he is just contemplating with admiration a bold stroke of his friend's, when Freddy, quite beside himself, rushes into the room and into his father's arms.

"Why, what is it? what is the matter, old fellow?" the captain says, stroking his cheek kindly.

"Os—ostler Frank——" Freddy begins, but without another word he bursts into a fresh howl.

Startled by such sounds of woe from her son, Katrine hurries in, to find the captain seated in a huge leather arm-chair, the boy between his knees, vainly endeavouring to soothe him. Rohritz stands half smiling, half sympathetically, beside them, chalking his cue, while the parrot rattles at the bars of his cage and tries to out-shriek Freddy.

"What has happened? Has he hurt himself? What is the matter?" Katrine asks, in great agitation.

"N—n—no!" sobs Freddy, his fingers in his eyes, and the corners of his mouth terribly depressed; "but os—ostler Frank——"

Ostler Frank is the second coachman and Freddy's personal friend.

"Ostler Frank is an ass!" exclaims the captain,

beginning to trace the connection of ideas in his son's mind; "an ass. You must not let him frighten you."

"What did he tell you?" asks Katrine, standing beside her husband. "How did he frighten you? He has not dared to tell you a ghost-story? I expressly forbade it."

"Oh, no, Katrine: 'tis all about some stupid nonsense, not worth speaking of," replies the captain,—"a mere nothing."

"I should like to know what it is, however," Katrine says, growing more uneasy.

"He—told—me—papa must fight a duel; and when—they—fight a duel—they are killed!" Freddy screams, in despair, nearly throttling his father in his affection and terror.

"I should really be glad to have some intelligible explanation of the matter," Katrine says, with dignity.

"Oh, it is the merest trifle," the captain rejoins, changing colour, and tugging at his moustache.

"The affair is very simple, madame," Rohritz interposes. "Les felt it his duty, lately,—the day before yesterday, in fact,—to chastise an impertinent scoundrel in Hradnyk, and has conscientiously kept at home since, awaiting the fellow's challenge,—of course in vain. What he should have done would have been to emphasize in a note the box on the ear he administered."

"Yes, that's true," says the captain: "it is a pity that it did not occur to me."

Freddy has gradually subsided. As during his tearful misery he has done a great deal of rubbing at his eyes with inky fingers, his cheeks are now streaked with black, and he is sent off by his mother with a smile, in charge of a servant, to be washed.

"Might I be informed," she asks, after the door has closed upon the child, and with a rather mistrustful glance at her husband, "what the individual at Hradnyk did to provoke the chastisement in question?"

"'Tis not worth the telling, Katrine," stammers the captain. "Why should you care to know anything about it?"

"You are very wrong, Les, to make any secret of it," Rohritz interposes. "The scoundrel undertook to use certain expressions which irritated Les, with regard to you, madame."

"With regard to me?" Katrine exclaims, with a contemptuous curl of her lip. "What could any one say about me?"

"What, indeed?" the captain repeats. "Well, I will tell you all about it some time when we are alone, if you insist upon it. It was a silly affair altogether, but I took the matter to heart."

"You Hotspur!" Katrine laughs.

Rohritz has just turned to slip out of the room

and leave the pair to a reconciliatory *tête-à-tête*, when the door opens, and a servant announces that the sleigh is ready.

"Where are you going?" Katrine asks, hastily, in an altered tone, as the servant withdraws.

"I was going to Glockenstein, to take the 'Maître de Forges' to the grass-widow; she asked me for it yesterday; but if you wish, Katrine, I will stay at home."

"If I wish," Katrine coldly repeats. "Since when have I attempted to interfere in any way with your innocent amusements?"

"I only thought——you have sometimes seemed to me a little jealous of the grass-widow."

Rohritz could have boxed his friend's ears for his want of tact. Katrine's aristocratic features take on an indescribably haughty and contemptuous expression.

"Jealous?—I?" she rejoins, with cutting severity, adding, with a shrug, "on the contrary, I am glad to have another woman relieve me of the trouble of entertaining you."

Tame submission to such words from his wife, and before a witness, is not the part of a hot-blooded soldier like Jack Leskjewitsch.

"Adieu, Rohritz!" he says, and, with a low bow to his wife, he leaves the room.

For an instant Katrine seems about to run after him and bring him back. She takes one step towards the door, then pauses undecided. The sharp, shrill sound of sleigh-bells rises from without through the wintry silence: the sleigh has driven off. Katrine goes to the window to look after it. With lightning speed it glides along, the centre of a bluish, sparkling cloud of snow-particles whirled aloft by the trampling horses. It is out of sight almost immediately.

Her head bent, Katrine turns from the window, and leaves the room with lagging steps.

*   *   *   *   *   *   *

The *menu* for dinner comprises the captain's favourite dish of roast pheasants, but six o'clock strikes and the master of the house has not yet arrived at home.

" Would it not be better to postpone the dinner a little for to-day?" Katrine asks Rohritz, for form's sake. They wait one hour,—two hours: the captain does not appear. At last Katrine orders dinner to be served. Unable to eat a morsel, she sits with an empty plate before her, hardly speaking a word.

The meal is over, coffee has been served, Freddy has played three games of cards with his tutor and then disappeared with a very sleepy face.

Katrine and Rohritz sit opposite each other, each taking great pains to appear unconcerned. One quarter of an hour after another passes without a word exchanged between them. Suddenly Katrine rises, goes to the window, opens first the inner shutter and then the peep-hole in the other.

"Listen how the wind roars!" she says, in a hoarse, subdued voice, to Rohritz. "And the snow is falling as if a feather bed had been cut in two."

Rohritz is really unable to smile, as he would have been tempted to do at any other time, at the contrast between Katrine's deeply tragic air and her very commonplace comparison: he is rather anxious himself.

"Hark! just hark how the wind whistles! I hope Jack has not got wedged in a snow-drift."

Rohritz makes some reply which Katrine does not heed. In increasing agitation she paces the room to and fro.

"The worst place is the bit of road near the quarry," she murmurs to herself. "If he goes a hand's-breadth too far on one side, then——"

"Les has a remarkable sense of locality, and is the best whip I know," Rohritz remarks, soothingly.

She is silent, compresses her lips, listens at the window, hearkens to the raging wind, which drives the snow-flakes against the shutters and tears and rattles at the boughs of the giant linden until they shriek from out their long winter sleep.

How much we are able to forgive a man when we are anxious about him!

"I would rather send some one to meet him," she stammers. "I am exceedingly anxious."

She reaches out her hand for the bell-rope, when suddenly from the far distance, like mocking, elfin laughter, comes the tinkle of sleigh-bells. Katrine holds her breath, listens. The sleigh approaches, draws up before the door. Rohritz goes out into the hall. Katrine hears a man stamping the snow from his boots, hears the captain's fresh, cheery voice as he answers his friend's questions. Her anxiety is converted into a sensation of great bitterness. She cannot rally herself too much for her childish anxiety, cannot forgive herself for behaving so ridiculously before Rohritz. Whilst she has been fancying her husband lost in a snow-drift, he beyond all doubt has been admirably entertained with the grass-widow.

The door opens; the captain appears alone, without his comrade.

"Still up, Katrine?" he asks, in a gentle undertone, approaching his wife, and with an uncertain, half-embarrassed smile he adds, "Rohritz told me you were anxious about—about me." As he speaks he tries to take his wife's hand to draw her towards him; but Katrine avoids him.

"Rohritz was mistaken," she rejoins, very dryly. "For a moment I thought you might have fallen into the quarry, because I could not see any apparent reason for your late return. But as for anxiety——" Without finishing the sentence, she shrugs her shoulders.

The captain smiles bitterly, and passes his hand across his forehead.

"Yes, he was evidently mistaken; it was an attempt to bring us together," he murmurs; "his sentimental representation did at first seem rather incredible to me. But what one wishes to believe one does believe so easily! I was foolish enough to delight in the hope of a kindly welcome from you; but, in fact, in comparison with the reception you. have vouchsafed me the weather outside is genial."

He seats himself astride of a low chair, and begins to drum impatiently upon the back of it.

"It seems to me quite late enough to go to bed," says Katrine, taking a silver candlestick from the mantel-piece. "It is a quarter-past ten."

Suddenly the captain grasps her by the wrist. "Stay!" he says, sternly.

"You have come back in a very bad humour," Katrine remarks, with a contemptuous smile. "The grass-widow must have proved unkind. Your delay in returning led me to suppose the contrary."

The captain looks at his wife with an odd expression. Was it possible she could take sufficient interest in him to be jealous?

"I have not seen the grass-widow," he rejoins, after a short pause.

"That is, you did not find her at home?　How very sad!"

"I did not go to Glockenstein."

"Ah, indeed!　I thought——"

"You are quite right," he said, with an air of bravado.　"After the very kind and choice words with which in the presence of an auditor you dismissed me, I certainly whipped up the horses in order to reach Glockenstein with all speed.　When angels will have nothing to do with us, we are fain to go for consolation to the devil: he is sure to be at hand.　Frau Ruprecht would have received me with open arms; I am by no means"—with a forced laugh—"so insignificant in her eyes; for her I am quite a hero, and—what would you have? she is stupid, but she is pretty and young, and an amount of consideration from any woman flatters a poor fellow who is never without the consciousness of his inferiority in the eyes of his clever wife at home."

"Ah! really?" Katrine sneers.　"May I beg you to make a little haste with your explanations? —the lamp is beginning to burn dimly."

"It burns quite well enough for what I have to say," replies the captain.　"I whipped up my horses, as I said,—I was positively in a hurry to fall at the Ruprecht's feet; but, just at the last moment, so many different things occurred to me! Glockenstein was in sight, but I turned aside, and then drove over to Reitzenberg's to settle with him about the wood."

" Ah! It seems to have been a very protracted business discussion."

" I took supper with Reitzenberg, and played a game of cards afterwards."

" Hm! Since, then, you have perhaps sufficiently explained the reason of your delay, will you permit me to withdraw ?" Katrine asks.

" Apparently you do not believe me. And yet you ought to know that falsehood is not to be reckoned among my bad qualities."

" True; but"—Katrine shrugs her shoulders— " no man hesitates to improvise a little when there's a lady in the case. I should like to know, however, why you take so much trouble in the present instance for me, who have so little interest in such things." And, taking the candlestick once more from the chimney-piece, she asks, " Can I go now? Have you finished?"

" No," he exclaims, angrily, " I have not finished, and you will hearken to me. Matters are come to a worse pass than you fancy; our whole existence is at stake. You know how my sister Lina's marriage turned out, and you are in a fair way to plunge me into the same misery into which Franz Meineck was thrust by his wife."

" Your comparison of me to your sister seems to me rather forced," Katrine replies. " I know it is not pleasant to hear one's relatives criticised by another, however we may disapprove of them ourselves, but I must defend myself. Your sister neglected her household and her children, giving herself over to a ridiculous ambition; whilst I——" She hesitates, deterred from proceeding by something in the captain's look:

"Whilst you——" he begins. "I know perfectly well what you would say. Your household is perfectly attended to, you are an ideal mother, and daintily neat. In a word, you would have been for me the ideal wife if you had ever shown me a particle of affection."

"I have always done my duty by you."

"Your hard, prescribed, bounden duty."

"You could not expect anything more of me. When we married it was agreed between us that each should be satisfied with a sensible amount of friendship."

He has risen, and is gazing at her keenly, searchingly.

"That is true; you are right," he says, bitterly. "The sad thing about it is that I had forgotten it!"

"I cannot understand how you—I must say I never have observed—that you——"

"Indeed? You never have observed that I have long ceased to keep my part of our compact!" the captain exclaims. "Really? Women are fabulously blind when they do not choose to see. Do you suppose I should have allowed the reins to be taken from my hands, do you suppose I should have resigned my authority over you, have lost the right of disposing of my own child, and have abandoned my profession, if—if I had not fallen in love with you like a very school-boy! There! now despise me doubly for my confession, and until you see me stifling in the mire, like poor Franz Meineck, console yourself with the conviction that you have done your duty by me."

He makes her a profound bow, then turns and leaves the room.

CHAPTER XXX.

A SLEEPLESS NIGHT.

" UNTIL you see me stifling in the mire, like poor Franz Meineck, console yourself with the conviction that you have done your duty by me."

Strange how deeply these words are impressed upon Katrine's soul! She does not sleep during the night following upon the captain's explanation, no, not for a quarter of an hour.

She tosses about restlessly in bed; a moonbeam which has contrived to slip through a crack in her shutters points at her with uncanny persistency, like an accusing ghostly finger. The little clock on her writing-table strikes twelve; the sixth of January is past, the seventh of January has begun. The seventh of January! It was her wedding-day. On the seventh of January nine years before, without a spark of love for Jack Leskjewitsch, but with the angry memory of humiliation suffered at another's hands, she had donned her gown of bridal white and her bridal wreath had been placed upon her head. In her inmost soul she had compared her bridal robes to a shroud, and so cold, so white, so stern, had she looked on that day that those who helped to dress her for the sacred ceremony had often said later that they had seemed to themselves to be preparing a corpse for burial, while all who witnessed the marriage declared that no funeral could have been sadder.

She had first known Jack on her father's, the Freiherr von Rinsky's, estate in M——. Quartered at the castle, Jack had soon ingratiated himself with its gouty old master. Katrine did not dislike him, —nay, she rather liked him. Her pride, which had been suffering from the destruction of her illusions ever since the winter she had spent with her aunt in Pesth three years before, turned with a bitterness that bordered on disgust from all the homage paid her by men. Jack Leskjewitsch had always been attentive to her without ever making love to her,—which attracted her. When he asked her to marry him he did it in so dry, odd a way that from sheer surprise she did not at once say no.

She replied that she would take his offer into consideration. Living beneath the same roof with a young stepmother whom she did not like, and who ruled her father, the suit of a wealthy, thoroughly honourable man was not to be lightly rejected. Yet if he had wooed her passionately and tenderly she would surely have refused to listen to him. This, however, he did not do.

When she confessed to him that a bitter disappointment had paralyzed all the sentiment she had ever possessed, that he was not to expect any love from her, he received the confession with the utmost calmness, and replied that he too had nothing to offer her save cordial friendship.

"Those of my friends who married for love are one and all wretched now. Let us try it after another fashion," he had said to her. And thus, almost with a laugh, without the slightest emotion, they had been betrothed on a gray, rainy November day, when the winds were raging as if they had sworn to blow out the sun's light in the skies, while the last field-daisies were hanging their heads among the faded meadow-grass as if tired of life.

Six weeks afterwards they were married, and took the usual trip to Rome and from one hotel to another.

The pale moonbeam still pointed at her like an accusing finger; its silver light fell upon her past and revealed many things which she had heedlessly forgotten during the nine years which now lay behind her.

She had married poor, very poor,—had brought her husband nothing save her trousseau.

All the material comfort of her existence came from him. To show him any special gratitude for that would indeed have been petty; but, putting it aside, with how much consideration he had always treated her! how carefully he had removed from her path all need for trouble and exertion, with the tenderness which rude soldiers alone know how to lavish upon their wives. She had complained of the inconveniences of the nomadic life of the army; but who had drained all those inconveniences to the dregs? He! He had taken all trouble upon himself. In their wanderings she and the child had been cared for like the most frail and precious treasures, upon the transportation of which it was impossible to bestow too much thought. It had always been, " Spare yourself, and look out for the boy!" and either "It is too hot," or "It is too cold: you might be ill, or you might take cold; but do not stir. I will see to it; rely upon me!"

Yes, she had indeed relied upon him; he looked after everything, without any words, without annoying her with restlessness, quietly, simply, and as if it could not have been otherwise.

And what had she done for him in return for all his care and consideration? She had kept his home in order, had treated him with more or less friendliness, had never flirted in the least with any other man, and had presented him with a charming child.

But no; she had not even presented him with it: she had jealously kept it for herself, had grudged him every caress which the boy bestowed upon his father; she had spoiled the child in order that she might hold the first place in his heart. Yet, oddly enough, in spite of all her indulgence the boy was fonder of his fiery, irritable, good-humoured, but strict papa whose nod he obeyed, than of herself, whom the young gentleman could wind around his finger. She confessed this to herself, not without bitterness.

When, the previous autumn, Erlach Court had come to her by inheritance from a grand-uncle, she was filled with a desire to break off all connection with an army life. Without the slightest consideration for her husband, she had left him and forced him for her sake to adopt an existence that was contrary to all his habits and tastes. The moonbeam still penetrated into her room: it grew brighter and brighter, and at last lit up the most secluded corner of her heart.

"Until you see me stifling in the mire, like poor Franz Meineck, console yourself with the conviction that you have done your duty by me."

Again and again the words echoed through her soul.

"I have done my duty by him," she repeated to herself, with the obstinacy with which we are wont to clutch a self-illusion that threatens to vanish. "I have done my duty."

Suddenly she trembles from head to foot, and, hiding her face in the pillow, she bursts into tears.

The boundless egotism, in all its petty childishness, which has informed her intercourse with her husband flashes upon her conscience.

How is it that she has never perceived that he has long since ceased to perform his part of their agreement? Little tokens of affection full of a timid poetry hitherto heedlessly overlooked now occur to her. Why had she not understood them? Why had she never felt a spark of love for him? Her cheeks burn. She had continually reproached her husband with never being done with his illusions, and she—— In a secret drawer of her writing-table there is at this very moment, shrivelled and faded, a gardenia which she has never been able to bring herself to destroy. She springs up, lights a candle, hastens to her writing-table, finds the ugly brown relic,—and burns it. When she lies down in bed again the admonitory moonbeam has vanished, but through the cold black of the winter night filters the first weak shimmer of the dawn. The dreamy ding-dong of a church bell among the mountains ringing for early mass has the peaceful sound of a sacred morning serenade as it floats into her room.

It is barely six o'clock. She folds her hands, a fervent prayer rises to her lips, and, with a still more fervent, unspoken prayer in her heart, her brown head sinks back upon the cool white pillow, and she falls asleep.

CHAPTER XXXI.

GLOWING EMBERS.

"Papa is lazy to-day," Freddy remarks the next morning, breaking the silence that reigns at the breakfast-table and looking pensively at his father's empty chair. It is late, Freddy has drunk his milk, and Rohritz and the tutor are engaged with their second cup of tea. The host, usually so early, has not yet made his appearance.

"You ought not to make such remarks about papa," Katrine corrects her son on this occasion, although she is usually very indulgent to Freddy's impertinence. "Run up to his room and tell him I sent you to ask whether he took cold last evening, and if he would not like a cup of tea sent to him." In two minutes the boy returns, shouting gaily, "Papa sends you word that he does not want anything; he has nothing but a bad cold in his head, and he is coming presently."

In fact, the captain follows close upon the heels of his pretty little messenger.

"I was troubled about you," Katrine says, receiving him with a sort of timid kindness which seems painfully forced.

"Indeed? Very kind of you," he makes reply, in a very hoarse voice,—"but quite unnecessary."

"You seem, however, to have taken cold," Rohritz interposes.

"Pshaw! 'tis nothing. I lost my way in the dark last night, and got into a drift this side of K——: that's all.—Well, Katrine, am I to have my tea?"

"I have just made you some fresh; the first was beginning to be bitter," she makes excuse. "Wait a moment."

The captain is about to reply, but a fit of coughing interrupts him.

"Papa barks as Hector does at the full moon," Freddy remarks, merrily.

Katrine frowns. Why does Freddy seem so thoroughly spoiled to-day?

"I told you just now that it is very wrong in you to speak in that way of your father."

"Let him do it; papa knows what he means," the captain replies, turning to his little son sitting beside him rather than to his wife. "You're fond enough of papa,—love him pretty well,—eh, my boy?"

"Oh, don't I?" says Freddy, nestling close to his father; "don't I?" That any one could doubt this fact evidently amazes him. The captain talks and plays merrily with the boy, never addressing a single word to Katrine.

Breakfast is over. For an hour Katrine has been sitting in her room, some sewing which has dropped from her hands lying in her lap, listening and waiting for his step,—in vain. Another quarter of an hour glides by: her heart throbs louder and louder, and tears fill her eyes. Suddenly she tosses her work aside, rises, and with head erect, looking neither to the right nor to the left, walks with firm, rapid steps along the corridor to the captain's room. At the door she pauses,—pauses for one short moment,—then boldly turns the latch and enters. Is he there? Yes, he is standing at the window, looking out upon the quiet, white landscape. Rather surprised, he looks back over his shoulder at his wife, for he knows it is she: he could recognize her step among a thousand.

"Do you want anything?" he asks, dryly.

"N—no."

The captain turns again to the snowy landscape.

"What are you gazing at so steadily?" Katrine asks him. "Is there anything particularly interesting to be seen out there?"

"No," he replies; "but when the room is cheerless, one looks out of the window for diversion."

A pause ensues.

"What shall I say to him? what can I say to him?" she asks herself, uneasily. The blood mounts to her cheeks; she stands rooted to the spot, not venturing to approach him. At last, she begins with all the indifference at her command, "You have forgotten our wedding-day to-day, for the first time. Strange!"

"Very," the captain rejoins, with bitter irony.

Another pause ensues. Katrine is just about to withdraw, mortified, when the captain again turns to her.

"I did not forget. No, I do not forget such things; and, if you care to know, I had provided the yearly, touching surprise in celebration of the anniversary; but I suppressed it at the very last moment."

"And why?"

"Why? A woman of your superior sense should be able to answer that question herself. After having been laughed at eight times for my well-meant attentions, I said to myself finally that it was useless to serve for the ninth time as a target for your sarcasm."

She comes a step nearer to him.

"I had no desire to laugh to-day."

"Indeed! Hm! then you can open the packet on my writing-table. I had the boy photographed for you, and the picture turned out very well."

She opens the packet. 'Tis a perfect picture, —Freddy himself, bright, wayward, charming, one hand upon his hip, his fur cap on his head.

"He is a beauty, our boy!" she exclaims, smiling down upon the picture in its simple frame.

"Our boy!" the captain murmurs. "You are immensely gracious to-day; you usually speak of him as if he belonged to you only."

Katrine blushes a little, but, without apparently noticing this last remark, says, "He begins to look like you, the dear little fellow!"

"Indeed? Tis a pity——"

"You really would do better to sit by the fire and warm yourself than to stand shivering at that cold window."

"The fire has gone out, and there is small comfort in sitting by the ashes."

"You ought to have made the fire burn afresh."

"I tried to," he replied, with significant emphasis, "but I failed."

"Really!" she says, laughing archly in the midst of her vexation; "you must have tried very awkwardly. If I am not mistaken, there are embers enough under the ashes to set Rome on fire. I should like to see."

She kneels upon the hearth, scrapes together the embers, and with great skill and precision piles three logs of wood on top of them. One minute later the wood is burning with a clear flame.

"Jack!" she calls, very gently.

He starts, and looks round.

"Jack, is the fire burning brightly enough for you now?" she asks.

As in a dream he approaches her.

"Now sit down," she says, in a tone of gay command, pulling forward a large, comfortable arm-chair, "and warm yourself."

He obeys, looking down at her half in surprise, half in tenderness, as she kneels beside him, slender, graceful, wonderfully fair to see, with the reflection from the fire crimsoning her cheeks and lending a golden lustre to her light-brown hair.

Her breath comes quick, as it does when there is something in the heart, longing for utterance, which will not rise to the lips. She had thought out so many fine phrases early this morning in which to clothe her repentance, but they all stick fast in her throat.

The bell rings for lunch. Good heavens! is this moment to pass without sealing their reconciliation?

He sits mute. The wood in the chimney crackles loudly, sometimes with a noise almost like a pistol-shot.

Katrine still kneels before the fire, growing more and more restless. On a sudden she throws back her head, and, casting off the unnatural degree of feminine gentleness which has characterized her all the morning, she exclaims angrily, her eyes flashing through burning tears, " What would you have, Jack ? How far must I go before you come to meet me ?"

" Oh, Katrine, my darling, wayward Katrine !" the captain almost shouts, clasping her in his arms. " At last I know that 'tis no deceitful dream mocking me !"

A light tripping step is heard in the corridor. Both spring up as Freddy's merry little face appears at the door :

" Lunch is growing cold."

* * * * * * *

In the evening, as the couple are sitting in the drawing-room in the twilight, Katrine says,—

" If only there were no such thing as war !"

" What makes you think of that ?" asks the captain.

" Why, because I should beg you to go back to the service, if I were not so mortally afraid of a campaign."

" No need to take that into consideration," the

captain rejoins, "for in case of war I should go back immediately: not even you could prevent me, Kitty. But tell me, could you really summon up courage enough?"

"Could I not? It will be very hard eventually to part from the boy, but sooner or later we must send him to the Theresianeum, and—to speak frankly—even a separation from Freddy would not distress me so much as to see you degenerate in an inactive life."

"You really would, then, Kitty?—would voluntarily subject yourself again to all the inconveniences and petty miseries of the soldier's nomadic life?"

"Try me," and her large eyes are very serious and determined as they look into his own, "try me, and you shall see what a comfortable home I will make for you in the forlornest Hungarian village."

"Ah, you angel!" her husband exclaims, taking her soft little hand in his and pressing it against his cheek. "What a pity it is that we have lost so much time in all these nine years!"

"A pity indeed," she admits, "but 'tis never too late to mend,—eh?"

At this moment Rohritz enters the room, as is usual at this hour every afternoon, to get a cup of tea. He observes, first, that the pair have forgotten to ring for the lamp, and, secondly, that they stop talking upon his entrance; in short, that, for the first time, he has intruded.

"You have come for your tea," says Katrine. "I had positively forgotten that there was such a thing. Ring the bell, Jack."

Before the evening is over Edgar has made a very important discovery,—to wit, that however cordially one may rejoice when two human souls after long and aimless wanderings come together and are united, any prolonged association with a couple so reconciled is considerably more tedious than with an unreconciled pair; wherefore he leaves Erlach Court on the following day.

CHAPTER XXXII.

THÉRÈSE, THE WISE.

In Thérèse's boudoir are assembled four people, Thérèse, her husband, her brother Zino, and Edgar, —Edgar, who on the previous day, to the great surprise of his relatives in Paris, was persuaded to transfer himself from the Hôtel Bouillemont, whither he had gone upon his arrival, to the Avenue Villiers and the shelter of his brother's hospitable roof.

"Thérèse, exhausted, more breathless than usual,

is lying on a lounge, wrapped in a thick white coverlet, shivering, coughing, feverish, with every symptom of a violent cold, and disputing vehemently with her husband as to whether, as he maintains, she caught the said cold on Monday at the Bon-Marché, or, as she maintains, on Tuesday in his smoking-room.

"No one could take cold in my smoking-room; it is the only room in the house where the temperature is a healthy one," Edmund declares. "Judge for yourself, Edgar; there's no getting a sensible word out of Zino. How could any one catch cold in my smoking-room? I know perfectly well how she caught it. Day before yesterday —Monday—there were bargains in Oriental rugs advertised at the Bon-Marché. My wife rushes there in such a storm——"

"That means, I drove there in an hermetically-closed coupé," Thérèse defends herself.

"Pshaw! the damp air always penetrates into every carriage," her husband cuts her words short. "The fact is, she rushed to the Rue du Bac, where she did not buy a single rug, but instead a dozen umbrellas, and then came home in a state of exhaustion,—such exhaustion that I had positively to carry her up-stairs, because she was unable to stir; and now she blames my smoking-room for her cold! It is absurd!" And, by way of further expression of his anger, for which words do not suffice, Edmund rattles the tongs about among the embers on the hearth.

"Have some regard for my nerves, Edmund," Thérèse entreats, stopping her ears with her fingers. "You make more noise than one of Wagner's operas. Twelve umbrellas!" Then turning to Edgar, "To place the slightest dependence upon what my husband says——"

But before she can finish her sentence Edmund breaks in again:

"It makes no difference; it might have been three umbrellas and six straw bonnets: it is all the same. Every Parisian woman suffers from the bargain-mania, but I have never seen the disease developed to such a degree as in my wife. She buys everything she comes across, if it is only a bargain,—old iron rubbish, new plans of Paris, embroideries, antique clocks, and bottles of rock-crystal as——christening-presents for children who are not yet born!"

"*A propos* of presents," Thérèse observes, reflectively, "do you not think, Zino, that the chandelier of Venetian glass I bought last year would be a good wedding-present for Stella Meineck?"

"Is she betrothed, then?" Zino inquires, naturally.

"As good as," Thérèse assents.

"To whom?" Capito asks, sitting down, both hands in his trousers-pockets, and crossing his legs.

"To Arthur de Hauterive,—a brilliant match," says Thérèse.

"Cabouat de Hauterive," murmurs Zino, ironically stroking his moustache, and stretching his legs out a little farther. "A brilliant match if you choose, but rather a scaly fellow,—eh?"

"I should like to know what objection you can make to him," Thérèse asks, crossly.

Zino shrugs his shoulders up to his ears, and then straightens them again, without taking any further pains to clothe in words his opinion of Monsieur Cabouat.

"He is not a thorough gentleman," says the elder Rohritz.

"He is a thorough snob," says Zino.

"One question, if you please." Edgar suddenly and unexpectedly takes part in the conversation: he has hitherto seemed quite absorbed in contemplation of a photograph on the mantel-piece of his little niece. "Has Fräulein Meineck agreed to the match?"

"Yes, to my great surprise," his brother replies. "I did not expect it of her."

"It was no easy task to bring her round," Thérèse declares; "but I went to work in the most sensible manner. 'Have you any other preference?' I asked Stella yesterday, after telling her that Monsieur de Hauterive was ready to lay his person and his millions at her feet and had begged me to ascertain for him beforehand that his suit would not be rejected."

"And what was Stella's reply?" Edmund asks.

"She started and changed colour. 'Dear child,' I said, 'it is perfectly natural that you should have some little fancy: we have all had our enthusiasms for the man in the moon; *cela va sans dire;* such trifles never count. The question is, Have you a passion for some one who returns it and who you have reason to hope will marry you?'

"'No!' she answered, very decidedly.

"'Then do not hesitate an instant, dear child,' I exclaimed; and when she did not reply I laid the case before her, making clear to her how un-justifiable her refusal of this offer would be. 'You have no money!' I exclaimed. 'You propose to go upon the stage. That is simply nonsense; for, setting aside the fact that you have scarcely voice enough to succeed, a theatrical career for a girl with your principles and prejudices is impossible. Look your future in the face, dear heart. Your little property must soon, as you cannot but admit, be consumed; that meanwhile the fairy prince of your girlish dreams should appear as your suitor is not within the bounds of probability. You must choose between two courses, either to earn your living as a governess or to give lessons; since you do not wish to leave your mother, you must adopt the latter. Fancy it!—running about in galoshes and a water-proof in all kinds of weathers, looked at askance by servants in the halls, tormented by your clients and pupils, no gleam of light anywhere, except in an occasional ticket for the theatre, either given to you or purchased out of your small savings, and finally in your old age a miserable invalid existence supported chiefly by the alms of a few charitable pupils. This is the future that awaits you if you refuse Monsieur de Hauterive. On the other hand, if you accept him, how delightful a life you will lead! You can assist your mother and sister largely, and will have nothing to do except to treat with a reasonable degree of consideration a good husband who exacts no passionate devotion from you, and to be the mistress, with all the grace and charm natural to you, of one of the finest houses in Paris. Why, you cannot possibly hesitate, my darling.'"

All three gentlemen have listened with exemplary patience to this lengthy exordium,—Edmund with a gloomy frown, and Zino with the half-contemptuous smile which he has taught himself to bestow upon the most tragic occurrences, while Edgar's face tells no tale, as during his sister-in-law's long speech it has been steadily turned away, gazing into the fire.

"And what did the little Baroness have to say to your brilliant argument in favour of a sensible marriage?" Zino asks, after a short pause.

"For a moment she sat perfectly quiet: she had grown very pale, and her breath came quick. Then she looked up at me out of those large, dark eyes of hers, which you all know, and said,—

"'Yes, you are right. I will be sensible.'

"I took her in my arms, and exulted in my victory. I confess I had a hard battle; but you must all admit that I was right."

"I admit that you went resolutely to work," says her husband, gloomily.

"What do you think, Edgar?"

"Since I have no personal knowledge of Monsieur Cabouat de Hauterive, my opinion is of no value," Edgar replies, dryly.

"Well, you at least think I was right, Zino?" Thérèse exclaims, rather piqued.

"Certainly," he replies, "since I have lately become quite too poor to indulge in expensive pleasures, and consequently cannot marry for love. I shall be glad at least to know Stella well taken care of."

"*Mauvais sujet!*" Thérèse laughs. "I see it is high time to marry you off, or you'll be committing some stupidity. I must marry you all off,—you too, Edgar—ah, *pardon*, I believe I did promise to leave you unmolested; but I have such a superb match for you."

"Who is it?" asks Zino. "I am really curious."

"Natalie Lipinski."

"*Pardon*, there you are reckoning without your host," the Prince says, almost crossly. "Natalie does not wish to marry."

"So say all girls, before the right man appears."

"You're wrong," Zino interposes. "I know of three people—hm! people of some importance—to whom Natalie has given the mitten. Two of them I cannot name: the third—well, I myself am the third. She refused me point-blank."

"*Tiens!* now I guess the reason of your lasting friendship for Natalie: you are ever grateful to her for that refusal!" Thérèse laughs. "You and Natalie!—it is inconceivable."

"She pleased me," the Prince confesses. "'Tis strange: you're sure to over-eat yourself on delicacies; you never do on good strong bouillon. Natalie always reminds me of bouillon. She is the only girl for whom ever since I first knew her —that is, ever since I was a boy—I have felt the same degree of friendship. *Ça!*" he takes his watch out of his pocket; "she begged me not to fail to come to the Rue de la Bruyère to-day. Will not you come too, Edgar? She would be delighted to see you."

Edgar lifts his brows with a bored expression. Before he finds time in his slow way to answer, Thérèse interposes:

"Do go, Edgar, please! You must know that Monsieur de Hauterive is to make his declaration to

Stella to-day.   I advised him to speak to her before
he preferred his suit to her mother: it is the fashion
in Austria.   Stella would be sure to value such a con-
cession to Austrian custom.   Yes, Edgar, go to the
Lipinskis' and watch little Stella and her adorer.
If I were not so utterly done up I would go too, I
am so very curious."

CHAPTER XXXIII.

STELLA'S FAILURE.

LIKE most of the salons of foreigners in Paris,
even of the most distinguished, that of the Lipinskis produces the impression of a social menagerie.   Artists, Americans, diplomatists, stand out
in strong relief against a background of old Russian acquaintances.   French people are seldom met
with there.   Scarcely three months have passed
since the Lipinskis took up their abode in Paris,
and they have not yet had time to organize their
circle.   The agreeable atmosphere of every-day
intimacy which constitutes the chief charm of every
select circle is lacking.   The Russians and the
elderly diplomatists gather for the most part about
the fireplace, where Madame Lipinski holds her
little court.

She is an uncommonly distinguished, graceful old lady, who had been a celebrated beauty in the best days of the Emperor Nicholas's reign, and had played her part at court. One of the Empress's maids of honour, she had preserved in her heart an undying, unchanging love for the chivalric, maligned Emperor, so sadly tried towards the end of his life. She wears her thick white hair stroked back from her temples and adorned by a rather fantastic cap of black lace; her tiny ears, undecorated by ear-rings, are exposed,—which looks rather odd in a woman of her age. As soon as she becomes at her ease with a new acquaintance she tells him of the annoyance which these same tiny ears occasioned her at the time when she was maid of honour. The Empress condemned her to wear her hair brushed down over her cheeks, merely because the Emperor once at a ball extolled the beauty of her ears.

"She was jealous, the poor Empress," the old lady is wont to close her narrative by declaring, and then, raising her eyes to heaven, she says, with a deprecatory shrug, "Of me!" What she likes best to tell, however, is how the Emperor once, when he honoured her with a morning call, had with the greatest patience kindled her fire in the fireplace, whereupon she had exclaimed, "Ah, Sire, if Europe could behold you now!"

The artistic element collects about Natalie.

On the day when Edgar and Zino are sent to the Lipinskis' to observe Stella and Monsieur Cabouat, the artistic element is represented by a pianist of much pretension and with his fingers stuck into india-rubber thimbles, and besides by Signor della Seggiola.

Della Seggiola, without his gray velvet cap, in a black dress-coat, looks freshly washed and—immensely unhappy. His comfortable, barytone self-possession stands him in no stead in this cool atmosphere: he has no opportunity to produce the jokes and merry quips with which he is wont to enliven his scholars during his lessons. Restless and awkward, he goes from one arm-chair to another, is absorbed in admiration of a piece of Japanese lacquer, and breathes a sigh of relief when he is asked to sing something, which seems to him far easier in a drawing-room than to talk.

The pianist, on the contrary, needs a deal of urging before he consents to pound away fiercely at the Pleyel piano as though he were a personal enemy of the maker.

"I have a great liking for artists," Madame Lipinski, after watching the barytone through her eye-glass, declares to her neighbour Prince Suwarin, who is known in Parisian society by the nickname of *memento mori*, "but they seem to me like hounds,—delightful to behold in the open air, but mischievous in a drawing-room. One always dreads lest they should upset something. Natalie disagrees with me : she likes to have them in the house; she is exactly my opposite, my daughter."

In this Prince Capito agrees with her, and hence his regard for Natalie.

It is about half-past ten when Edgar and Zino enter the Lipinski drawing-room. After Edgar has paid his respects to both ladies of the house,—a ceremony much prolonged by Madame Lipinski,—he looks about for Stella, and perceives her directly in the centre of the room, seated on a yellow divan from which rises a tall camellia-tree with red blossoms, beside Zino. He is about to approach her, when he feels a hand upon his arm. He turns. Stasy stands beside him, affected, languishing, in a youthful white gown, a bouquet of roses on her breast, and a huge feather fan in her hand.

"What an unexpected pleasure!" she murmurs.

As just at this moment a young lady, a pupil of the pianist, has seated herself at the piano, to play a bolero, Edgar is obliged to keep quiet, and cannot help being detained beside the wicked old fairy; nay, he is even pinned down in a chair beside her.

The assemblage listens in silence to the young performer's first effort; but when the Spanish dance is followed by a Swedish 'reverie' the silence ceases. The hum of conversation rises throughout the room,—conversation conducted in that half-whisper which reminds one of the low murmur of faded leaves. The first to begin it was Zino.

"I do not understand how such delicate hands can have so hard a touch," he whispers, leaning a little towards Stella, with a significant glance towards the narrow-chested little American at the piano. "Dummy instruments ought always to be provided for these drawing-room performances of young ladies: there would be just as much opportunity for the performers to display their beautiful hands, and the misery of the audience would be greatly alleviated."

Stella laughs a little, a very little. She is melancholy to-night. Zino thinks of the sword of Damocles suspended above her fair head, and pities her. For a moment he is compassionately silent; then, espying Anastasia, he says, "I should like to know how the Gurlichingen comes here. She is a person of whom, were I Natalie, I should steer clear."

"To steer clear of the Gurlichingen against her will is almost as difficult as to steer clear of an epidemic disease; she steals upon us perfectly unawares," says Stella, with a slight shrug.

"Of all antipathetic women whom I have ever encountered, the Gurlichingen is the most antipathetic," the Prince boldly asseverates. "Her smile is peculiarly agreeable. It always reminds me of Captain White's Oriental pickles,—'the most exquisite compound of sweet and sour.' At Nice they called her the death's-head with forget-me-not eyes. To-night she looks like a skeleton at a masquerade. Just look at her! If she only would not show all her thirty-two teeth at once!"

"Where is she?" asks Stella, slightly turning her head. So great has been her dread of perceiving somewhere her menacing destiny, Monsieur de Hauterive, that hitherto she has not looked about at all.

"There, between Rohritz and that flower-table, there——"

By 'Rohritz' Stella has been wont for weeks to understand the husband of Thérèse; she has not yet heard of Edgar's arrival in Paris. She raises her eyes, and starts violently. He is here in the same room with her, and has not even taken the trouble to bid her good-evening. Good heavens! what of that? How many minutes will pass before Monsieur de Hauterive comes to ask her to redeem Thérèse Rohritz's pledged word? and then—— The blood mounts to her cheeks.

"*Sapristi!*" Zino thinks to himself, "can it be possible that my brother-in-law has been keener of vision than my very clever sister?"

"Do you not think, Baron Rohritz," Stasy meanwhile remarks to the victim still fettered to her side, "that Prince Capito pays too marked attention to our little friend Stella?"

"That is his affair," Edgar replies, coldly.

"And what does your sister-in-law say to Stella's conduct with Capito?"

"My sister-in-law evidently has no fault whatever to find with the young lady, for this very day she praised her in the warmest terms."

"Yes, yes," Stasy murmurs; "Thérèse, they say, has taken Stella under her wing."

"She is very fond of her."

"Yes, yes; all Paris is aware that Thérèse,"—to speak all the more familiarly of her distinguished acquaintances the less intimate she is with them is one of Stasy's disagreeable characteristics,— "that Thérèse has set herself the task of marrying Stella well. If this be so she ought to advise the girl to conduct herself somewhat more prudently, or the little goose will soon have compromised herself so absolutely that it will be impossible to find a respectable match for her. Do you know that for Stella's sake Zino has joined della Seggiola's class?"

"Would you make Stella Meineck responsible for Prince Capito's eccentricities?"

"Granted that it was not in consequence of her direct permission,—I do not say it was. But she makes appointments with him in the Louvre; and"—Stasy's eyes sparkle with fiendish triumph —"she visits him at his lodgings. A very worthy and truthful friend of mine has rooms opposite the

Prince's in the Rue d'Anjou, and she lately saw
Stella, closely veiled, pass beneath the archway
of his——"

"Absurd!" Rohritz exclaims, indignantly; and,
without allowing her to finish, he leaves her very
unceremoniously to go to Stella. But before he
can make his way among the various trains, and
the thicket of furniture of a Parisian drawing-
room, to the yellow divan, some one else has taken
the place beside Stella just vacated by Zino,—a
handsome, broad-shouldered man of about forty,
well dressed, correct in his appearance, but not distinguished, although it would be impossible to describe what is lacking. There is something brand-
new, stiff, shiny, about him. Between him and a
dandy of the purest water, like Capito, for instance, there is the same difference that is to be
found between a piece of genuine old Meissner
porcelain and some of modern manufacture.

"Who is the man with the red face and peaked
moustache beneath the camellia there?" Edgar
asks his old acquaintance Prince Suwarin, whom
he has just met.

"That is a certain Cabouat de Hauterive, a
millionaire, who is very fond of pretty things," replies Suwarin. "A little while ago he bought a
superb Rousseau for his gallery, and now, they
say, he intends to buy a pretty wife for his house.
But he is absolutely lacking in the very *A, B, C* of

æsthetic knowledge. The picture-dealer, Arthur Stevens, selected his Rousseau for him. I should like to know who found a wife for him. Whoever it was had good taste, I must say. The stupid fellow brags to all his acquaintances of the beauty of his new acquisition. She's a countrywoman of yours, if I'm not mistaken,—the young girl there beside him. She is simply divine!"

In fact, she is exquisitely lovely. How can Stasy presume to slander her so brutally? Truly it would be difficult to imagine anything more modest, more innocent, than the slender creature beside that broad-shouldered parvenu! Her elbows pressed close to her sides, her hands in her lap, with drooping head she sits there deadly pale, and evidently trembling with dread, as if awaiting sentence of death.

"It is a crime to force a young girl thus," Rohritz mutters between his set teeth. "I would not for the world have Thérèse's work to answer for. Fool that I am!—fool!"

Every drop of blood in his veins boils; for a moment it seems as if the sight of that pale, sad, child-like face must rob him of all self-control, as if thus at the last moment he must snatch her from the glittering, terrible fate to which she has devoted herself and bear her off in his arms, far, far away, to a peaceful green country where in the dreamy evening twilight stands a white castle in the shade of a mighty linden, where the odour of the linden-blossoms mingles on the evening breeze with the fragrance of the large, pale roses which look up from the dark verdure to the blue evening skies, where the music of gently-rustling leaves blends sadly with the sobbing ripple of the Save!

None but a maniac, however, would in our civilized century yield to such an impulse. Edgar is by no means a maniac: he is even too well bred to show the slightest outward sign of his agitation. Calmly, his eye-glass in his eye, he stands beside Suwarin and answers intelligibly and connectedly his questions as to the new Viennese ballet.

Stella Meineck has less self-control. While Monsieur in the most insinuating minor tones is preluding the momentous question, she is vainly trying to convince herself of all that should force her to receive his suit with joyful gratitude from the hand of fate as a gift of God. She recalls the petty poverty of the life that lies behind her, the endless, monotonous misery of the future in galoches and water-proof that lies before her, the hotel-bill that is not paid, the golden brooch she has been obliged to sell to buy two pair of new gloves,—everything, in short, that is hopeless and comfortless in her life. Oh, she will be sensible, will accept his offer. There,—now he has put the great question, so distinctly, so clearly, that no pretence of misunder-

standing that might delay the necessity for her reply
is possible. She catches her breath; her heart beats
as if it would break; black misty clouds float before
her eyes; there is a sound in her ears as of the rushing of a far-distant stream. She raises her head,
and is about to speak, when her eyes meet Edgar's;
and if instant death were to be the consequence of
her refusal, her consent is no longer possible.

"You are very—very kind," she stammers, imploringly, "Monsieur de Hauterive, but I cannot—
I cannot—forgive me, but—I cannot."

A moment more, and she is sitting alone beneath
the camellia-bush.

CHAPTER XXXIV.

ROHRITZ DREAMS.

"She has given him the sack."

"So it seems."

"A pretty affair! How pleased Thérèse will
be!"

The speakers are Capito and Edgar as they leave
the Rue de la Bruyère, where the small hotel which
the Lipinskis have rented is situated, and walk
along under the blue-black heavens glittering with

v

millions of stars, to the more animated part of Paris.

"Yes, Thérèse will be pleased," Edgar murmurs, repeating Zino's words.

"It serves her right," Zino says, laughing. "I must confess, Stella ought not to have let matters go so far; but I cannot help liking it in her that she refused the fellow. Natalie and I were looking at her; it was immensely funny,—and yet so sad. Ah, that poor, distressed, pale face! After it was all over, Natascha—she has lately grown very intimate with Stella—called the girl into a little private boudoir, where the poor child began to sob bitterly. Natascha kissed her and comforted her, I brought her a cup of tea, and we gradually soothed her."

"Disgusting creature, that Cabouat!" growls Rohritz.

"In my opinion he is an awkward, common snob," says Zino, "and if I am not mistaken he will shortly prove himself to be so in the eyes of every one. The affair cannot fail to be unpleasant, since he has been boasting everywhere that he intended to marry a most beautiful Austrian, a friend of Madame de Rohritz, a charming young girl, very highly connected, and with no dowry."

"He is at perfect liberty to say that at the last moment he changed his mind," Rohritz remarks, casually.

"I rather think he'll not content himself with that. *Ça*, you are coming with me to the masked ball at the opera?"

"Not exactly. I am going to bed."

"Indolent, degenerate race!" Zino jeers. "What is to become of Paris, if this indifference to all gaiety gets the upper hand? I dreamed last night of a white domino: I am going to look for it." So saying, he leaves Edgar, and has walked on a few steps, when he hears himself recalled.

"Capito! Capito!"

"What is it?"

"Pray get me an invitation to the Fanes' ball; it is short notice, but——"

"All right: that's of no consequence at an American's ball," Zino replies, and hurries on to his goal. The two men turn their steps in opposite directions. Capito hastens back into the heart of Paris, where the garish light from gas-jets and lamps illuminates a night life as busy as that of the day, and Rohritz passes along the Boulevard Malesherbes, towards the Rue Villiers. Around him all is quiet; the few shops are closed; an occasional pedestrian passes, his coat-collar drawn up over his ears, and humming some *café-chantant* air, or a carriage with coach-lamps sparkles along the middle of the street like a huge firefly. The street-cars are no longer running: the street is but dimly lighted. The Dumas monument looms, clumsy and awkward, on its huge pedestal in the little square on the Place Malesherbes.

A thousand delightful thoughts course through Rohritz's brain. What a pleasant hour he has had talking with Stella at the Lipinskis'! At first she was stiff towards him, but gradually, slowly, she thawed into the loveliest, most child-like confidence. He will wait no longer. At the Fanes' ball, the next evening but one, he will confess all to her. What will she reply? Blind as are all mortals to the future, he looks back, and seeks her answer in the past. Slowly, slowly, he passes in review all the lovely summer days which he has spent with her, to that evening when he carried her in his arms through the drenching rain across the slippery, muddy road. Again he sees the windows of the little inn gleam yellow through the gloom; he hears Stella's soft word of thanks as he puts her down on the threshold. The picture changes. He sees a large, watery moon gleaming through prismatic clouds, sees a little skiff by the shore of a dark, swollen stream, and in the skiff, at his—Edgar's—feet, kneels a slender girl in a light dress, trembling with distress, her eyes imploringly raised to his, her delicate hands clasping his arm.

He bends over her. " Stella, my poor, dear, unreasonable child!" He has lifted her, clasps her in his arms, presses his lips upon her golden hair, her eyes, her mouth—— With a sudden start he rouses from his dream to find that he has run against a passer-by, who is saying, crossly, "*Mais comment donc?* Is not the pavement wide enough for two?" And, looking up, Edgar perceives that he has already passed ten numbers beyond his brother's hôtel.

CHAPTER XXXV.

A SPRAINED ANKLE.

"MY DEAR ROHRITZ,—

"Accidents will occur in the best-regulated families! As I was escorting my cousin in a ride yesterday, my horse slipped and fell on the ice, and I sprained my ankle. Was there ever anything so stupid! If it could be called a misfortune for which one could be pitied; but no, 'tis a mere tiresome annoyance. Ridiculous! And I am engaged to dance the cotillon at the Fanes' with Stella Meineck. Old fellow as I am, I had really looked forward to this pleasure. *Eh bien!* all the massage in the world will not enable me to put my foot on the ground before the end of a week. Have the kindness, as they say in your native Vienna, to dance the cotillon in my stead with our fair star. Send me a line to say that you agree, or come and tell me so yourself.

"Is Thérèse going to the ball? Tell her from me to be nice to Stella, and not to reckon it against her that, in spite of a moment of indecision induced by the distinguished eloquence of my very clever little sister, she has behaved nobly and honestly throughout,—in short, just as was to be expected of her. Adieu! Yours forever,

" Capito."

Such is the letter Edgar receives the second morning after the Lipinskis' soirée, while he is breakfasting with his · brother in the latter's smoking-room.

"Zino?" asks Edmund, looking up from his 'Figaro,' the reading of which is as much a part of his breakfast as are the fragrant black coffee and the yellowish Viennese bread with Norman butter.

"Read it," Edgar replies, as he scribbles with a lead-pencil on a visiting-card, "I am quite at your disposal," and hands it to the waiting servant.

"He's a fool!" the elder Rohritz remarks, handing back the note to his brother. "He knows perfectly well that you do not dance."

"But one can talk through a cotillon," Edgar says, with as much indifference as he can assume.

"You have consented?"

"I could not do otherwise. Stella is a stranger in Paris: it might be a source of annoyance to her

to have no partner for the cotillon. If at the last
moment she should find a more desirable partner
than myself, I am of course ready to retire. *A propos*, is Thérèse going to the ball? Her cold is
better?"

"Yes."

"What kind of ball is it?"

"A kind of public ball in a wealthy private
house," given by immensely wealthy Americans,
who know nobody, whom nobody knows, and
who arrange an entertainment from the Arabian
Nights, that they may be talked of, mentioned in
'Figaro,' and laughed at in society.   Only three
weeks ago there was no end of ridicule heaped
upon Mrs. and Mr. Fane, unknown grandees from
California, when it was reported that they wished
to give a ball.   Nobody dreamed of accepting
their invitation; but Mrs. Fane was clever enough
to induce a couple of women of undeniable
fashion to be her 'lady patronesses,' and when
the rumour spread that the Duchess of —— had
accepted there was a perfect rage for invitations.
Every one declared, '*Cela sera drôle!*' Every one
is going.   With the best Parisian society there
will of course be found people whom one sees nowhere else.   I wonder how many of the guests will
take sufficient notice of the host and hostess to
recognize them in the street the next day? But it
will certainly be a beautiful ball, and an amusing

one. Stella is going with the Lipinskis, I believe.
I am curious to see how she will look in a ball-dress,
—charming, of course, but rather too thin."

In the course of the morning Edgar drops in
upon Capito, and finds him, in half-merry, half-
irritated mood, stretched upon a lounge which is
covered by a bearskin, the head of the animal
gnashing its teeth at the Prince's feet. Of course
Capito's rooms form a tasteful chaos of Oriental
rugs, Turkish embroideries, interesting bibelots,
and charming pictures. Throughout their arrangement, from the antique silken hangings veined with
silver that cover the walls, to the low divans and
chairs, there runs a suggestion of effeminate, Oriental luxury, in whimsical contrast with the proverbially vigorous personality of the Prince, hard-
ened as it has been by every species of manly sport
and exercise. The atmosphere is heavy with the
fragrance of a gardenia shrub in full bloom, the
odour of cigarettes, and the aroma of some subtle
Indian perfume. A tall palm lifts its leaves to the
ceiling. Half a dozen French novels, two guitars,
and a mandolin lie within Zino's reach. He wears
a queer smoking-jacket of blue silk faced with
red, and his foot is swathed in towels.

"I'm delighted to see you! Sit down. 'Tis
most annoying, this sprain of mine. But what do
you say to the pleasure to which you have fallen
heir?"

"In fact, I never dance," Rohritz makes reply, "but, to oblige you——" Edgar's eyes are wandering here and there through the room, and suddenly rest upon a certain object.

"Ah, 'tis my Watteau that attracts you!" Capito observes. "A pretty little picture. I bought it at the Hôtel Drouot a while ago for a mere song, —five thousand francs."

"Five thousand francs! Ridiculous," says Rohritz. "The picture is really lovely. But it was not the Watteau alone that attracted my attention, but——" He points to two or three pictures which are turned with their faces to the wall.

"Ah! ah!" the Prince laughs. "You wish to know what led to that prudential measure? Well, I have had a visit from ladies."

"From whom?" Rohritz asks, absently.

"Unasked I should probably have told you, but in view of such ill-bred curiosity I am mute," Zino replies, still laughing.

"Hm!—evidently a woman of character," Rohritz observes, indifferently.

"Of course: 'tis the only kind with whom I can endure of late to associate. If you but knew how bored I was at the opera ball the other night! I was made ill by the bad air. The feminine element must always play a large part in my life; but, you see, of late I can tolerate none but the most refined, the most distinguished of the species.

We are strange creatures, we men of the world : in the matter of cigars, wine, horses, we always require the best, while with regard to women we are sometimes satisfied with what——"

The arrival of a fresh caller, one of Capito's sporting friends, interrupts these interesting reflections.   Rohritz takes his leave.

The same day he is driving by chance through the Rue d'Anjou, when his attention is attracted by a slender, graceful, girlish figure hurrying along, evidently anxious to reach her destination.

Is not that Stella?   He leans out of the carriage window, but it is dark, and she is closely veiled. And yet he could swear that it is she.   She vanishes in the Hôtel ——, in the house where he called upon Zino Capito this very day.

For one brief moment all the evil that Stasy said of Stella confuses his brain; then he compresses his lips : he cannot believe evil of her.   A malicious chance has maligned her.   She must have a double in Paris.

CHAPTER XXXVI.

LOST AGAIN.

How Stella has looked forward to this ball ! how carefully and bravely she has cleared away all the obstacles which seemed at first to stand in the way of her pleasure! how eagerly and industriously she has gathered together her little store of ornaments, has tastefully renovated her old Venetian ball-dress! how she has exulted over Zino's note, in which with kindly courtesy he has begged her to accord to his friend Edgar Rohritz the pleasure he is obliged to deny himself! And now—now the evening has come; her ball-dress lies spread out on the sofa of the small drawing-room at the ' Three Negroes;' but Stella is lying on her bed in her little bedroom, in the dark, sobbing bitterly. For the second time she has lost the *porte-bonheur* which her dying father put on her arm three—nearly four years before, and which was to bring her happiness. She noticed only yesterday that the little chain which she had had attached to it for safety was broken, but the clasp seemed so strong that she postponed taking it to be repaired, and to-day as she was coming home, about five o'clock, fresh and gay, her cheeks flushed, her eyes sparkling with the excitement of anticipation, and laden with all sorts of packages, she perceived that her bracelet was gone. In absolute terror, she went from shop to shop, wherever she had made a purchase, always with the same imploring question on her lips as to whether they had not found a little *porte-bonheur* with a pendant of rock-crystal containing a four-leaved clover,—a silly, inexpensive trifle, of no value to any one save herself. But in vain!

Almost beside herself, she finally returned to her home, and told her mother of her bitter distress; but the Baroness only shrugged her shoulders at her childish superstition, and went on writing with extraordinary industry. She has lately determined to edit an abstract of her work on 'Woman's Part in the Development of Civilization,' for a book-agent with whom she is in communication, and who undertakes to sell unsalable literature. It seems that the abstract will fill several volumes! In the midst of Stella's distress, the Baroness begins to bewail to her daughter her own immense super-abundance of ideas, which makes it almost impossible for her to express herself briefly. And so Stella, after she has hearkened to the end of her mother's lament, slips away with tired, heavy feet, and a still heavier heart, to her bedroom, and there sobs on the pillow of her narrow iron bedstead as if her heart would break.

There comes a knock at the door.

"Who is it?" she asks, half rising, and wiping her eyes.

"Me!" replies a kindly nasal voice, a voice typical of the Parisian servant. Stella recognizes it as that of the chambermaid.

"Come in, Justine. What do you want?"

"Two bouquets have come for Mademoiselle,— two splendid bouquets. Ah, it is dark here; Mademoiselle has been taking a little rest, so as to be fresh for the ball; but it is nine o'clock. Mademoiselle ought to begin to dress: it is always best to be in time. Shall I light a candle?"

"If you please, Justine."

The maid lights the candles.

"Ah!" she exclaims in dismay when she sees Stella's sad, swollen face, "Mademoiselle is in distress! Good heavens! what has happened? Has Mademoiselle had bad news?—some one dead whom she loves?"

Any German maid at sight of the girl's disconsolate face would have suspected some love-complication; the French servant would never think of anything of the kind in connection with a respectable young lady.

"No, Justine, but I have lost a *porte-bonheur*,— a *porte-bonheur* that my father gave me a little while before he died,—and it is sure to mean some misfortune. I know something dreadful will happen to me at the ball. I would rather stay at home. But there would be no use in that: my fate will find me wherever I am: it is impossible to hide from it."

"Ah," sighs Justine, "I am so sorry for Mademoiselle! But Mademoiselle must not take the matter so to heart: the *porte-bonheur* will be found; nothing is lost in Paris. We will apply to the police-superintendent, and the *porte-bonheur* will be found. Ah, Mademoiselle would not believe how

many lost articles I have had brought back to me!
Will not Mademoiselle take a look at the bouquets?" And the Parisian maid whips off the cotton
wool and silver-paper that have enveloped the
flowers. "*Dieu! que c'est beau!*" cries Justine, her
brown, good-humoured face beaming with delight
beneath the frill of her white cap. "Two cards
came with the flowers; there——"

Stella grasps the cards. The bouquet of gardenias and fantastic orchids comes from Zino; the
other, of half-opened, softly-blushing Malmaison
roses and snowdrops, is Edgar's gift.

In their arch-loveliness, carelessly tied together,
the flowers look as if they had come together in the
cold winter, to whisper of the delights of spring and
summer,—of the time when earth and sunshine,
now parted by a bitter feud, shall meet again with
warm, loving kisses of reconciliation.

Zino's orchids and gardenias lie neglected on the
cold gray marble top of a corner table; with a
dreamy smile, in the midst of her tears, Stella buries
her face among the roses, which remind her of
Erlach Court.

"Mademoiselle will find her *porte-bonheur* again;
I am sure of it; I have a presentiment," Justine
says, soothingly. "But now Mademoiselle must
begin to make herself beautiful. Madame has
given me express permission to help her."

*   *   *   *   *   *   *

At this same hour a certain bustle reigns in the dressing-room of the Princess Oblonsky. Costly jewelry, barbaric but characteristically Russian in design and setting, gleams from the dark velvet lining of various half-opened cases in the light of numberless candles. In a faded sky-blue dressing-gown trimmed with yellow woollen lace, Stasy is standing beside a workwoman from Worth's, who is busy fastening large solitaires upon the Princess's ball-dress. The air is heavy and oppressive with the odour of veloutine, hot iron, burnt hair, and costly, forced hot-house flowers. Monsieur Auguste, the hair-dresser, has just left the room. Beneath his hands the head of the Princess has become a masterpiece of artistic simplicity. Instead of the conventional feathers, large, gleaming diamond stars crown the beautiful woman's brow. She is standing before a tall mirror, her shoulders bare, her magnificent arms hanging by her sides, in the passive attitude of the great lady who, without stirring herself, is to be dressed by her attendants. Her maid is kneeling behind her, with her mouth full of pins, busied in imparting to the long trailing muslin and lace petticoat the due amount of imposing effect.

Although half a dozen candles are burning in the candelabra on each side of the mirror, although the entire apartment is illuminated by the light of at least fifty other candles, a second maid, and

Fräulein von Fuhrwesen, now quite domesticated in the Princess's household, are standing behind the Princess, each with a candle, in testimony of their sympathy with the maid at work upon the petticoat.

Yes, Sophie Oblonsky is going to the Fanes' ball: she knows that Edgar will be there.

At last every diamond is fastened upon the ball-dress, among its trimming of white ostrich-feathers. The task now is to slip the robe over the Princess's head without grazing her hair even with a touch as light as that of a butterfly's wing. This is the true test of the dressing-maid's art. The girl lifts Worth's masterpiece high, high in the air: the feat is successfully accomplished. In all Paris to-night there is no more beautiful woman than the Princess Oblonsky in her draperies of brocade shot with silver, the diamond *rivière* on her neck, and the diamond stars in her hair. The Fuhrwesen kneels before her in adoration to express her enthusiasm, and Stasy exclaims,—

"You are ravishing! Do you know what I said in Cologne to little Stella, who, as I told you, was so desperately in love with Edgar Rohritz? 'Beside Sonja the beauty of other women vanishes: when she appears, we ordinary women cease to exist.'"

"Exaggerated nonsense, my dear!" Sonja says, smiling graciously, and lightly touching her friend's cheek with her lace handkerchief. "But now hurry and make yourself beautiful."

"Yes, I. am going. I really cannot tell you how eagerly I am looking forward to this ball. I feel like a child again."

"So I see," Sonja rallies her. "Make haste and dress; when you are ready I will put the diamond pins in your hair, myself." And when Stasy has left the room the Princess says, turning to Fräulein von Fuhrwesen, "I only hope Anastasia will enjoy herself: it is solely for her sake that I have been persuaded to go to this ball; I would far rather stay at home, my dear Fuhrwesen, and have you play me selections from Wagner."

CHAPTER XXXVII.

THE FANES' BALL.

YES, the Fanes' ball is a splendid ball, one of the most beautiful balls of the season, and fulfils every one's expectations. Not one of the artistic effects that puzzle newspaper-reporters and delight the public is lacking,—neither fountains of eau-de-cologne, nor tables of flowers upon which blocks of ice gleam from among nodding ferns, nor mirrors and chandeliers hung with wreaths of roses, nor the legendary grape-vine with colossal grapes. The crown of all, however, is the conservatory, in which, among orange-trees and magnolias in full bloom, gleam mandarin-trees full of bright golden fruit. There are lovely, secluded nooks in this Paradise, where has been conjured up in the unfriendly Northern winter all the luxuriance of Southern vegetation. Large mirrors here and there prevent what might else be the monotony of the scene.

The company is rather mixed. It almost produces the impression of the appearance at a first-class theatre of a troop of provincial actors, with here and there a couple of stars,—stars who scarcely condescend to play their parts. Most of the guests do not recognize the host; and those who suspect his presence in the serious little man in a huge white tie and with a bald head, whom they took at first for the master of ceremonies, avoid him. His entire occupation consists in gliding about with an unhappy face in the darkest corners, now and then timidly requesting some one of the guests to look at his last Meissonier. When the guest complies with the request and accompanies him to view the Meissonier, Mr. Fane always replies to the praise accorded to the picture in the same words : "I paid three hundred thousand francs for it. Do you think Meissoniers will increase in value ?"

The hostess is more imposing in appearance than her bald-headed spouse. Her gown comes from Felix, and is trimmed with sunflowers as big as dinner-plates,—which has a comical effect. Thérèse Rohritz shakes her head, and whispers to a friend, "How that good Mrs. Fane must have offended Felix, to induce him to take such a cruel revenge!" But except for her gown, and the fact that she cannot finish a single sentence without introducing the name of some duke or duchess, there is nothing particularly ridiculous about her.

Yet, criticise the entertainment and its authors as you may, one and all must confess that rarely has there been such an opportunity to admire so great a number of beautiful women, and that the most beautiful of all, the queen of the evening, is the Princess Oblonsky. Anywhere else it would excite surprise to find her among so many women of unblemished reputation; but it is no greater wonder to meet her here than at a public ball. Anywhere else people would probably stand aloof from her; here they approach her curiously, as they would some theatric star whom they might meet at a picnic in an inn ball-room.

Perhaps her beauty would not be so completely victorious over that of her sister women were she not the only guest who has bestowed great pains on her toilette. All the other feminine guests who make any pretensions to distinction seem to have entered into an agreement to be as shabby as possible. As it would be hopeless to attempt to rival the Fane millions, they choose at least to prove that they despise them.

One of the shabbiest and most rumpled among many dowdy gowns is that worn by Thérèse Rohritz, who, pretty woman as she is, looks down with evident satisfaction upon her faded crêpe de Chine draperies, remarking, with a laugh, that she had almost danced it off last summer at the balls at the casino at Trouville.

Her husband is not quite pleased with such evident neglect of her dress on his wife's part, nor does he at all admire Thérèse's careless way of looking about her through her eye-glass and laughing and criticising. He must always be too good an Austrian to be reconciled to what is called *chic* in Paris. There is the same difference between his Austrian arrogance and Parisian arrogance that there is between pride and impertinence. He thinks it all right to hold aloof from a parvenu, to avoid his house and his acquaintance; but to go to the house of the parvenu, to be entertained in his apartments, to eat his ices and drink his champagne, to pluck the flowers from his walls, and in return to ignore himself and to ridicule his entertainment, he does not think right. But whenever he expresses his sentiments upon this point to his wife, Thérèse answers him, half in German, half in

French, "You are quite right; but what would you have? 'tis the fashion."

The only person at the ball who is honestly ashamed of her modest toilette is Stella, and this perhaps because the first object that her eyes encountered when she appeared with the Lipinskis, a little after eleven, was the Oblonsky in all her brilliant beauty and faultless elegance. By her side, her white feather fan on his knee, sits—— Edgar von Rohritz. Stella's heart stands still; ah, yes, now she knows why she has lost her bracelet. All the tender, child-like dreams that stole smiling upon her soul at sight of his flowers die at once, and Stasy's words at the Cologne railway-station resound in her ears: "Yes, it is ridiculous to think of rivalling the Princess: when she appears we ordinary women cease to exist."

"Yes, it is ridiculous to think of rivalling the Princess," Stella repeats to herself, "particularly for such a stupid, awkward, insignificant thing as I am."

She cannot take her eyes off the beautiful woman. How she smiles upon him, bestowing her attention upon him alone, while a crowd of Parisian dandies throng about her, waiting for an opportunity to claim a word. There is no doubt in Stella's mind that he is reconciled with Sophie Oblonsky.

A man will forgive a very beautiful woman

everything, even the evil which he has heard of
her, nay, he may find a mysterious charm in her
transgressions, if she takes pains to win his favour
with intelligence, prudence, and the necessary degree of reserve. This piece of wisdom Stella has
gained from the French romances of which she
has read extracts out of pure ennui as they appear
daily in ' Figaro' and the ' Gaulois.'

That a man must find it difficult to shake off an
old friend who approaches him with imploring hu-
mility, that he cannot well refuse when she requests him to bring her an ice, and that should she
hand him her fan he cannot possibly lay it down
on a table with a proudly forbidding air and then
take his leave with a formal bow,—all this Stella
never takes into consideration; and this is why she
is so wretchedly unhappy as she seats herself beside Natalie Lipinski on a plush ottoman, near a
table of flowers.

A young Russian, a friend of the Lipinskis,
begs Natalie for a waltz, and she takes his arm
and goes into the adjoining dancing-room. Stella
is left alone, beside old Madame Lipinski, who is
just getting ready to relate something extremely
entertaining about the Emperor Nicholas, when
Rohritz suddenly perceives Stella. With a smiling
remark he hands the white feather fan to a gentleman standing beside him, and hastens towards
the young girl, paying his respects, of course, first

to the elder lady, and then to her. If he has reckoned upon her old-time child-like, confiding smile, he is disappointed. She answers him stiffly, and thanks him for his flowers without cordiality. "How pale she looks!" he says to himself. "What can be the matter with her? Can she have cried her eyes out because she must dance the cotillon to-night with me instead of with Zino Capito?"

"'Tis very hard that poor Capito should be disabled just at this time," he remarks.

"Yes, because the burden of dancing the cotillon with me devolves upon you," Stella replies, betraying, for the first time since he has known her, a degree of sensitiveness that is almost ridiculous. "I am, of course, perfectly ready to release you from the obligation."

"That would be a readiness to rob me of a pleasure to which I had looked forward eagerly," he replies, gravely.

"You had looked forward to it?—really?" Stella asks, with genuine surprise in her eyes. "Really?" And she looks down with a shake of the head at her poor white dress, at her entire toilette, in which nothing is absolutely modern save the long gloves that reach to her shoulders.

It is rather remarkable that these gloves are the only thing about her with which Edgar Rohritz finds fault.

"What charming dimples that Swedish kid must

hide!" he says to himself. A seat beside Stella hitherto occupied by an Englishwoman with very sharp red elbows is vacated. Edgar takes possession of it.

"Yes, I had looked forward to it," he says, "although I do not dance, and you will consequently be obliged to talk with me through the cotillon."

A pause ensues. She looks down; involuntarily he does the same. His eyes rest upon her foot that peeps out beneath the hem of her ball-dress. He recalls how once, on a meadow beneath a spreading oak, kneeling before her he had held that foot in his hands. What a charming, soft, warm little foot it was! She suddenly perceives that he is looking at it; she withdraws it hastily, and with a half-wayward, half-distressed air pulls her skirt farther over her knee. Of course he does not smile, but he wants to. And he could reproach this girl for accidentally in the outline of her features recalling a woman who from all that he could discover concerning her was more to be pitied than blamed. It was odious, cruel; more than that, it was stupid!

Leaning towards her, and speaking more softly than before, he says, gravely, "And I hope that during the cotillon you will confide to me, as an old friend, why you look so sad to-night."

Any other girl would have understood that these

words from a man of Edgar's great reserve of character were to pave the way for a declaration.

Stella understands nothing of the kind.

"Why I am so sad?" she replies, simply. "Because——"

At this moment Natalie approaches on the arm of a blonde young man.

"Count Kasin wishes to be presented to you, Stella," she says.

The young man bows, and begs for a dance. Stella goes off upon his arm, not because she has any desire to dance, but because it would be disgraceful for a young girl to sit through an entire ball.

"Who is that young lady?" asks an Englishman of Edgar's acquaintance.

"She is an Austrian,—Baroness Stella Meineck."

"Strange how like she is to that famous Greuze in the Louvre,—' *La Cruche cassée*' ! She is charming."

The words were uttered without any thought of evil, but nevertheless Edgar feels for a moment as if he would like to throttle the Hon. Mr. Harris.

And why is he suddenly reminded of the girl whom he had seen this afternoon in the twilight hurrying along the street to vanish in the house where Zino has his apartments? How very like she was to Stella!

*   *   *   *   *   *   *

An hour has passed. Stella has walked through two quadrilles, has walked and polked with various partners, as well as she could,—that is, conscientiously and badly, just as she learned from a dancing-master eight years before, and, try as she may, she is conscious that she never shall take any real pleasure in this hopping and jumping about. Now, when the rest are just beginning fairly to enjoy the ball, she is tired,—quite tired. With her last partner, a good-humoured, gentlemanly young Austrian diplomatist, she has become so dizzy that in the midst of the dance she has begged to be taken back to Madame Lipinski. But Madame Lipinski has left her place; some one says she has gone to the conservatory; and thither Stella and her partner betake themselves.

They do not find Madame Lipinski, but Stella feels decidedly better. The green, fragrant twilight of the conservatory has a soothing effect upon her nerves. The air is cool, compared with that of the ball-room ; the roughened surface of the mosaic floor affords a pleasant change after the slippery smoothness of the dancing-room. Stella sinks wearily into an inviting low chair.

"Are balls always so terribly fatiguing?" she asks her companion, with her usual frankness.

He bows.

"I did not mean to be rude," she hastily explains, "but you must confess that it is much pleasanter to

talk comfortably here than to whirl about in there,"
—pointing with her fan in the direction of the
dancing-room.

The attaché, quite propitiated, takes his place
upon a low seat beside her, and prepares for a
sentimental flirtation. To his great surprise, Stella
seems to have as little enthusiasm for flirting as
for dancing.

"A charming spot!" he begins. "The fragrance of these orange-blossoms reminds me of
Nice. You have been at Nice, Baroness?"

"I have been everywhere, from Madrid to Constantinople," Stella sighs; "and I wish I were at
home. My head aches so!"—passing her hand
wearily across her brow.

"Shall I get you an ice, or a glass of lemonade?"
he asks, good-naturedly.

"I should be much obliged to you," Stella replies.

"Hm! it does not look as if she were very
anxious for a *tête-à-tête* with me," he thinks, as he
leaves her.

He has gone: she is alone among the fragrant
flowers and the larged-leaved plants. Softened,
but distinctly audible, the sound of hopping and
gliding feet reaches her ears, while, now sadly
caressing and anon merrily careless, the strains
of a Strauss waltz float on the air. For a while
she sits quite wearily, with half-closed eyes, thinking of nothing save "I hope the attaché will stay

away a long time!" Mingling softly and tenderly with the music she hears the dreamy murmur of a miniature fountain. Why is she suddenly reminded of the melancholy rush of the Save, of the little canoe by the edge of the black water? Suddenly she hears voices in her vicinity, and, raising her eyes to a tall, broad mirror opposite, she beholds, framed in by the gold-embroidered hangings of a heavy portière, a striking picture,—the Princess Oblonsky and Edgar. They are in a little boudoir separated from the conservatory by an open door. Without stirring, Stella watches the pair in the treacherous mirror. Edgar sits in a low arm-chair, his elbow on his knee, his head propped on his hand, and the Princess is opposite him. How wonderfully beautiful she is!—beautiful although she is just brushing away a tear.

"It always makes me so ugly to cry!" Stella thinks, not without bitterness.

The Princess's gloves and fan lie beside her; her arms are bare. With an expression of intense melancholy,—an expression not only apparent in her face and in the listless droop of her arms, but also seeming to be shared by every fold of her dress,—she leans back among the soft-hued, rose-coloured and gray satin cushions of a small lounge.

"Strange, that we should have met at last!— at last!" she sighs. Stella cannot distinguish his reply, but she distinctly hears the Princess say,

"Do you remember that waltz? How often its notes have floated towards us upon the breath of the roses in the long afternoons at Baden! How long a time has passed since then! How long——"

A black mist rises before Stella's eyes. She puts up her hands to her ears, and, thrilling from head to foot, springs up and hurries away,—anywhere, anywhere,—only away from this spot,—far away!

* * * * * * *

At the other end of the conservatory she is doing her best to regain her composure and to keep back the tears, when suddenly she hears a light manly tread near her and the clinking of glasses.

"Ah! 'tis Binsky: he has found me," Stella thinks, most unjustly provoked with the good-humoured attaché.

"I really believe, Baroness, you are playing hide-and-seek with me," the young diplomatist addresses her in a tone of mild reproof.

There is nothing for it but to turn round. Beside the attaché, in all the majestic gravity of his kind, stands a lackey with a salver, from which she takes a glass of lemonade.

After the servant has withdrawn, Count Binsky says, with a laugh, "I have been looking for you, Baroness, in every corner of the conservatory. I must confess to having made interesting discoveries during my wanderings. Look here,"—and he shows her a white ostrich-feather fan with yellow tortoise-shell sticks broken in two,—"I found this relic in the pretty little boudoir near the place where I left you. Now, did you ever see anything so mutely eloquent as this broken fan?—the tragic culmination of a highly dramatic scene! I should like to know what lady had the desperate energy to reduce this exquisite trifle to such a state."

"Perhaps there is a monogram on the fan," says Stella, her pale face suddenly becoming animated. "Look and see."

"To be sure. I did not think of that," the young man replies, examining the fan. "'S. O.' beneath a coronet."

"Sophie Oblonsky," says Stella.

"Of course,—the Oblonsky." The attaché is seized with a fit of merriment on the instant. "The Oblonsky,—the woman who had an affair with Rohritz long ago. She seemed to me this evening to have a strong desire to throw her chains about him afresh, but"—with a significant glance at the fan—"Rohritz evidently had no inclination to gratify her. Hm! she must have been in a bad humour,—the worthy Princess!" The attaché laughs softly to himself, then suddenly assumes a grave, composed air, remembering that he is with a young girl, before whom such things as he has alluded to should be forbidden subjects and his merriment suppressed. He glances at Stella. No need to worry himself; she does not look in the least horrified: her white teeth just show between her red lips, merry dimples play about the corners of her mouth, and her eyes sparkle like black stars.

She really does not understand how five minutes ago she could have wished the poor attaché at the North Pole. She now thinks him extremely amusing and amiable. She feels so well, too,—so very well. Is it possible that there may be no evil omen for her in the loss of her bracelet? Nevertheless, try as she may to hope that it may be averted, a shiver of anxiety thrills her at the recollection of her lost amulet.

"If the ball were only over!" she thinks.

CHAPTER XXXVIII.

FOUND AT LAST.

THE hour of rest before the cotillon has come; the dancing-room is almost empty. Only a few gentlemen are selecting the places which they wish reserved for themselves and their partners, and a couple of lackeys are clearing away from this battle-field of pleasure the trophies left behind, of late engagements, shreds of tulle and tarlatan, artificial and natural flowers, here and there a torn glove, etc. Edgar tells himself that his hour has come,

the hour when he may indemnify himself for ennui
hitherto so heroically endured.   Meanwhile, he
goes to the buffet to refresh himself with a glass
of iced champagne, and in hopes of finding Stella.

The supper-room is in the story below the ball-
room.   The different stories are connected by an
extremely picturesque staircase, decorated with
gorgeous exotics and ending in a vestibule, or
rather an entrance-hall, hung round with antique
Flemish draperies.

The buffet is magnificent, and the guests who are
laying siege to it, especially the more distinguished
among them, are conducting themselves after a very
ill bred fashion.   Edgar perceives that several of
them have taken rather too much of Mr. Fane's
fine Cliquot.

He looks around in vain for Stella.   In one corner he observes the Oblonsky, with bright eyes and
sweet smiles, surrounded by a throng of languishing adorers; farther on, Stasy, in pale blue, with
rose-buds and diamond pins in her hair, in a state
of bliss because an American diplomatist is holding her gloves and a Russian prince her fan; he
sees Thérèse taking some bonbons for the children.
Stella is nowhere visible.   He thinks the champagne poor, doing it great injustice, and, irritated,
goes to the smoking-room to enjoy a cigar.   The
first man whom he sees in the large room is Monsieur de Hauterive.   His face is very red, and he

is relating something which must be very amusing, for he laughs loudly while he talks. The men standing around him do not seem to enjoy his narrative as much as he does himself. A few offensive words reach Edgar's ears:

" *La Cruche cassée*—Stella Meineck—an Austrian —these Viennese girls—mistress of Prince Capito! I have it all from the Princess Oblonsky!"

" Would you have the kindness to repeat to me what you have just been telling these gentlemen ?" Rohritz says, approaching the group and with difficulty suppressing manifestation of his anger.

" I really do not know, monsieur, by what right you interfere in a conversation about what does not concern you," Cabouat manages to reply, speaking thickly. " May I ask who——"

Edgar hands him his card. The other gentlemen are about to withdraw, but Edgar says, " What I have to say to Monsieur de Hauterive all are welcome to hear: the more witnesses I have the better I shall be pleased. I wish to call him to account for a slander, as vile as it is absurd, which he has dared to repeat, with regard to a young lady, an intimate friend of my family. You said, monsieur——"

" I said what every one knows, what ladies of the highest rank will confirm, what the Princess Oblonsky has long been aware of, and the proof of which I obtained to-day."

"Might I beg to know in what this said proof consists?" Edgar asks, contemptuously.

Monsieur de Hauterive, with an evil smile upon his puffy red lips, draws from his vest-pocket a golden chain to which is attached a crystal locket containing a four-leaved clover.

With a hasty movement Edgar takes the trinket from him, and searches for the star engraved upon the crystal.

"You know the bracelet?" asks de Hauterive.

"Yes," says Edgar.

"I found it on the staircase of Prince Capito's lodgings. When I rang the Prince's bell his servant informed me that the Prince was not at home. As I was perfectly aware that he had been confined to a lounge for two days with a sprained ankle, I naturally supposed that the Prince had special reasons for wishing to receive no one. What conclusion do you draw?"

Edgar's tongue is very dry in his mouth, but he instantly rejoins, "My conclusion is that Mademoiselle de Meineck, visiting a friend, a lady, who, as I happen to know, has lodgings in that house, lost her bracelet on the landing, and that Prince Capito has no desire to receive Monsieur de Hauterive."

"Your judgment strikes me as kind, rather than acute," says Monsieur de Hauterive. "Will you kindly tell me the name of the friend lodging in Number — ?" he adds, with a sneer.

Edgar is silent.

"I thought so!" exclaims de Hauterive. "And you would debar me from mentioning what any unprejudiced person must admit, that——" But before he can utter another word his cheek burns from a blow from Edgar's open palm.

The next moment Rohritz leaves the smoking-room, and goes out into the vestibule, longing for solitude and fresh air.

There, among the antique hangings, the Australian ferns, and the Italian magnolias, among the bronze, white-toothed negroes that bear aloft lamps with ground-glass shades shaped like huge flower-cups, he stands, the little bracelet in his hand. He feels stunned; red and blue sparks dance before his eyes, and his throat seems choked. He would fain groan aloud, or dash his head against the wall, so great is his distress. He cannot believe it; and yet all a lover's jealous distrust assails him. He is perfectly aware that his defence of Stella was pitiably weak, his invention of a female friend lodging in Number — clumsy enough; he knows that everything combines to accuse her.

Has he been deceived for the second time in his life? Whom can he ever trust, if those grave, dark, child-like eyes have been false? And suddenly in the midst of his torment he is possessed by overwhelming pity.

"Poor child! poor child!" he says to himself.

"Neglected, dragged about the world, without any one to care for her, fatherless, and the same as motherless!" Should he judge her? No, he will defend her, hide her fault, protect her from the whole world. But a stern voice within asks, "What protection do you mean? Will you—dare you offer her the only thing that can save her from the world,—your hand?" He is tortured. No, he cannot. And yet how desperately he loves her! Why did he not take her in his arms when she lay at his feet in the little skiff, and shield her next his heart forever? He must see her; an irresistible longing seizes him; yes, he must see her, —insult her, mistreat her, it may be,—but clasp her in his arms though he should kill her.

"Why are you standing here, like Othello with Desdemona's handkerchief?" he suddenly hears his brother ask, close beside him.

He starts, closes his fingers over the bracelet, and tries to assume an indifferent air.

"Where is Stella?" inquires Thérèse, who is with her husband.

"How should I know?" asks Edgar.

"But some one must know! some one must find her!" she exclaims, in a very bad humour. "The Lipinskis have gone home, and have placed her in my charge, and I must wait until she is found before we too can go home. Ah, do you want to dance the cotillon with her? Pray find her, and

as soon as you have done so we must go home,—
instantly!   I do not want to stay another moment."   And, in a state of evident nervous agitation, Thérèse suddenly turns to her husband, and
continues, "I cannot imagine, Edmund, how you
could bring me to this ball!"

"That is a little too much!" her husband exclaims, angrily. "Had I the faintest desire to
come to this ball? Did I not try for two long
weeks to dissuade you from coming? But you
had one reply for all my objections: 'Marie de
Stèle is going too.' Since you are so determined
never, under any circumstances, to blame yourself,
blame the Duchess de Stèle, not me."

"Marie de Stèle could not possibly know that a
Russian diplomatist would bring that woman to this
ball and present her as his wife."

"Neither could I," rejoins her husband.

"A man ought to know such things," Thérèse
retorts; "but you never know anything that everybody else does not know, you never have an intui-
tion; although you have been away from your own
country for fifteen years, you are the very same
simple-minded Austrian that you always were."

"And I am proud of it!" Edmund ejaculates,
angrily.

"Be as proud as you please, for all I care," says
Thérèse, as, at once angry and exhausted, she sinks
into a leathern arm-chair. "But now, for heaven's

sake, find Stella Meineck, that we may get away at last."

Edgar has already departed in search of her. He passes through the long suite of rooms, for the most part empty because all the guests are in the dining-rooms at present.

"They neither of them know anything yet," he says to himself, bitterly, and his heart beats wildly as he thinks, "If she can only explain it all!"

He searches for a while in vain. At last he enters the conservatory. A low sound of sobbing, reminding one of some wounded animal who has crept into some hiding-place to die, falls upon his ear. He hurries on. There, in the same little boudoir where he had lately been with the Princess Oblonsky, Stella is cowering on a divan in the darkest corner, her face hidden in her hands, her whole frame convulsed with sobs.

"Baroness Stella!" he says, advancing. She does not hear him. "Stella!" he says, more loudly, laying his hand on her arm. She starts, drops her hands in her lap, and gazes at him with such terrible despair in her eyes that for an instant he trembles for her reason. He forgets everything,—all that has been tormenting him; his soul is filled only with anxiety for her. "What is the matter? what distresses you?" he asks.

"I cannot tell it," she replies, in a voice so hoarse, so agonized, that he hardly knows it for hers. "It is something horrible,—disgraceful! It was in the dining-room—I was sitting rather alone, when I heard two gentlemen talking. I caught my own name, and then—and then—I would not believe it; I thought I had not heard aright—then the gentlemen passed me, and one of them looked at me and laughed, and then—and then—I saw an English girl whom I knew at the Britannia, in Venice —she was with her mother, and she came up to me and held out her hand with a smile, but her mother pulled her back,—I saw her,—and she turned away. And then came Stasy——" Her eyes encounter Rohritz's. "Ah! you have heard it too!" She moans and puts her hands up to her throbbing temples. Her cheeks are scarlet; she is half dead with shame and horror. "You too!" she repeats. "I knew that something would happen to me at this ball when I found I had lost my bracelet again, but I never—never thought it would be so horrible as this! Oh, papa, papa, I only hope you did not hear,—did not see; you could not rest peacefully in your grave." And again she buries her face in her hands and sobs.

A short pause ensues.

"She is innocent; of course she is innocent," an inward voice exclaims exultantly, and Rohritz is overwhelmed with remorse for having doubted her for an instant. He would fain fall down at her feet and kiss the hem of her dress.

"Be comforted: your bracelet is found," he whispers, softly. "Here it is!"

She snatches it from him. "Ah, where did you find it?" she asks, eagerly, her eyes lighting up in spite of her distress.

"I did not find it. Monsieur de Hauterive found it on the first landing of the staircase at Number —, Rue d'Anjou," he says, speaking with difficulty.

"Ah, I might have known! I must have lost it when I went to see my poor aunt Corrèze, and when I dropped my bundles on the stairs!" She is not in the least embarrassed. She evidently does not even know that Zino's lodgings are in the Rue d'Anjou.

"Your aunt Corrèze?" asks Rohritz.

"Do you not know about my aunt Corrèze?" she stammers.

"Yes, I know who she is."

"She was very unhappy in her first marriage," Stella goes on, now in extreme confusion, "very unhappy, and—and—she did not do as she ought; but she married Corrèze four years ago,—Corrèze, who abused her, and who is now giving concerts in America. She recognized me in the street from a photograph of me which papa sent her from Venice. She was so sweet to me, and yet so sad and shy, and she had her little daughter with her, a beautiful child, very like her, only with black hair. Papa once begged me to be kind to her if I ever met her, for his sake. What could I do? I could not ask her to come to us, for mamma will not hear her mentioned, and has for years burned all her letters unanswered. Once or twice I arranged a meeting with her in the Louvre; then she was taken ill, and could not go out, and wanted to see me. I went to see her without letting mamma know. It was not right, but—papa begged me to be kind to her——" Her large, dark eyes look at him helpless and imploring.

"Poor child! your kind heart was sorely tried," he murmurs, very gently.

"I am so glad to be able to tell some one all about it," she confesses: she has quite forgotten her terrible, disgraceful trial, in the child-like sensation of delightful security with which Rohritz always inspires her. The tears still shine upon her cheeks, but her eyes are dry. She tries to fasten the bracelet on her wrist; Rohritz kneels down beside her to help her; suddenly he possesses himself of the bracelet.

"Stella," he whispers, softly and very tenderly, "there is no denying that you are very careless with your happiness. Let me keep it for you: it will be safer with me than with you."

She looks at him, without comprehending; she is only aware of a sudden overwhelming delight,— why, she hardly knows.

"Stella, my darling, my treasure, could you consent to marry me?—could you learn to enjoy life at my side?"

"Learn to enjoy?" she repeats, with a smile that is instantly so deeply graven in his heart that he remembers it all his life afterwards. "Learn to enjoy?" She puts out her hands towards him; but just as he is about to clasp her to his heart she withdraws them, trembling, and turns pale. "Would you marry a girl at whom all Paris will point a scornful finger to-morrow?" she sobs.

"Point a scornful finger at my betrothed?" he cries, indignantly. "Have no fear, Stella; I know the world better than you do: that finger will be pointed at the worthless woman whose wounded vanity invented the monstrous slander. There is still some *esprit de corps* among the angels. Those in heaven do not permit evil to be wrought against their earthly sisters. One kiss, Stella, my star, my sunshine, my own darling."

For an instant she hesitates, then shyly touches his temple with her soft warm lips.

"One upon your gray hair," she murmurs.

They suddenly hear an approaching footstep. Rohritz starts to his feet, but it is only his brother, who says, as he advances towards them,—

"Where the deuce are you hiding, Edgar? My wife is frantic with impatience."

"Thérèse must be merciful," Edgar replies, with a smile. "When for once one finds the flower of happiness in his pathway, one cannot say, ' I have no time to pluck you ; my sister-in-law is waiting for me.' "

" Aha!" Edmund exclaims, with a low bow. "Hm ! Thérèse will be vexed because I was right, and not she; but I rejoice with all my heart,—not because I was right, but because I could wish you no better fortune in this world."

*   *   *   *   *   *   *

Stella's betrothal to Edgar is now a week old. Thérèse was vexed at first at her own want of penetration, but it was an irritation soon soothed. She is absorbed in providing the most exquisite trousseau that money and taste combined. can procure in Paris.

Zino, too, was vexed, first that Stella should have been subjected to annoyance on his account, and in the second place because his temporary lameness prevented his challenging de Hauterive. " It was tragic enough not to be able to dance the cotillon with our star, but not to be able to fight for the star is intolerable."

Thus Capito declares in a long congratulatory epistle to Edgar, adding, in a postscript, " The ladies in whose honour certain pictures were turned, as you lately observed, with their faces to the wall, were the Lipinskis, mother and daughter. I am betrothed to Natalie."

The Princess Oblonsky has left Paris for Naples ;

the Fuhrwesen accompanied her. Monsieur de
Hauterive is said to have followed her. Stasy is
left behind in Paris, where she meditates sadly
upon the ingratitude of human nature. She is no
longer an ardent admirer of the Oblonsky.

And the lovers?

The scene is the little drawing-room with the
blue furniture and bright carpet at the "Three
Negroes." The Baroness is sitting at her writing-
table, scribbling away with all her wonted energy
at something or other which is never to be finished;
the floor around her is strewn with torn and crumpled sheets of paper.

From without come the sound of heavy and light
wheels, the echo of heavy and light footsteps. But
through all the noise of the streets is heard a dreamy,
monotonous murmur, the slow drip of melting snow.
A thaw has set in, and the water is dripping from
the roofs. Sometimes the Baroness pauses in her
writing and listens. There is something strangely
disturbing to her in the simple sound: she does not
clearly catch what the water-drops tell her; she no
longer understands their speech.

Beside the fire sit Edgar and Stella. His left arm
is in a sling. In the duel with small-swords which
took place a couple of days after the Fanes' ball
he received a slight wound. Therefore there is an
admixture of grateful pity in Stella's tenderness for
him. They are sitting, hand clasped in hand, de-

vising schemes and building airy castles for the future,—the long, fair future.

"One question more, my darling," Rohritz whispers to his beautiful betrothed, who still conducts herself rather shyly towards him. "How do you mean to arrange your life?"

"How do I mean—have I any decision to make?"

"Indeed you have, dearest," he says, smiling. "My part in life is to see you happy."

"How good and dear you are to me!" Stella murmurs. "How could you torment me so long, —so long?"

"Do you suppose I was happy the while, dear love?" he whispers. Her reproach touches him more nearly than she thinks. How could he hesitate so long, is the question he now puts to himself. What has he to offer her, he with his weary, doubting heart, in exchange for her pure, fresh, untouched wealth of feeling? "But to return to my question," he begins afresh. "Will you live eight months in society and four months in the country?—or just the other way?"

"Just the other way, if I may."

"Jack Leskjewitsch wrote me at the close of his note of congratulation—the most cordial of any which I have had yet—that his wife wishes to sell Erlach Court, and thus deprive him of all temptation to retire for a second time to that Capua from a military life. Shall I buy Erlach Court for you, Stella,—for you ?—for your special property ?"

" It would be delightful," she murmurs.

" Let us be married, then, here in Paris at the embassy, and meanwhile have everything in readiness for us at Erlach Court. We can then make a tour through southern France to our home for our wedding journey."

But Stella shakes her head : " No, our wedding journey must be to Zalow, to visit papa's grave. You see, when he gave me the four-leaved clover that you have round your neck now he said, ' And if ever Heaven sends you some great joy, say to yourself that your poor father prayed the dear God that it might fall to your share !' So I must go to him first to thank him : do you not see ?"

Edgar nods. Then, looking at the girl almost mournfully, he says,—

" Is the joy really so great, my darling ?"

She makes no reply in words, but gently, almost timidly, she puts her rounded arm about him and leans her head on his breast.

Meanwhile, the Baroness looks round. 'Tis strange how the monotonous melody of the falling water-drops interferes with her work. A kind of wondering melancholy possesses her at sight of the lovers : she turns away her head and lays her pen aside.

*　　*　　*　　*　　*　　*　　*

" The world was all before them where to choose their place of rest, and Providence their guide," she murmurs to herself. " 'Tis strange how well the words suit the beginning of every young marriage. And yet they are the last words of ' Paradise Lost.' "

THE END.

PRINTED BY J. B. LIPPINCOTT COMPANY, PHILADELPHIA.

WORKS OF FICTION, SELECTED FROM THE CATALOGUE OF J. B. LIPPINCOTT COMPANY, 715–717 MARKET ST., PHILA.

MRS. LEITH ADAMS (MRS. LAFFAN).

12mo, half cloth, 50 cents.   Paper cover, 25 cents.

Madelon Lemoine.   **Aunt Hepsy's Foundling.**
Geoffrey Stirling.

"Mrs. Adams's stories are among the best works of fiction.   There is a great deal of graphic description, with incident, and fine portraiture of character.   We commend them as good specimens of pure and high-toned romance, well worth the reading."—*Phila. Evening Bulletin.*

F. ANSTEY.

A Fallen Idol.   16mo, half cloth, 50 cents.   Paper, 25 cents.

"Mr. Anstey's new story will delight the multitudinous public that laughed over 'Vice Versa.' . . . . The boy who brings the accursed image to Campion's house, Mr. Bales, the artist's factotum, and, above all, Mr. Yarker, the ex-butler who has turned policeman, are figures whom it is as pleasant to meet as it is impossible to forget."—*London Times.*

WILLIAM ARMSTRONG.

Thekla.   A Story of Viennese Musical Life.   12mo, cloth, $1.00.

"The story of Thekla is one of simple beauty.   It deals with the life of a young girl, who rejoices in the possession of a glorious voice, and with it earns her livelihood and many warm friends.   There are several very masterly bits of work in the book."—*Baltimore American.*

JOSEPHINE W. BATES.

A Blind Lead.   The Story of a Mine.   12mo, extra cloth, $1.25.

A Nameless Wrestler.   Square 12mo, cloth, $1.00.   Paper, 50 cents.

"It is certainly a powerful book.   We took up 'A Blind Lead' indifferently enough, but we had read a few pages only before we found it was no ordinary work by no ordinary writer.   There are no dull pages. and the interest is continuous from the first chapter to the last."—*Boston Advertiser.*

FRANCES COURTENAY BAYLOR.

12mo, extra cloth, $1.25 per volume. Complete set of three volumes in box, $3.75.

A Shocking Example, and other Sketches.

Behind the Blue Ridge.

On Both Sides, containing "The Perfect Treasure" and "On This Side."

"Few of our women writers have ventured upon so wide a range of character or been more successful."—*New York Herald.*

HARRIETT PENNAWELL BELT.

Marjorie Huntingdon. 12mo, cloth, $1.25.

A Mirage of Promise. 12mo, cloth, $1.25.

"Her characters are interesting and at the same time ennobling. They are pictured in the most intense situations with a touch of the true artist."—*Ohio State Journal.*

EDGAR C. BLUM.

Bertha Laycourt. 12mo, cloth, $1.25.

"It is a book suitable for any household; interesting and instructive for all classes of readers, moral in tone, beautiful in language."—*Williamsport Republican.*

PETER BOYLSTON.

John Charáxes. A Tale of the Civil War in America. 12mo, cloth, $1.25.

"'John Charáxes' is called a tale of the civil war in America, by Peter Boylston. It is very well understood, however, from internal evidence, that the story is the work of the celebrated lawyer and jurist, George Ticknor Curtis, now a man approaching the limit of three score years and ten, and still in his intellectual vigor capable of giving to the world the result of his long experience of life. No one who knows Mr. Curtis could doubt that the views of society, politics, and religion expressed in this novel are his."—*Hartford Courant.*

CHARLOTTE BRONTÉ.

Brontë Novels. Library Edition. Large crown 8vo. Per volume, $1.50. Per set, 7 volumes, $10.50.

Handy Edition. Each containing a Frontispiece. 16mo. Per volume: half cloth, 50 cents; half morocco, $1.00. Complete in Sets of 7 volumes: half cloth, $3.50; half morocco, $7.00.

CHAPLAIN JAMES J. KANE, U.S.N.

Ilian; or, The Curse of the Old South Church. 12mo, cloth, $1.25.

" This is a book worthy of more than passing notice. The tale is absorbingly interesting, the glimpses of Northern and Southern social life are evidently given by one who knows, and the naval episodes are almost worthy of Clark Russell himself.—*New York Truth.*

CAPT. CHARLES KING, U.S.A.

Laramie; or, the Queen of Bedlam. A Story of the Sioux War of 1876. 12mo, cloth, $1.00.

The Colonel's Daughter; or, Winning His Spurs. 12mo, cloth, $1.25.

Marion's Faith. 12mo, cloth, $1.25.

Kitty's Conquest. 16mo, cloth, $1.00.

The Deserter, and From the Ranks. (No. 1 of *American Novel Series.*) Square 12mo, cloth, $1.00. Paper, 50 cents.

" Captain King has caught the true spirit of the American novel, for he has endowed his work fully and freely with the dash, vigor, breeziness, bravery, tenderness, and truth which are recognized throughout the world as our national characteristics. Captain King's narrative work is singularly fascinating."—*St. Louis Republic.*

MRS. E. LYNN LINTON.

Patricia Kemball. 12mo, cloth, $1.25.

The Atonement of Leam Dundas. Illustrated. 8vo, cloth, $1.25.

The World Well Lost. Illustrated. 8vo, cloth, $1.25.

" Mrs. Linton's stories are vigorous, brilliant, and refined in style and dramatic effect. She is not only an able writer, but she is a deep thinker as well."—*Boston Gazette.*

ANNIE BLISS McCONNELL.

Half Married. 12mo, cloth, $1.25.

" A lively story of military and civil life. The heroine is a typical soldier's daughter of the United States army, and we become curiously attached to her. The pages sparkle with humorous selections and sprightly remarks."—*Philadelphia Ledger.*

VIRGINIUS DABNEY.

The Story of Don Miff, as Told by his Friend John Bouche Whacker. 12mo, cloth, $1.50.

Gold That Did Not Glitter. 12mo, cloth, $1.00.

"This is a very original and interesting book. It is hard to find a page that does not arrest attention by some striking thought or odd conceit, some flash of wit, or what is better still a delicious waggery, and when the attention is thus arrested it is hard to lay the volume down."—*Baltimore American.*

CHARLES DICKENS.

The Standard Edition. Profusely illustrated. 8vo, cloth, per volume, $2.50. Complete sets, 30 volumes, cloth, $60.00.

Library Edition. 12mo. With the Original Illustrations. 30 volumes. In sets. Cloth, $45.00.

Handy Edition. 32 volumes. 16mo. Per volume, half cloth, 50 cents. Half morocco, $1.00.

Diamond Edition. Complete in 14 volumes. Square 18mo. Cloth, per set, $10.00. Paper, per volume, 35 cents. Same in 7 volumes, cloth, $7.50.

People's Edition. 15 volumes. 12mo, cloth, $15.00.

"DUCHESS" NOVELS.

16mo, uniform style, half cloth, per volume, 50 cents. Paper, 25 cents.

Phyllis.	Mrs. Geoffrey.
Molly Bawn.	Portia.
Airy Fairy Lilian.	Loÿs, Lord Berresford, and
Beauty's Daughters.	other Stories.
Faith and Unfaith.	Rossmoyne.
Doris.	A Mental Struggle.
"O Tender Dolores."	Lady Valworth's Diamonds.
A Maiden All Forlorn.	Lady Branksmere.
In Durance Vile.	A Modern Circe.
The Duchess.	The Honourable Mrs. Ver-
Marvel.	eker.
Jerry, and other Stories.	Under-Currents.

"In all her stories the 'Duchess' shows the same excellent qualities. She is bright, spirited, vivacious, and invents a dramatic situation capitally. She begins at you with so much dash and sparkle that you find yourself in quite a glow at having found a genius."—*Iowa Gate City.*